The Many Meanings of Meilan

by Andrea Wang

Kokila

KOKILA
An imprint of Penguin Random House LLC, New York

First published in the United States of America by Kokila,
an imprint of Penguin Random House LLC, 2021
First paperback edition published 2022

Visit us online at penguinrandomhouse.com

THE LIBRARY OF CONGRESS HAS CATALOGED THE HARDCOVER EDITION AS FOLLOWS:
Names: Wang, Andrea, author.
Title: The many meanings of Meilan / Andrea Wang.
Description: New York: Kokila, [2021] | Includes bibliographical
references. \ | Summary: "A family feud before the start of seventh grade
propels Meilan from Boston's Chinatown to rural Ohio, where she must tap
into her inner strength and sense of justice to make a new place for herself"—
Provided by publisher.
Identifiers: LCCN 2021002355 | ISBN 9780593111284 (hardcover) |
ISBN 9780593111291 (ebook)
Subjects: CYAC: Families—Fiction. | Identity—Fiction. | Moving,
Household—Fiction. | Taiwanese Americans—Fiction.
Household—Fiction. | Taiwanese Americans—Fiction.
Classification: LCC PZ7.1.W3645 Man 2021 | DDC [Fic] —dc23
LC record available at https://lccn.loc.gov/2021002355

Printed in the United States of America
ISBN 9780593111307

1st Printing

LSCH

Design by Jasmin Rubero
Text set in Palatino

For my family—related, created,
and chosen. You give my life meaning.

Chapter One

I thought I knew all of my grandmother's stories, but I was wrong. Somehow, I forgot to ask Nǎinai about the most important one of all.

Now Tiffi is demanding to hear it. I'm good at inventing bedtime stories, but it feels wrong to make up the story of how our family bakery got its name. There is meaning behind every name. But with Nǎinai gone and the rest of my family too broken to talk about her, I'm left to fill in the gaps on my own.

I take a deep breath and gather my thoughts.

"Long ago," I start, "there was a fènghuáng who lived in a tall—"

"Meilan," Tiffi whines and pokes my arm. "I thought you were going to tell me the story about the phoenix and the bakery."

"I am," I say, moving my arm out of my youngest cousin's reach. "Fènghuáng is the name of the Chinese phoenix. Anyway, the fènghuáng lived in the top of a tall paulownia tree—"

"What's a polly-knee?" This time, Tiffi slides her foot out from under the covers and taps my knee with her toe. She giggles.

I send a quick prayer to the goddess Guānyīn for patience. Tiffi is just a normal, incredibly curious five-year-old, I remind myself. "The paulownia tree is also called the Chinese parasol tree. The leaves grow as big as dinner plates, and fairies like to use them as parasols to shade them from the sun." That last part isn't true, of course, but what's the point of telling tales if you can't add fairies to them? I poke Tiffi back gently. "Now, do you want to hear this story or not? I'm totally happy to watch TV and eat all the leftover butterfly cookies while you go to sleep."

Tiffi pouts. "Those are MY butterfly cookies! Māma said she made them just for me!" When I raise my eyebrows, she sighs and squirms deeper under the blanket. "I want to hear the story! I won't keep asking questions, I promise." She looks up at me through her thick black lashes and says, "Well, not unless you keep using big words like polly-knee that I don't know."

Even though I can't see her mouth, a dimple appears just above the edge of the blanket, and I know she's grinning at me. I grin back. She's as feisty as her mom, whom I call Third Aunt, but as sweet as the caramelized sugar on those butterfly cookies.

"So, back to that *parasol* tree," I begin again. "The fènghuáng lived at the very top, so she could see all of China, from the mountains whose peaks wore crowns of clouds, to where the mighty Yellow River flowed into the deep blue sea, where dragons lived. But it had been months since she had seen a dragon, and the fènghuáng knew that she had to leave her beloved home."

A furrow appears between Tiffi's eyes. "Like Năinai had to leave us," she says softly.

Tears sting my eyes, and I turn away. Our grandmother died just a few months ago, after a sudden and mysterious illness. Third Aunt is convinced that Năinai was attacked by a jiāngshī, a vampire-zombie-like monster who sucks the life force out of its victims at night. She's been hanging up eight-sided mirrors and buying peach wood carvings ever since. Bàba said that is nonsense, but he used a not-very-nice word in Mandarin that made Māma scold him. Still, half of me believes Third Aunt's explanation. Somehow, it's more comforting to blame a monster than to think that Năinai's body was too tired from years of hard work to keep on living.

"Biǎojiě," Tiffi says, "are you okay? Did mentioning the dragons scare you?"

I blink, coming back to the small pink room and Tiffi under her knock-off Disney princess blanket. I'd spent all of Tiffi's bath time coming up with a good story to answer her question, and I'm curious to see how she'll react. Xing, our middle cousin, loves all my stories. But she's also my best friend, so it's her duty to like them. Tiffi never thinks about anyone's feelings but her own. She's a lot like her mom that way.

"I'm fine. Don't worry," I tell Tiffi. "Chinese dragons, lóng, aren't scary—they're good creatures who protect us. Just like the fènghuáng. She was such a peaceful creature that she only ate bamboo seeds and drank the morning dew so she wouldn't hurt any plants or animals. But the dragon who usually brought the rains to her valley home had fallen in love with another dragon who lived in the faraway mountains. He'd gone to be with her and forgotten his duties to the valley. Without the life-giving rain, the bamboo forest died and the morning dew dried up. Weakened by hunger and thirst, the fènghuáng was at last forced to leave her home and search for another place to live.

"She looked to the east but only saw enormous plumes of choking dark fog, creeping out in all directions from the big cities the way a drop of calligraphy ink spreads in water. To the south, a white tiger battled huge balls of writhing snakes—writhing means wriggling and slithering—their fangs filled with venom so poisonous that one tiny prick could kill the biggest and fiercest rhinoceros. Up north, past the grasslands and the Mongolian desert, a qílín wearing gold armor struggled to stomp out waves of giant red ants that set fire to everything in their path."

"That's terrible!" Tiffi makes a face. "I hate snakes and ants! Did the fènghuáng help fight them?"

"She didn't have enough life energy, unfortunately. Instead, the fènghuáng decided it was time to return to her original celestial home near the sun. Celestial means in the heavens. The fènghuáng had the power to give blessings to human beings. Before she left, she wanted to reward one more human—the most deserving person she could find. That meant finding a person who possessed all the Five Virtues: benevolence, honesty, wisdom, integrity, and propriety."

Tiffi's eyebrows pinch together in confusion. She is only five, after all, and Māma has been drilling the virtues into me for twice as many years. "Can you imagine how hard that task must have been? To find someone who did good things for other people, was honest, smart, never did anything bad, and had perfect manners?" My little cousin nods solemnly. She is never bad on purpose, but she can definitely be a handful. There is a reason Xing and I have secretly nicknamed her Typhoon Tiffi.

"There was only one direction that the fènghuáng could safely travel in—west. And as she flew, she felt the tug of a human heart. A very special heart that belonged to a young woman who had endless love for her family. The fènghuáng drank in the love of this young woman for her family and felt refreshed. Her wings felt lighter than ever before, and her belly no longer ached with hunger.

"The fènghuáng flew on, determined to find the young woman and give her a gift to honor her for her character. Her golden-yellow wings glowed in the sunlight as she flew over mountains and plains and, finally, another wide, turbulent ocean. She came to rest on the crimson awning above a small shop on a busy street in a foreign land. The shop was closed, the dusty windows covered with newspaper. On the sidewalk below, a woman stood as still as a stone in a stream as people flowed around her. She stared at the vacant shop, hope and longing on her face. Four children played in the gutter behind her—three boys and a girl."

"Mommy," Tiffi murmurs. She's almost asleep. Time to wrap it up.

"Yes, the little girl was your mommy, and the woman was Nǎinai," I tell her. "Your mommy was searching for pennies while the two older boys tossed pebbles into the storm drain. The smallest child was still in diapers. He sat on the curb and played with a bit of red string. As the fènghuáng watched, the woman turned around to make sure her children were safe. The tug that the fènghuáng had felt ever since she'd left her home suddenly disappeared, washed away by a surge of love. That's how she knew that this mother was the young woman she had been searching for.

"The fènghuáng spread her golden wings wide and, with her beak, plucked out a feather. She trilled a short song—five musical notes that only the young woman seemed to be able to hear. The woman turned around, her eyes growing large with wonder as she saw the colorful bird perched on the edge of the awning. The fènghuáng released the golden feather, which floated softly down into the woman's outstretched hand. The moment it touched her palm, the feather curled and spun itself into a heavy gold coin. Her task complete, the fènghuáng leaped into the air, the wave of gratitude from the woman buoying her up toward her heavenly home."

I lean over my sleeping cousin and kiss her forehead lightly. "And that, Biǎomèi, is why our bakery is called the Golden Phoenix."

I flick the switch on Tiffi's dumpling-shaped nightlight and turn off the overhead light before closing the door behind me. *A butterfly cookie would go really well with the book I brought with me to read,* I think to myself. Smiling, I head for the kitchen.

As I reach the end of the hall, a hand shoots out from behind the doorway and grabs my upper arm tightly. Then, a voice.

"Where is the gold?"

Chapter Two

It takes everything to stop myself from screaming and waking up Tiffi. I breathe deeply and stare into Third Aunt's piercing eyes. "Hi, Sān Āyí," I manage to say. "You're home early."

She waves one hand as if to shoo away a gnat, the multiple rings on her fingers glittering like a tiny constellation of stars. "Food was bad. They overcook the shrimp, put too much sauce on vegetables. They even took head off fish!" She huffs with irritation. "Āiyā, I will have to burn much incense to get rid of this bad luck." Still holding on to my arm, Third Aunt drags me to the sofa opposite the kitchen area and takes a seat, pulling me down beside her. The plastic covering crinkles and squeaks under our weight.

"But this is not what I want to talk to you about, Lánlán," she says, using my family nickname. "I want to know about your dream."

I'm having a hard time following my aunt's train of

thought. "Um, what dream?" I have a lot of dreams, but I'd never tell Third Aunt about any of them. Whenever Māma thinks I'm talking too much, she says, "The mouth is the doorway to disaster."

"Your dream!" She shakes my arm impatiently. The gemstones on her rings dig into my flesh. "About the fènghuáng who dropped the piece of gold into your Nǎinai's hand." She leans in until I can see every pore underneath the heavy makeup she wears. "What else happened in your dream?"

Oh no. How long had she been listening? "That wasn't a dream, that was just a story I made up for Tiffi so she could fall asleep."

"Story, dream, same same." Third Aunt finally releases my arm so she can wave both bejeweled hands simultaneously. "I always knew Dà Gē was hiding something from me."

Alarm bells sound in my head at the mention of my father, Third Aunt's eldest brother. The two of them have never gotten along. "No, he's not hiding anything. There's no gold coin. There's no fènghuáng. I made it all up."

The look my aunt gives me is as sharp as a warrior's arrow. "If you just make it up, then how you know about that day?"

"What day?"

"That day," she repeats. "When Māma took me, Dà Gē, Èr Gē, and Dìdi to look at the empty bakery. How you know I was looking for coins? How you know Dìdi was wearing red string bracelet?"

I stare at her, horror slowly creeping up my back like cold corpse fingers. "I didn't. How could that really have happened? Weren't you a lot older when Gōnggong and Nǎinai moved here?"

She ignores my logic. "I think maybe YOU think have dream, but I think you have vision. You see the truth."

"The truth?" I stammer.

Third Aunt leans back and gives me a long look. Then she abruptly stands, rummages in the cabinet by the TV, and pulls out a small brown cardboard box. When she sits down again, her whole attitude has changed. She opens the box, revealing fancy chocolates wrapped in gold foil, and offers them to me. I shake my head. Nice Third Aunt is much scarier than Loud Third Aunt.

"Go on, Lánlán, have one," she urges sweetly. "I know is hard for you. You love your bàba. But truth is, bakery make much more money than your bàba say. So much money, he changed it for gold pieces so it cannot lose value. Just like the gold coin that the fènghuáng dropped into my māma's hand."

"No, that didn't actually happen. I told you, it's just a story."

Third Aunt smiles and nods. "Okay, okay. Like you say, just a story. Tell me more. Tell me where it is."

"Where what is?"

Her mask slips. "The gold!" she snaps. "Did the fènghuáng show you where Dà Gē hid the gold? Or maybe he gave it to your mother to hide?"

I've had enough of this. I'm freaked out, and Third Aunt isn't listening to anything I say. Bàba and his brothers always try to calm her down when she gets like this; they usually start agreeing with her just to get her to stop. But they're not here right now, and if I start agreeing, she'll just keep insisting that I tell her where the made-up gold is. And then what do I say? There's no treasure. I know every inch of our apartment, and there's nowhere my parents could've hidden something like a pile of gold coins. Plus, if we had any gold, Māma and Bàba wouldn't complain about the cost of internet service going up. They haven't bought anything new for themselves in a long time, either.

"Sān Āyí," I say, trying to sound respectful and reasonable. "There truly isn't any gold. Or extra money. Bàba and Māma haven't hidden anything from you. I didn't have a vision—I just used my imagination to create a bedtime story." Gently, I take the box of chocolates out of her hands and put it on the coffee table. "Please. I need to go home. I have school tomorrow."

Third Aunt blinks at the mention of school, so far removed from tales of magical birds and hoards of gold. Slowly, she puts her calm face on again. "Of course," she says. "I keep you too long already."

As I move toward the door, it opens suddenly, startling me. Third Uncle comes in, his cheeks ruddy. It's not that cold out for November, so he must have been drinking at their dinner.

"I had to park three blocks away!" he complains in Mandarin before catching sight of me. "Lánlán," he says. "You're still here?"

"I'm leaving right now," I tell him quickly. "Sān Āyí and I were just, um, chatting."

I grab my Docs and slip out the door without putting them on. I glance back and see Third Aunt stashing the box of chocolates in the back of the cabinet again. She's the one hiding gold, not Bàba.

The arguments begin the next day.

I head to the bakery before school, dodging Second Aunt as she slides a large tray of roast pork buns into the oven. Māma is in the front, helping the early customers buying their breakfasts. She turns and frowns at me when I reach into the glass display case to grab my own breakfast.

"What?" I ask, pulling out one earbud, music still spilling into my other ear. "There weren't any leftovers upstairs."

Māma shakes her head at me and gives Mrs. Zhang her change, thanking the woman and congratulating her on her new job. While the next customer decides what to order, Māma comes over to me. "Méiguānxì," she says in a low voice. "Take what you want."

"Then why are you frowning at me?"

She leans closer, pretending to tuck my hair behind my ear, murmuring in Mandarin. "I am not frowning at you. I want you to go into the office and tell Bàba and Sān Āyí to shut the door and keep their voices down." She peers back at the line of customers, who all suddenly look intensely interested in the almond cookies in the window. "Everybody can hear!"

Now I can hear them, too, even over Alicia Keys singing about girls who can't be themselves.

"I have a right to see the books!" Third Aunt shouts in Mandarin. In the kitchen, Second Aunt bangs the oven door shut, making me jump.

"Go!" Māma urges. She gives me a tiny shove.

I snatch a random pastry out of the case and hurry into the kitchen. My steps slow as I approach the tiny office at the back, my father's and aunt's sharp voices crack through the air like whips. My knees feel as wobbly as the custard in the dàntà in my hand.

I peek through the doorway of the office from a couple of feet away. Bàba is behind his desk, leaning over it, his left hand placed firmly on top of a thick bound ledger. That must be the book Third Aunt wants to examine. I can't see my aunt from my position—she must be on the opposite side of the desk. There's no room in the office for her to be anywhere else.

Bàba's voice is loud and frustrated. "I still don't understand," he continues in Mandarin. "You've never been interested in seeing the books before."

"Well, I want to look at them now," Third Aunt insists.

"Jiāyù, what is this really about? Do you even know how to read an accounting ledger?"

Third Aunt gives a shriek that can probably be heard by the old men playing xiàngqí in Mary Soo Hoo Park. "Just because you are the eldest does not mean you are the best person for the job! Our mother knew I am better at math, but still she gave control to you, her favorite!"

Bàba scoffs. "You think she would leave her life's work in your grasping hands? She told me that she trusted you only when she could see you."

This was getting ugly. I never knew Nǎinai had a favorite child, or that she didn't trust her only daughter. I take a deep breath and step into the office, my boot accidentally hitting the door with a loud thump. They both turn to stare at me, their faces fixed into matching scowls.

I say the first thing that pops into my head. "Um, Gōnggong is still sleeping." It's a lie, and they both know it. My grandfather is used to getting up before dawn. "Is it okay if I shut the door?" Both of their faces change colors—my father's face pales as he realizes the whole bakery has been listening to their argument. Third Aunt's face gets redder, like the tip of a stick of burning incense when you blow on it. Great. Now she's mad at me for hiding the location where Bàba has supposedly stashed a pile of gold *and* for interrupting her demand and preventing her from getting what she wants.

She shoots one last glare at Bàba. "We have not finished talking about this." She shoulders past me and flounces out the door.

I glance helplessly at my father. "Sorry, Bàba."

He doesn't look at me. "Go to school, Lánlán," he says. "And close the door."

I back out of the office, pulling the door shut as I go, as quiet as a sparrow in the grass.

Chapter Three

Xing is surprised when I step out of the cobblestone alley next to the bakery. "What are you still doing here? You're going to be late for school!"

I glance at the time on my phone and sigh. "Well, it's Māma's fault, so she'll just have to deal with me getting a tardy. At least we get to walk together today." Xing's a year younger, so she's still at the elementary school, which starts a half hour later than the middle school. This summer, Xing promised she would get up early and walk with me to school since our two schools are across the street from each other. But when Nǎinai died, Xing had to stay and take care of Tiffi in the morning so Third Aunt could work in the bakery. I know she's doing her duty, but I miss her company.

We hurry down Beach Street and turn the corner onto Harrison. Shopkeepers wave at us as they lift the metal gates of their storefronts. Mrs. Chiang, who owns the shoe shop and puts aside a pair of red Dr. Martens for me every year, calls out, "Huā Měilán! You're late for school!" She sounds half-amused, half-scolding. I wonder if she'll ask Māma about it later. Sometimes it's not so great that everybody knows everybody—the gossip in this tight-knit community can be brutal.

How long will it take before all of Chinatown knows about Third Aunt and Bàba's argument? I wish the boba café was open this early—a matcha slush would calm me down.

Xing glances at me. "So, what happened this morning? I came down the front stairs to avoid the crowd, and I heard Third Aunt yelling."

"Since when is she not yelling?"

Xing grins. "True. But seriously, what's going on?"

I didn't see Xing after babysitting for Tiffi last night, so I fill her in on the bedtime story, how Third Aunt overheard me, and how she grilled me about where my father was hiding the gold I'd made up. "And this morning she was shouting at Bàba to let her see the books. Māma made me interrupt their argument. That's why I'm late."

Xing looks confused. "What books?"

"I think she means the record that Bàba keeps of how much money the bakery makes every day, how much is spent on ingredients, all that." I bite my lip. "I think she wants to find proof that Bàba is stealing money from the bakery."

My cousin gasps. "That's awful! How can she think that?"

"Right?" I walk faster, trying to burn off my anger and the sneaking suspicion that my fènghuáng story has started something serious. Xing hurries to keep up with me.

We're passing the St. James the Greater Church when a hoarse voice calls out, "Hey! Lánlán!" I stop and smile at Old Yang, who is sitting on the steps of the church as usual, his dog beside him. "Nàonào and I were afraid you weren't coming today. What did you bring us?" he says in his rolling Beijing dialect.

Guilt washes over me as I reply, "Oh no! I'm so sorry, I forgot! There was a lot going on at the bakery this morning." Every Friday, I grab a bag of leftover pastries for Old Yang and Nàonào. Māma started the tradition when I began kindergarten, and I kept it up even after she stopped walking me to school.

The old man's face falls. "No matter, no matter," he says kindly. "Maybe tomorrow, eh?"

But Nàonào isn't as forgiving. The brindled brown dog,

who looks like a Labrador retriever-pit bull-dachshund mix, trots over and pushes her snout against my hand. I raise my hand and realize that I'm still clutching the dàntà from earlier. The pastry shell is crushed into the custard part, but the waxed paper baking cup has kept it from leaking out . . . mostly. "Um, you wouldn't want this, would you?" I feel bad enough giving Old Yang day-old pastries, never mind squished ones.

Old Yang laughs. "Of course she does! She's a dog!"

I laugh, too, and hand the mangled tart to him. He breaks off a piece for himself and puts the rest on the ground for Nàonào, who wolfs it down in one bite and looks up for more. Old Yang waggles his finger at the dog and pops his piece into his mouth, humming with satisfaction. "I'll bring you better ones tomorrow," I promise them.

"Do you know," the old man says, "that the first thing I bought from your nǎinai was a dàntà?"

Xing pulls at my sleeve. "Come on, Meilan, we have to go." She makes a face at Nàonào, who is licking my hand clean. "That's gross."

Xing has never been friendly to Old Yang and Nàonào. She claims it's because she's scared of dogs, but I've seen her play with her friends' dogs lots of times. I think it's because the old man and his dog are homeless, and they don't get a chance to wash very often. I move my arm, and she lets go. "Don't you want to hear about Nǎinai?" Now that I can't talk to her in person, every little tidbit about my grandmother feels precious.

"No," she says. "Maybe you don't care about being tardy, but I do."

"Then go ahead," I tell her. "I want to listen to this story."

"You and your stories!" she huffs. "They're going to get you in trouble someday." She marches off, arms swinging.

I push Xing's comment to the back of my mind and take a seat on the gray stone steps next to Old Yang. Nàonào sits on my boots as if to stop me from going anywhere. I stroke the patch of white fur on her chest. "When did you meet Nǎinai?"

"Many years ago," he replies. "I had a job then, catching and selling fish. I had to get up very early to haul my nets and take the fish to the market. I would walk past your family's bakery on my way. Always, there was a light on in the back, in the kitchen." The old man pauses to smile at me. "Your grandparents got up before the sun to work, like me."

For some reason, this surprises me. Not that Gōnggong and Nǎinai got up really early to start baking—my parents, aunts, and uncles still do that. But I never realized that Old Yang used to have a job. He and Nàonào have been roaming the streets of Chinatown since I can remember.

Old Yang continues, "It is a hard life, being a fisherman. One morning, I was feeling very sad. Only four small fish were caught in my nets—too small to sell at the market. All I had to feed my family that day were those four tiny fish. Just as I passed the bakery, your nǎinai was setting a tray of dàntà in the window. Even out on the street, I could smell their aroma!"

I smile. "Waking up to the smell of baking pastries is one of the best things in the world."

"Ah, you are so lucky," Old Yang says. "Your nǎinai looked up and saw me staring at the dàntà through the window. The bakery wasn't open yet, but she unlocked the door and beckoned me inside. I could not resist following my nose even though I had very little money. But your grandmother would not let me pay. She put three dàntà in a small bag for me to take home and told me to keep my coins. I was too proud to accept. In the end, she took one of the fish as payment. I went home with three fish and three dàntà, and my family was very happy. Your nǎinai was a good bargainer, but that day I got the better deal." He grins mischievously, and for a moment, I catch a glimmer of a young Old Yang.

There's a lump in my throat from thinking about Nǎinai and how she started giving pastries to Old Yang before I was born. Third Aunt said her mother treated her differently, but I can't imagine it. Nǎinai was always so loving and encouraging to me and Xing. She took care of everyone. I also can't help but wonder where Old Yang's family is now and what happened to make him homeless. I swallow and say, "Thank you for telling me this story about Nǎinai. I better go—I'm already really late for school."

Maybe I should tell my family Old Yang's story. Maybe it would inspire them to stop fighting.

Chapter Four

Old Yang's story about Năinai doesn't change a thing. Four weeks later, my family is still arguing. It's mostly over money, but it could be about anything, even grudges from years ago. Even worse, Māma told me to stop telling stories. Actually, what she said when I went to babysit Tiffi was, "Maybe only read book to Tiffi at bedtime," but I knew what she meant. She doesn't have to worry— I've learned my lesson. I'm never telling another story again, made-up or otherwise.

Today, there's a line outside our bakery—the usual after-school rush plus grownups wanting to order cakes for the holidays. I can picture the kids inside, crowding the glass counter, debating how many roast pork buns and egg tarts to get. I duck into the alley before anyone can see me and beg for freebies. Warm, yeasty air scented with sugar immediately envelops me when I enter.

Two men sit on tall stools in front of a stainless steel table in the bakery kitchen. One rolls dough into small, perfect circles, spinning the dough with his left hand while flicking the rolling pin with his right. He's wearing a blue dress shirt with the sleeves rolled up under his apron. The faded logo of a rock band peeks out from behind the apron of the other man, who cradles each circle of dough, puts a dollop of sweet bean paste in the center, and expertly twists the dough around it. It's like a dance—and pastry flowers magically bloom in their hands.

"Chén Shūshu, Lǐ Shūshu. Nǐmén hǎo ma?" I greet them using the title that means "mother's younger brother." They're not really my uncles, but Māma insists that I address everyone respectfully. They've also known me since I was born.

They both grin at me, and Lǐ Shūshu waves one floury hand toward the metal racks against the opposite wall. "Just come out," he says in Mandarin.

I grab one of the piping hot bōluóbāo, thank both bakers, and push through the door next to the racks. The apartment hallway is cool and dim. I pop bits of the bun's sweet, crumbly topping into my mouth as I climb the stairs. It doesn't taste like pineapple, it just looks like it.

Xing grabs my arm as soon as I step onto the third

floor. "Hey!" I protest, crumbs showering the cracked tiles. It must be early release day for her.

"Come on, Meilan," Xing urges. She pulls me toward her apartment and away from mine.

"What's going on?" I ask, just before a wave of angry voices rolls down the hall from my apartment. "Ugh. Another discussion?"

Xing leads me into the little utility closet. It's where we go when we need to get away from our parents. It's also between our two apartments, making it a perfect place to listen to conversations happening in our living rooms.

Bàba's voice is muffled, but his impatience is clear. "I thought we were here to discuss the holiday work shifts. Why are you bringing up last Friday?"

"You took the whole day off," Third Aunt accuses. "So you will have one more vacation day than the rest of us."

"It was not vacation. I was attending Meilan's parent-teacher conference. Then I had meetings with our bank and suppliers." I don't have to see my dad's face to know that he's scowling. He always scowls when he talks to Third Aunt. "When your daughter goes to school, you will also be able to take time off to talk to her teachers. This is a pointless argument."

"The point is, you are used to giving yourself more than you give to your own brothers and sister."

Bàba snaps, "That is ridiculous! When have I given myself more? I have always put the three of you first."

"Our mother's silver hairpin," she responds. "You gave it to your wife."

"Only because you said you didn't want it!"

"I would have liked to have it," a third voice says. It's Second Aunt, Xing's mom. Beside me, Xing's eyes grow wide.

"You see!" Third Aunt exclaims. "You did not even ask Èr Gē or his wife. Just like you did not ask before taking money from our family's business and exchanging it for gold. Gold that you have hidden from us."

"Do not make me laugh," Bàba says icily. "There is no gold. My daughter already told you that it was only a story from her imagination."

My stomach lurches. "I can't believe she's still talking about my story!"

"You know she thinks it's real. Third Aunt believes in fairies and visions." Xing nudges my shoulder. "Just like you."

"I do not! I know when something is made-up. Especially if I'm the one who made it."

Xing puts her hands up as if conceding. "Okay, okay. I'm just saying your stories are really convincing."

"Tiffi asked why the bakery is named Golden Phoenix. What was I supposed to do? I mean, it's not as if . . ." I stop.

"Not as if you could ask Năinai," Xing finishes softly. She reaches out and twines her fingers with mine. We listen to the raised voices, the pipes coming up from the bakery below warm against our backs.

"Dà Gē," Second Uncle says. "I have long told you of my desire to go to medical school. Even though our mother is gone, I still hope to make her proud. If there is extra money, please share with us so we may pursue our dreams." His voice is strained. Xing's father is closest in age and friendship to Bàba. It must be hard for him to be caught between his siblings.

Fourth Uncle, the youngest of Gōnggong and Năinai's children, doesn't even try to keep his tone respectful. "Don't bother beseeching his conscience, Lăo Èr. If Dà Gē has been stealing money from us, do you think he will admit it? He has always been arrogant, thinking he knows best how we should spend our money. I bet he got tired of us having different ideas, so he started saving it for himself. He kept us chained to the bakery for his own selfish desires."

"Yes," Third Uncle says, "we should listen to Lǎo Yāo—he knows the most about psychology."

"Is that right?" Māma scoffs. "Then why can't he figure out who is bluffing at the poker table? And what about you? You should have no say in what happens to the bakery. Half the time you are too busy partying to work, and the other half you are too hungover."

"Ouch," Xing murmurs. "That was kind of harsh."

I have to agree with her, even though Māma's right. She rarely loses her patience, but when she does, her words burn the hottest.

"Enough!" Bàba roars. "I have never stolen from any of you!"

"It is a good thing I overheard Lánlán," my Third Aunt says. "Children are always more honest."

I bury my face in my arms, trying not to cry. This is all my fault.

"C'mon," Xing says, standing and pulling me up beside her. "I have to get back. I'm supposed to be watching Tiffi."

I gasp. "You left Typhoon Tiffi by herself?"

"I had to come out and get you. I didn't want you to go home. It's like a pack of wolves in there." We hurry out of the closet and to the stairwell. Third Aunt's apartment is on the second floor, right below Xing's.

"Wait. Where's Gōnggong?"

Xing rolls her eyes. "Where do you think? Same place he's been since Nǎinai died." She looks at me curiously. "What are you going to do?"

Gōnggong lives right below my own apartment, so he must be able to hear this argument. I bet everybody in Chinatown can hear it, from the páifāng gate all the way down to the fancy new high-rise buildings on Washington Street.

I turn toward our grandfather's apartment. "He's supposed to be the head of the family now, right? I'm going to make him come upstairs and help."

Xing puts her hand on mine so I can't knock on Gōnggong's door. She makes a face. "Don't you remember what happened the last time you tried that?"

I sigh. A few weeks ago, soon after the fighting began, I had asked Gōnggong to come out and stop the arguments. "He said, 'The bakery has lost its heart,' and shut the door in my face. And then I got in trouble with my parents."

I know Gōnggong is mourning, but I wish he would talk to the whole family, tell everyone that my bedtime story isn't real and there isn't any hidden gold. Or even better, that he'd come out and say it *is* true and open a large black lacquered box stuffed with gold coins. Because then everybody would be rich and happy, not sad and angry.

But that's just a fantasy. The reality is that Gōnggong has given up on the bakery, on his children, and even on us, his beloved grandchildren. Nǎinai always called our family "bābǎo fàn"—Eight Treasure Rice Pudding. The other Hua family members—her husband, three sons, one daughter, and three grandchildren—were the "treasures." But what I didn't understand then was that Nǎinai had been the sticky rice holding all the other ingredients together. Now she's gone, and the family is falling apart.

We get to Tiffi right before she jumps into a monster bubble bath, the water up to the rim of the tub. I drain the tub until it's only half-full before letting her get in while Xing checks the rest of the apartment.

We've just finished putting away all the toys and art supplies when Third Aunt appears in the doorway, my father behind her. Their faces are hard and icy. Bàba beckons to me. "Zǒu ba," he says.

Third Aunt won't look at me at all. She asks Xing to stay and entertain Tiffi while she cooks dinner. I should say something. But I don't. Māma says Third Aunt was born in the Year of the Ox and is stubborn. Nothing I say will change her mind. And then she and Bàba would know we were eavesdropping. Quickly, I say goodbye to my cousins and follow Bàba up the stairs.

In our tiny entry hall, I wait for Bàba to take off his shoes first. He doesn't ever leave the apartment in his slippers, even though we all live in the same building as if it's one big house. It's like he wants to keep the aunts and uncles separate. But Bàba doesn't bend down to unlace his shoes. He just stands there, a hand grasping the coat hook on the wall, his knuckles white.

A fluttery feeling like moth wings beats inside my chest. "Bàba?" I touch his elbow. "Are you okay?"

His shoulders stiffen. "The family has reached a decision. We will sell the bakery. And," He turns to me. "Māma, Gōnggong, you, and me . . ."

"What?"

"We are moving."

They aren't moths inside my chest. They're beetles, hundreds of them, their shells clicking against each other, pushing, pushing.

"Moving?" I whisper. "Just the four of us? Where?"

Bàba tries to smile. "This is Měi Gúo," he says, using the Mandarin name for the United States. Beautiful Country. "It is big. We will find a place where Gōnggong can go fishing every day and Māma can pluck peaches off the trees." He puts his hand on my shoulder. "You will see. It will be like one of your fairy tales."

I want to tell him that only the Disney versions end happily. The original fairy tales? Not so much.

But I don't.

Chapter Five

We leave Boston in July, the seagulls squawking over the garbage steaming in the alley, the taste of bitter melon in my mouth. It has taken six miserable months to sell the bakery, and the grown-ups are barely speaking to each other anymore. The entire Hua family stands awkwardly on the sidewalk in front of the bakery, its awning looming over us. Only Tiffi is happy, running from one aunt to another, chattering about how many shrimp dumplings she's going to eat. She thinks we're going to Fortune Palace for dim sum, the way we always do to mark a family event. Except for this time.

Xing and I hug goodbye, but not as tightly as before. At first, she'd been upset that her father had taken Third Aunt's side against my father, but neither of us could really blame him. After all, he wants to become a doctor and help people. Lately, it feels like Xing has been pulling away from me.

The fiery arguments have reduced our family to ashes.

In Greek mythology, the phoenix is consumed by fire and then reborn. But that isn't the Chinese bird. The Chinese fènghuáng is a symbol of harmony, not rebirth. Only, my phoenix tale destroyed any good feelings between my father and his siblings. I wonder what, if anything, will rise from the ashes of the Hua family.

I step away from Xing and look for my parents. Chén Shūshu and Lǐ Shūshu are there, too, clasping Gōnggong and Bàba's hands in farewell, not bothering to hide their tears. They'll continue on, working with the new owners. Gōnggong accepts their thanks and good wishes, but his voice and face are emotionless, like his soul is somewhere else. The tears in Bàba's eyes surprise me, but I realize that he cares about these men as if they were his true brothers.

Once, Nǎinai took out a box of old photos to entertain me and Xing. There was one photo that I found especially fascinating. In it, my father, Second Uncle, Chén Shūshu, and Lǐ Shūshu are kneading dough at the table in the bakery kitchen, with Gōnggong watching over them. They're teenagers, and they look so eager, all except for Second Uncle. He's holding up one hand covered in sticky, too-wet dough and frowning in disgust. Third Aunt is there, too, lounging against the office doorway in a fancy silk dress, smirking at the camera. Fourth Uncle isn't in the photo at all. When I asked Nǎinai why, she'd just made a *tsk* sound and changed the subject.

The Massachusetts Turnpike shoots us out of Boston like an arrow, dipping to the south before climbing to the northwest. The highway narrows from four lanes to three and then to two, the trees growing thicker and taller, creeping closer and closer to the road. Gōnggong's eyes are closed, and his arm is draped over the boxes between us in the back seat, but I'm not sure he's asleep. His face isn't relaxed like it would be if he were, his back is too straight, and there are too many wrinkles on his forehead. I wonder what he's thinking about, but then I realize it's probably the same as me. Everything we're leaving behind.

Bàba and Māma chatter excitedly in Mandarin about the last time we went on vacation five years ago. We had driven up to Acadia National Park in Maine with Xing and her parents.

"Remember, Lánlán?" Māma says. "The view from the top of the mountain was like a painting."

"I was only seven. I don't remember anything." I reply in English even though my parents expect me to speak

Mandarin to them. Being stuck in the car has made me crabby. And a liar. Because I do have a memory of that trip—a long car ride, a lot like this one, except that now Xing isn't here to talk or sing or play I Spy with me.

There is a pause, and then Bàba says, "How can you forget Xing complaining about hiking?"

Māma laughs. "Such a small girl with such a loud voice! She scared all the birds away with her complaints!"

"Good thing you came up with that story! Or else we never would have reached the top!" Bàba smiles at me in the rearview mirror.

"Story? What story?"

"Something about fairies," Māma says. Her tone is a little dismissive.

"They lived in the rocks, I think," Bàba adds.

Rock fairies. I remember now.

That had been a good day. My fairy tale had motivated Xing to stop whining, do what the family wanted, and hike to the top. If only my latest story could have resulted in something so positive.

Later that afternoon, we slowly wind through the streets of Albany, New York, and stop in front of a tidy white house. There are pots of red flowers on the front step and a fú character embroidered in gold on a red silk background that hangs upside down on the door, letting good fortune pour into the house.

"Where are we? Whose house is this?" I feel the familiar flutter and scrape of beetle wings reacting to my nervousness. Bàba and Māma haven't said much about where we're moving to or where they'll work, only that they'll figure it out. I can't believe they don't have a plan and that they're just going to start over from nothing. I said as much to Bàba, and he just smiled and said, "Did it before, can do it again." He seems to think he's on some great adventure.

Bàba turns off the engine and steps out of the car, stretching his arms high over his head. He comes around to my side and opens my door. "Come out, come out. This my friend's house. Professor Hsieh. We go to high school together in Taiwan."

"You *went* to high school together," I correct my father. His English is better than Māma's because she didn't come to the US until after college, but he's gotten rusty. In Chinatown you can go for months without speaking much English. We're not in Chinatown anymore.

He shrugs. Nothing seems to annoy him since we left. "Yes, yes, that is what I said." He helps Gōnggong out of the car and then goes to give Māma a hand with our suitcases.

Professor Hsieh turns out to be a woman that I recognize from the holiday cards she sends us every year. She greets us warmly and shows us to our rooms. Gōnggong gets the guest bedroom to himself, while Māma and Bàba have an air mattress in an office near the front hall. There's a sort of bed made from stacked blankets on the floor of her daughters' room for me.

"Your parents said that you have a sleeping bag?" Professor Hsieh asks. I nod, and she smiles. "Good. I hope you'll be comfortable here. Josephine and Julianna are looking forward to meeting you. They're at a violin lesson right now, but they'll be back before dinner." She looks at me intently for a moment. "Would you like to rest now? Come downstairs whenever you are ready." I nod again, and she leaves, closing the door gently behind her.

I know I should go downstairs and sit with the grown-ups. I should drink tea and nibble snacks and answer questions about school. But I can't. Instead, I lie down on the blankets and take deep breaths until the beetles settle down.

"Jiějie! Jiějie!"

I wake abruptly to two girls squealing and clutching my shoulders. They're a little older than Tiffi, maybe seven or eight. This must be Josephine and Julianna, but I have no idea who is who. I struggle to remember if their last holiday card identified them but come up empty. The one on my right is in unicorn pajamas and the other wears sloth pajamas. I sit up, and they let go of me. "Um, hi. I'm Meilan."

They don't bother to introduce themselves. "We know!" Unicorn pj's giggles. "You slept right through dinner, and now it's our bedtime! Will you tell us a story?"

"What? A story? Now?" My brain is still fuzzy from sleep.

"Please!" the sloth-covered one begs. "Māma says that your stories have won awards!"

I shake my head. "That was two years ago, and it was just a school thing."

"Tell us a story anyway. I bet it'll be a really good one."

Their wide eyes and eager faces remind me too much of Tiffi. "I'm sorry," I say. "I don't tell stories anymore." I ignore the pang near my heart and get up and go downstairs.

I eat some leftovers at the kitchen table, listening

to the adults chatting in the family room. Bàba and Māma laugh more than I've heard in a long time. Even Gōnggong says a few things. Then Bàba asks how far away Niagara Falls is, and they all start planning for us to go there.

The girls are asleep when I sneak back into the room, and the food in my stomach feels like a brick. I feel bad for not being a good guest. Why am I the only one who isn't happy to be here? Don't my parents realize that we basically got thrown out of our family? They're acting like this trip is a treat, but to me it feels like misery.

~

The next morning, we say goodbye to the Hsiehs and spend half a day in the car. In a parking lot near the falls, Māma pulls out a thermos of hot water and passes around Styrofoam cups of instant ramen and disposable chopsticks. We slurp our noodles and soup in silence, looking out the car windows at the crowds of tourists. After lunch, we plunge into the stream of people and let them carry us to the waterfalls. Māma and Bàba take a ton of pictures while Gōnggong stands with his back to the railing, his eyes darting from face to face in the mass of people milling around us.

At first, I think he's just noticing how many Asians

there are in the crowd. Or, more specifically, how many of them are Chinese. But as flashes of hope followed by dimmed frowns cross his face over and over, I realize what my grandfather is doing.

He's looking for Năinai.

I turn around and stare at the green water pouring over the edge and crashing into the pool below, where it churns up brown foam. The spray from the waterfall lightly mists my face, and when I lick it off my top lip, I wonder why it tastes salty.

Finally, Māma and Bàba get tired of taking photos, and we walk to a souvenir shop a few blocks away. The owner is a friend of Professor Hsieh's, and he gives me a small pin with a photo of the Horseshoe Falls on it.

The man and his wife, whom I'm told to call Uncle and Auntie Yuan, live in a tiny apartment above their shop. They don't have any children, which is kind of a relief.

After dinner, I sit in my sleeping bag on the floor of the basement below the shop, tucked up against the warped wooden paneling on the wall. The thin carpet smells musty, and I can't focus on my book. I try not to look at the spiderwebs in the corners. I try not to think about my old bed with the silk quilt Năinai made for me, or of Xing lying in her own bed just down the hall. I try not to remember the warmth and chatter rising up from the bakery below, up the stairwell and through the walls.

It's just the four of us now, on our own, on the road. Four is an unlucky number, as unlucky in Chinese culture as the number thirteen is in this country. I stick the Horseshoe Falls pin on my backpack next to the kawaii cactus pins I got from a tiny shop in Harvard Square. We're like the water in the Niagara River—rushing away from the source of our strength and dropping over the edge only to splash down in some strange place. Where will we end up? I don't think even Bàba knows.

Chapter Six

For the next month, we are like the Hakka—the guest people of China that Māma told me about, who migrated from place to place. I discover that my parents have more friends scattered across the entire eastern United States than I ever knew about.

After we leave Niagara Falls, we visit one of Gōnggong's old friends in New York City, where he talks as much as he did before Nǎinai died. That's when I realize we're not just leaving behind good memories— maybe we are leaving bad ones behind, too.

In New Jersey, Māma makes us tour the castle-like brick buildings of Princeton University even though I won't go to college for six more years. Bàba insists on stopping in Philadelphia to see the Liberty Bell, which is a lot smaller than I expected.

In Baltimore, my parents decide to splurge and have lunch at a café overlooking the harbor. "I come one crab-cake, sauce on side," Māma orders.

at did you say?" the waitress asks. Māma repeats
order. The waitress shakes her head, a frown crossed
with a smirk on her pasty face. "Learn to speak English."

My parents' cheeks are flushed, but they won't make
a scene.

I glare at the waitress. "Our English is fine," I say.
Because it is.

Their English isn't "broken," like some people claim.
It's a translation of what they would say in Mandarin,
word for word. Sometimes I think English is the broken
language, with all the exceptions to grammar and spelling rules, words borrowed from other languages, and
messy conjugations.

My voice catches on a lump of beetles, but I push
through it. "My mother would like the crabcakes with
the sauce on the side, like she said." I order for the rest
of us, too, and shut my menu with a snap. The waitress
grabs our menus without a word and leaves. When the
food comes, another waitress serves us.

"It is good, Lan," Bàba says. I don't know if he means
the crabcakes or my speaking for them. But I notice that
they let me walk ahead and talk to the people in the
ticket booths at the museums in Washington, DC.

They're both quieter, at least during the day. At night,

they continue to stay up late, catching up with old friends on years' worth of news. When their friends ask questions about our future, like what kind of work they are looking for, Bàba says, "I'm going to become the next Chinese movie star," which makes everyone laugh, since he's never acted in his life. Māma tells them she's going to be a professional poker player in Las Vegas, which I think is a dig at Fourth Uncle except that she would be really good at it. I can never tell what she's thinking. When Bàba tells them about Năinai's passing and selling the bakery, that's when Gōnggong falls silent.

I wonder why we've never visited any of these people before, and then I realize the answer. The bakery. And the family. We always had the family around us. Now we don't.

The thought makes me yearn to call Xing, but I don't have a cell phone anymore. One more thing lost to the squabbles about money. Neither of my parents have called any of the aunts and uncles since we left. Asking to borrow their phones to call Xing feels like a betrayal.

Bàba zigzags across one state after another, chasing the setting sun. We climb up into the mountains of West Virginia, the trees changing from big leafy oaks to windswept spruces, the landscape a tapestry of different greens. I keep my window open so I can smell the sharp piney scent. The thin, cold air feels lighter and more alive than the heavy, wet air along the coast. Bàba takes deep breaths, too.

"Bìng cóng kǒu rù," Māma says in warning. Technically, her saying doesn't apply since I'm inhaling through my nose and not my mouth, but I understand that she thinks the cool air will make me catch a cold. I want to tell her that germs make people sick, not chilly temperatures. Instead, I take another long, slow breath.

Māma's voice gets sharper. "Lan, qiān jīn nán mǎi yì kǒu qì." Bàba shoots me an apologetic look, but I'm already rolling up my window. She's not worried about me, she's worried about Gōnggong, his mouth hanging open a little bit as he sleeps. She's right—a thousand pieces of gold couldn't buy another breath if he got sick. We can't lose him, too.

As the miles fall away, so does Māma's happy tourist attitude. Maybe it's because she doesn't have any friends who live this far west. Or maybe she's afraid that being too happy will make the gods angry. Or maybe she's actually worried about how she and Bàba will find jobs and make money. Only Bàba stays cheerful. He tells Māma we are on our very own "journey to the west," like in the ancient Chinese novel.

I say goodbye to July from the back seat of the car, my head resting against the stack of boxes, and wake up to August in a parking lot. It's the middle of the night. Yellow light from the lampposts streams through the windshield, and the car engine ticks softly, like an old clock winding down. Māma and Gōnggong are still asleep, but the driver's seat is empty.

Bàba stands in front of a small building, staring through the large glass windows. I get out of the car and stretch, then walk toward him, my footsteps crunching on the gravel. He turns and smiles as I approach. He points, and I follow the path of his hand to a sign in the window. HELP WANTED, it says in large red letters printed on a white background. Below, in black marker, someone has scrawled *Pastry Chef*. I take a step back and look up at the building. A wooden panel hangs above the door, the words REDBUD CAFÉ painted in cursive with a flowering tree carved above them.

I turn back to Bàba. "You want to work here?" I ask.

He nods enthusiastically. "Three signs," he says. I must look confused, because he holds up a finger. "First sign: They need a baker. I know how to do this job." He smiles again, holding up a second finger. "Second sign:

Name of café has 'red' in it. This is the luckiest color."

He's seeing extra meaning in the name of the restaurant, just like Third Aunt did in my story. Look where that got us.

But Bàba doesn't notice my frown. He holds up three fingers. "Third sign: moon." Startled, I look up and realize that streetlights aren't making the parking lot glow—it's the moon. It seems brighter out here in the countryside than back home in Boston. Bàba continues, "Full moon is a complete circle. It means that our journey is also complete."

I blink, trying to take it all in. "We're going to stop traveling? And live here?"

"Yes." Bàba's voice thrums with excitement. "Lan, I even found a house for us."

"A house?" I've never lived in a house before. Never had a yard. It seems like it would be lonely to have all that space separating each family.

"Yes," Bàba says again. "I drove all around this town while you were asleep. There is a house for rent. I saw the sign."

Bàba goes to wake up Māma so he can show her the three signs and convince her that this small town is our new home. I should be happy that we won't be guest people anymore. But the beetles scurry around and around in my stomach, upset and unsettled. Bàba said the house was a sign. That's a total of four signs. Four is the unluckiest number because the Mandarin word for it, sì, sounds the same as the word for death. I want to remind Bàba about that, but I don't.

While Māma exclaims over the full moon, I crawl back into the car. Bàba had called me Lan again. Just Lan. He hadn't even noticed, but I had. Somewhere on the dusty road between Boston and this unknown town, with the heat rising off the highway like a poisonous mist, my parents had started calling me Lan.

My parents have always called me Lánlán—repeating the second syllable of a child's name is a sign of affection in China. I feel a sharp ache inside, the bite of a hundred mandibles. We left Xing and Tiffi, the aunts and uncles, the bakery, Chinatown, and now—my childhood. Has my phoenix story changed the way my parents feel about me?

I look around at the dingy café, the dirt parking lot, the shuttered storefronts across the street. This is it, I guess. My fairy-tale ending.

Chapter Seven

The town is called Redbud, too, and we've officially lived here for a week. Māma and Bàba signed the landlord's papers, but it still feels like we're squatters in an abandoned house. It's going to take another week to get our furniture and the boxes holding the rest of our lives delivered from storage in Boston.

I can't wait for my stuff to get here. It's been worse than being guest people. At least my parents' friends' houses were homes, filled with their histories and memories. My room is on the first floor and is twice the size of my old room. All that empty space around my sleeping bag just makes it feel bigger, emptier, lonelier. I'm glad Gōnggong is in the bedroom next to mine. When I asked Bàba how we could afford such a large house, he smiled and said that Ohio didn't cost as much to live in as Massachusetts. I can see why—the town is super small, with only about a dozen shops on the main street. Chinatown might not have as much land as Redbud, but it has, like, five times the stores, restaurants, and people. And it's only a neighborhood of Boston, not a whole town by itself. How does Redbud survive? What is there for people to do?

I wonder who used to live in this house. Did another girl sleep in this room? There are two windows—one faces the street and the other looks out over the huge side yard. Did she stand here, like me, staring out at the yard, both scared and fascinated? It's not like I haven't been to lots of parks and gardens, but it's different when there's a huge empty space right outside my window. Especially at night, when I can't see anything. Anyone could be out there. Anyone could climb right in. Anyone like Gū Huò Niǎo, the bird demon. She shapeshifts into a beautiful woman and snatches children at night. Particularly girls, who then become bird demons just like her.

Tomorrow is the first day of school. I've never gone to a school where I know absolutely no one. I never expected to leave Boston. I thought our family would own Golden Phoenix Bakery forever, that Xing and I would run it together someday.

I go to the kitchen and grab a handful of uncooked rice grains from the giant bag on the floor. Back in my room, I raise the window and the screen and scatter the rice on the windowsill. The night air flows in and around me, whispering. I whisper back in Mandarin, "Gū Huò Niǎo, I'm here." I'd rather be a bird demon than stuck in a school full of strangers.

I wake to the sound of Māma making a fuss over the open window. It's still dark out. There is no bright light from the Golden Phoenix sign like there was in my old room. The nights here are filled with strange sounds, strange creatures hidden in the thick grass and twisting branches. But no Gū Huò Niǎo.

"Jié zú xiān dēng," Māma chirps. Another one of her Chinese proverbs. Something about victory and a foot being the first to climb. My feet are nice and toasty inside my sleeping bag. I groan and zip up further.

"Did you forget, Lan? Today is first day of school. We have to meet the principal soon." She's speaking English now. I'm glad she's practicing—she won't be able to speak Mandarin for any job in Redbud. And she needs a job, not just for the money, but also so I can get some time to myself again.

"Soon isn't for hours." I try not to sound whiny and fail.

"Come," she says briskly. "I will go make breakfast."

She gives the top of the sleeping bag a tug, but it doesn't budge. Māma frowns, and then her face softens. She smooths the hair away from my forehead. "Come," she says again. "Rise up. Maybe you understand this one better, since it is from the US, like you. Zǎo qǐ de niǎo'ér yǒu chóng chī."

"Yeah, yeah." I roll out of the bag and jam my feet into slippers. "Early bird. Worm. Got it."

I get ready, putting on black chinos and a floral top, the only clothes I brought that aren't faded jeans, leggings, or oversized T-shirts. I don't think I can stand hearing a third Chinese proverb from Māma this morning. The outfit doesn't go with my Dr. Martens, but by the time I put those on, it'll be too late for Māma to say anything. When I sit down to breakfast, she raises her eyebrows at my outfit and actually nods in approval. Mission accomplished.

"Gōnggong zǎo," I say, a little surprised that my grandfather is up and out of his room. The last few days, I'd heard him toss and turn on his makeshift bed of spare blankets, trying to get comfortable. He must have gotten better sleep last night, because he smiles and urges me to help myself to the food.

Māma has gone all out—in addition to the zhōu, she's

laid a variety of toppings and side dishes on the table for us. She must have brought all these ingredients with us in the car—there's no way the one tiny grocery store in Redbud would carry any of it. I put some salted peanuts, pork floss, and pickled vegetables in my rice porridge. I can only hope that the rest of the day goes as well.

Principal Reynard's office is not what I expected. Thick sheaves of paper are shoved into manila folders and stacked on his desk in messy piles nearly a foot high. Their sharp corners jut out like the yellow teeth of ancient beasts. Rolled-up posters are tossed in a corner like the long bones of the beasts' prey, gnawed clean. The windowsill behind his desk is crowded with mugs, trinkets, and plastic toys. Gifts from adoring students or bribes meant to appease an angry god, I wonder.

Principal Xu at my old school, An Wang Middle School, kept only a pot of lucky bamboo and a miniature Japanese rock garden on her windowsill. She let students use the tiny rake on the bed of white sand to draw ripples around the rocks and make it look like water. It calmed the kids down, she told me once, and then she could show them how actions created consequences— like a rock dropped into a pond.

Principal Reynard clears off a small square table in the corner next to the door. "Please, have a seat," he says. His voice is just as fake-cheerful as Māma's this morning. "Thank you so much for coming in early. Did you bring all the forms like we talked about over the phone?"

Māma pulls the papers out of her bag and sets them on the table. She clears her throat and speaks carefully. "Yes, they are all here. I also brought transcript from her old school. As you can see, she is very good student."

I wince. Why does Māma always have to suck up to white people? At the bakery, she was always telling the white tourists how they were so smart to choose that pastry, that they must be rich to be on vacation, or that she liked their hair or tie or shoes. I know she was trying to get them to buy more, but it was still so embarrassing. Besides, she's not selling pastries now, she's selling *me*. And confirming what people always think about Chinese parents—that all they care about is grades.

The principal nods, a lock of his reddish hair falling onto his forehead. He sweeps it back with one hand until it lies sleekly against his head. His hand travels down to stroke the goatee sprouting from his long chin. He glances at the form on top of the pile and then looks directly at me for the first time. His eyes are such a strange color—more orange than honey, like the amber beads on Māma's bracelet. "So, you must be Meilan." He stumbles over my name a little, pronouncing it MY-Lann. He draws out the second syllable in a nasal whine.

I almost say no. *Nope, that's not my name, you've got the wrong person, we're going back to Boston now, thank-you-very-much. There's been some huge mistake. I'll just grab my transcript and leave.* I wouldn't even be missing any school back home—classes at An Wang don't start for another two weeks. Māma catches my eye, so I quiet my inner me and nod at Principal Reynard. "Yes, sir."

I don't know where the *sir* came from; Ohio's not really that far south, but the principal looks like someone who wants to be called *sir*, and it just pops out. "It's actually May-LAHN, though." If I have to go to a school in the middle of nowhere, at least they can pronounce my name right.

Māma shakes her head the tiniest bit. Another one of her favorite sayings is: "People have faces just like trees have bark." So I'm not supposed to correct people, especially adults, because it hurts them like stripping the bark off trees. Hurt people will get a bad impression of me and then think badly of our whole family, which according to Māma is a fate worse than death. But all I'm

doing is telling someone how to say my name. How i.
that wrong?

Principal Reynard smiles widely, incredulously. His
canines are sharp and glisten slightly. His red hair, the
amber eyes, the beard, the long nose—it all reminds me
of the Chinese folktales about crafty and devious fox
spirits that can take on human forms during the day.
"Mulan?" he says. "Like the Disney movie?"

Sigh. Like I haven't heard that one a million times.
"No, sir. MAY-lahn, not MOO-lahn." I leave out the
tones, the rising and falling pitch of each syllable. Cor-
recting his pronunciation is bad enough in Māma's eyes.

"Well, now, that's . . ." Principal Reynard pauses, his
lips pressed together. "An *unusual* name. Your last name
is also rather unusual, isn't it? H-U-A." He spells it out
slowly for us, as though we don't know. "How do you
pronounce it? Hoo-ay?"

"Hwah," Māma says. "It means flower."

"Well, now," he says again. "That's nice."

He pins me with a steely stare; his eyelashes are red-
orange, framing his amber eyes in a glowing fringe. The
more I look at him, the more he resembles a fox. But is
he the good kind of fox spirit, or the kind that deceives
and tricks people? I'm not sure. Everything seems a little

ver since I stepped inside the school, a thin gray
s been creeping over everything, like someone is
y sliding a silk veil the color of smoke over my face.
ıb my eyes briefly and open them to find Principal
.eynard still inspecting me like a bug.

"Do you have any nicknames?" he asks.

What does that have to do with anything? I shake my head. "Everybody calls me Meilan." I don't mention that I used to have a family nickname but I lost it somewhere on the road.

"I see," Principal Reynard says. He makes a big show of rubbing the side of his nose thoughtfully. "Well, I'm just worried that kids here are going to tease you because of your unusual name." If he says "unusual" one more time, I'm going to scream. His fox-demon eyes and face are definitely stranger than my name. "You're coming in for seventh grade, smack dab in the middle of middle school." He smiles at his own wit. "Kids here have already formed their social groups. I don't want you to start off on the wrong foot by making them think you're a Disney princess."

"I won't tell them I'm a Disney princess," I say. "Besides, Mulan wasn't a princess—she was a warrior." We stare at each other for a long moment. Next to me,

Māma shifts in her chair, and the corner of her purse pokes me. My inner warrior shrinks, and I drop my gaze to the desk. "I don't mind if people call me Mulan."

Some of the iron in Principal Reynard's eyes leaks into his voice. "Regardless," he says, "I think it'd be better for everyone if we introduced you as Melanie instead." He smiles at Māma. "All right, Mrs. Hoo-ay? I really do think it will help *Melanie's* adjustment to Clifton Middle School."

My mother looks like she's about to fail an important test. She glances at me, then at Principal Reynard, then at the purse in her lap. "Meh-lah-nee?" She sounds out each syllable, her voice rising on the last syllable. The way she says it makes it sound like ní, the Mandarin word for dirt.

"Don't you think that's a beautiful name? I have a cousin named Melanie. And it sounds so similar to Meilan—just a little bit more . . . American." He clears his throat. "You know, names are very important. They can influence who gets into the top colleges, selected for the most impressive scholarships, even hired for the best jobs."

Oh, he's good. What parent doesn't want their kid to be "top," "best," and "most impressive?" Māma's face

She's sold. The two of them nod at each other,
principal flashes his sharp teeth.

all stand up. I get up too quickly, and my head
s. There's a sound like tearing silk, and for a moment
m afraid that my pants have split. I quickly run my arm
over my bottom like I'm smoothing out a skirt, relieved
to find that my pants are fine. Still, I'm a little disoriented.
I've just lost another name. First my family nickname,
now my real name. I look over at Māma. She'd been
wrong this morning. I'm not the bird; I'm the worm.

Chapter Eight

We follow Principal Reynard out to the main reception desk, where Mrs. Perry, the school secretary, sits. Māma and I stand awkwardly to one side while he thrusts my folder of forms at her. There's a boy about my age sitting in front of the desk, staring at Mrs. Perry unhappily. He looks over at me, his eyes traveling from my face down to my red boots, and his eyebrows raise all the way up under his blonde hair. Great. I'm clearly going to be the odd new girl. I must grimace or something, because his eyes widen. His green eyes. Does everyone here have eyes that aren't a normal shade of brown? Quickly, I relax all my face muscles so I have no expression at all.

Mr. Reynard clears his throat, and Mrs. Perry says to the boy, "Hold on just a minute, Logan." She takes the folder from the principal and looks through the forms, filled out in Māma's spiky handwriting. She glances at me, then up at him. "How do you pronounce her name?" she whispers.

He shrugs. "Just put down Melanie in the database. We agreed that it would be better if she had an American name." The principal makes no effort to lower his voice.

No, I want to shout. We did not agree. And my name *is* American. It's as American as Mr. Reynard's first name, whatever it is. And as American as Mrs. Perry's first name, which the sign on her desk says is Susan. Both their names came from other countries originally. But because they were probably European countries, and Europeans founded the United States, their names are considered American, while mine isn't.

Māma must sense that I'm about to argue, because she grips my arm, hard. If I speak up, I'll be stripping bark off her tree, too. I think of Chén Shūshu and Lǐ Shūshu and remind myself to be a dutiful and respectful daughter. I hold it all in, watching carefully, though, as Logan's eyes get a little wider, a little sharper.

Now I'm the odd new girl with such a strange name that the principal had to give me a new one so I'd have a tiny chance of fitting in with the other students. If this Logan boy tells all the other kids, that tiny chance will drop to zero.

Mr. Reynard is definitely a fox demon. Only a fox demon would be that devious, that crafty, to make me suffer while everyone believes that he's helping me. He saunters over to Māma. "Don't worry, Melanie is in good hands. Mrs. Perry here will set her up with a class schedule. I'm sure you have a lot of unpacking to do." His voice is dismissive. He shakes her hand briefly and retreats into his cluttered den.

"I'm fine," I say to Māma before she can come up with another inspirational Chinese saying. Māma squeezes my arm, more gently this time, and leaves.

I can feel the boy's eyes on me, but I deliberately avoid looking back at him. I stare at the industrial gray carpet under the secretary's navy-blue heels instead.

Mrs. Perry types a few things on her keyboard and clicks around with the mouse. I look up in time to see her shake her head. "I'm so sorry, Logan, but the Shale Team is full," she says. "The other students already have their schedules, and it wouldn't be fair to impose last-minute changes on anyone just to accommodate your desire to switch."

The boy slumps in his chair. The secretary gives him a little pat on the arm. "It's going to be okay, honey. It's only seventh grade. It's just a year, not forever. It will pass." I can tell Logan doesn't believe her, but he straightens up and tries to give her a smile. She smiles back at him. "Could you do me a favor? Could you take Melanie around today? She's new, and she actually has the same schedule as you."

They both turn to me, and with a shock, I realize that I'm the one Mrs. Perry is talking about. I'm Melanie now. And I'm stuck with this Logan boy who already thinks I'm weird.

The secretary hands me my schedule. "You're on the Chalk Team, same as Logan."

"Hi," I finally say.

Logan smiles again, and this time it doesn't look forced. Or am I imagining it? "Hi. Welcome to the Cliff."

"Logan Batchelder!" Mrs. Perry chides in an amused way.

"The Cliff?"

"Clifton Middle School—the Cliff. Where we live life on the edge." He shoulders a backpack and leads me down the hall. "Just be careful that you don't fall off!"

I have no idea what to make of this. Is he saying that I'm in danger? Or that all the students here are edgy and hip and I'm clearly not? I look down at my mom-approved outfit and sigh. Whatever he means, it doesn't sound good. I already feel like the earth beneath my feet is crumbling away.

Chapter Nine

The morning passes by in a blur. Logan walks me to my—our—first class, which my printed schedule says is Health. We don't talk on the way; he still seems upset by Mrs. Perry's refusing to switch him to another team. He introduces me to the teacher, Mrs. Shaughnessy, and tells her that my name is Melanie. I feel like I'm wearing another person's skin.

If Mr. Reynard is a fox demon, Mrs. Shaughnessy is a snake sprite, from the skintight ankle-length green dress she's wearing to the way she draws out the s's in her name. Her platinum-blond hair is pulled back into a bun so tightly that her cheekbones jut out. She reveals her evil nature by making me stand in front of the class while she questions me.

"Where are you from, Melanie?" she asks.

"Boston," I say, keeping my side turned toward the class so I don't have to look at them head-on. Logan sits down at the end of the front row and nods at me. I think he's trying to be encouraging. I can feel everyone else's stares. They must not get many new kids here.

Mrs. Shaughnessy raises her over-plucked, penciled eyebrows. "Massachusetts!" she says, overemphasizing all the s's again. "My, that's a long way away. What brings you to Ohio?"

I hesitate. What's the right answer? A bedtime story gone wrong? Bàba's three—no, four—signs? "Fate, I guess."

The teacher snorts, which startles me. "Fate! What a strange thing to say! You're certainly an odd one, aren't you?"

I have no answer for that. After a moment, she says, "Well, I think your family will like Redbud. We do grow excellent soybeans." The class snickers, and I feel my face flush. When Mrs. Shaughnessy points to an empty seat behind Logan, I sink into it and swing my hair so it covers most of my face.

I tune out while the teacher drones on about what we'll be learning this year and her expectations for us. In front of me, the collar of Logan's blue T-shirt rides up as he slouches in his chair. His hair has a little bit of a wave to it, like it would be curly if he let it grow a little longer.

I've always liked the name Logan. It reminds me of

the fruit that Mrs. Yao, the grocer, sells on tables on the sidewalk during the summer. Lóngyǎn. The small, round fruit with a shiny large black seed peeking through the creamy white flesh. The Mandarin name means dragon eyes, which sounds so poetic. When I was little, I would hold a fruit up to each eye and run around, roaring.

A dragon's piercing, powerful eyes would be very helpful right now. They could reveal which students are friendly, or which teachers are truly sprites or demons. Instead, the smoky veil over my eyes from earlier doesn't go away. All I can make out when I glance around the room is that there are no other Asian students. There aren't any brown or Black students, either. Is that why they call it the Chalk Team, because it was all white before I came along? Is the other seventh grade team like this? I've gone to Chinatown schools all my life, surrounded by Asian, Black, and brown faces. There were white kids, too, but not many. I never imagined there could still be classes like this one, where I'm one drop of paint on a white canvas.

When class ends, I wait until the other kids have rushed out the door before following. There are two Logans in the doorway. The one on the right is wearing blue, and the one on the left is in a green shirt with a tractor logo on it. I must look confused, because Blue Logan smiles tightly. Green Logan leans against the doorframe, with his arms crossed, staring at my feet. Does no one wear Dr. Martens in this town?

"This is my brother, Liam," Blue Logan says. "And yes, we're identical twins."

"Hi," I say to Liam.

"You're our new neighbor, huh?" Liam shoots a look at Logan. There's some kind of weird vibe between the two that I can't figure out.

I try to wrap my head around what Liam just said. "We're neighbors?"

Logan says, "We live in the house next to you. Our backyards touch. Or, I guess, it's really your side yard."

Our new house is on the corner of Wilson and Horace Streets, with the front door facing Wilson Street. There's a lawn around the whole house, but the largest yard is on the north side, next to my new bedroom window. "The one with the giant tree in the back?" That house is turned ninety degrees away from mine, with the front door on a different street. Bryant Street, I think it's called.

Logan nods, but before he can say anything, Liam asks, "Have you seen Old Mr. Shellhaus yet?"

"Ignore him." Logan glares at his brother.

I shake my head. "I don't know who that is."

"Didn't the lady who rented you the house tell you?" Liam smirks. "Old Mr. Shellhaus used to live there. Now his ghost does. Dropped dead right in the living room. No one knows what made him keel over."

"What?"

"You heard me," Liam says. "Your house is haunted. No one stays longer than a couple of months. That's why you got it so cheap."

"There's no ghost. He's just being superstitious. People leave because Redbud is boring." Logan tries to reassure me.

"*I'm* superstitious?" Liam retorts. "You're the one wearing your 'lucky shirt.'"

Logan's cheeks turn pink. "Come on." He motions me through the door. "I'm supposed to take you to your classes. We're going to be late for Social Studies."

Numbly, I follow him down the hall. A tall older Black boy passes by and acknowledges me with a brief what's-up nod, but I'm too distracted to ask Logan who he is. First a fox demon, then a snake sprite, and now a ghost. Bàba didn't know how right he was. We've stepped into a Chinese fairy-tale world.

Chapter Ten

In Social Studies, Ms. Brown smiles and says, "Welcome, Melanie!" She tells me to pick any seat I want. It's the strangest feeling. I have to resist the urge to turn around to see if there's some other girl behind me. The real Melanie. I don't even know how to be a Melanie. It feels like a distorted version of myself, one seen in a wavy antique mirror where the silver paint on the back has worn away in spots. According to Mr. Reynard, Melanie is the Redbud version of myself. The Ohio version. The acceptable version.

Quickly, I scan the faces of the other kids before choosing a seat in the back row next to the window. I'm pretty sure that most of them are the same ones from Health class last period, but they still stare as I walk past. This must be what it was like for the peanut mochi and steamed white radish cakes we used to sell in the bakery, stared at by non-Chinese tourists as something unknown and strange. Well, to me, in this land of farms and fields, all these kids look like white corn.

Mr. Lewis is the English teacher for third period. He hands out the first book we'll be studying. It's one of his favorites, he says. *A Wizard of Earthsea* by Ursula K. Le Guin. I study the cover, and it makes me nervous. There's a drawing of a large hawk, wings outstretched, talons ready to grab and slash. If I squint, it could be an angry fènghuáng. I haven't read or made up a story since that awful night. What will happen when I read this one?

Xing would probably tell me to not bother reading and just look up what it's about online. Thinking about Xing makes me tear up. I rub my eyes—the last thing I want to do is cry on my first day as the new girl. Being an outsider is temporary; being an outcast could be a life sentence. When I take my hand away from my eyes, though, the slight gray haze that's following me has thickened. Everything looks a little cloudier, a little blurrier around the edges. Māma always says that constant reading will ruin my eyesight. But then she turns around and tells me to study harder.

The haziness gets worse when I step inside the cafeteria. A kid in a blue shirt waves to me from the lunch line. Logan. It's probably part of his "buddy" duties to sit with me. I hold up my lunch bag and shake my head, letting him off the hook. Anyway, I don't want to sit with him if Liam is going to be there, teasing me about my house being haunted.

I scan the room, but all the voices crash against the inside of my head like a tsunami, threatening to swamp me.

It's not any different from An Wang's cafeteria, I scold myself. I am not some fragile flower; I can be Mulan, the warrior. But I'm not wearing any armor, not even the thin protection my real name gives me. I am a new-made creature, this Melanie, half this and half that, half here and half nowhere at all.

My eyes come to rest on a small group of brown faces. There are exactly five of them. If I mustered the courage to join their table, I'd be the only Asian kid.

I turn away and try to find the library, my favorite spot in any school. There's something so cozy and comforting about being surrounded by books. Now that the bakery has been sold, maybe I'll be a librarian someday, not that I'd ever tell my parents that.

Down another hall, I spot a door with a small sign that reads COURTYARD. I push through the door into a small sunlit space, maybe thirty feet square, bursting with life. Small trees crowd three of the corners, with a lopsided wooden shed in the fourth. Sunflowers crane their faces skyward against one wall, while vines dotted with small white flowers scramble merrily up a trellis against another wall. There are flowers carpeting the ground, too—marigolds and geraniums and purple flowers I don't recognize. A small brick path winds through the space and disappears under the shade from one of the trees. I can't resist, my feet moving as though I've been possessed by a spirit myself. It's as if the vivid colors of the flowers and leaves are burning through the veil that has been clouding my sight. I take a deep breath and feel my shoulders relax.

The path ends at a small stone bench under a maple tree. Dragonflies are carved onto the bench's legs and the words "All the flowers of all the tomorrows are in the seeds of today. —Chinese Proverb" are carved onto the seat. Sigh. Māma's sayings have found me even here. I sit down anyway and open my lunch bag. At least this proverb sounds hopeful.

I eat my fried rice cold, chewing slowly and looking at all the plants. The vines are peas, I realize, spotting a few pods hanging from the tendrils. I bet no one here knows that the tender leaves taste even better than the pods, especially when stir-fried with garlic. I can see desks and chairs through some of the windows set into the walls, and I hope one of my afternoon classes overlooks this lush garden.

Sitting there in the shade, I'm reminded of the small squares and tiny courtyards tucked away all through the Boston neighborhoods, with mossy cobblestones, worn bricks, and less charming memorials to dead old white men. I look up through the tree's branches to the impossibly clear blue sky beyond. I tell myself that the wetness on my face is from magical dewdrops sliding off the leaves above me. I tell myself that they're not tears.

Chapter Eleven

I'm relieved when it's finally Friday. After dinner, I go back to my room, shuddering when I pass the doorway opposite mine. So far, I haven't seen the ghost of Mr. Shellhaus, but a chill sweeps through me every time I have to cross the living room. I'm never going in there at night if I can help it.

I hear Bàba's slippered footsteps travel down the hall, and then he knocks on my door. The sound echoes eerily around my empty room.

"Come in," I call out.

He's carrying a small blue plastic bucket. It's the kind of bucket little kids use at the beach when they're making sandcastles. I had a red one with a white plastic handle and a matching white shovel. I didn't use it to hold sand, though. My favorite activity was to wade out at low tide and collect hermit crabs. Xing and I used to see who could get the most, and then we'd have a wild race where we'd dump them all out onto the sand and watch them scramble their way back to the ocean, going in circles and fighting, their miniature pincers held up like boxers' fists.

Bàba clears his throat, and I blink, returning to my room. There's nowhere to sit, so he leans against the radiator. "I bought a fishing rod for Gōnggong today," he says. "The store owner says there is a small pond near us that he can fish in."

"That's nice," I say cautiously, eyeing the bucket in his hand. Does he think the town pond will be the same as a beach on the Cape? Because it won't—not by any stretch of my imagination. Besides, I haven't played in the sand for ages.

He holds the blue bucket out to me. "Tomorrow is Saturday. I have to bake pies tonight to bring to the café early tomorrow morning." He pauses. "Many different pies."

When he doesn't continue, I try not to sigh. Māma is better about saying what she means, even if it's usually in the form of confusing Chinese sayings. Bàba takes forever, circling around and around like a marble in a drain until he finally spirals into the center and makes his point. Most of the time I can guess what he wants and cut the whole process short, but tonight I'm stumped.

Still, I try. "You want me to keep him company at the pond? The bucket is for if he catches something?"

"Yes, that is part of it," Bàba says, "But this bucket is too small to bring home much fish." He shakes the bucket at me, so I give in and take it.

"If it's too small to bring fish home, what's it for?"

"Bait."

"Bait?" I've read the word before and know what it means, but I don't actually know what it *is*. Or what it has to do with me.

Bàba nods. "Gōnggong needs bait to catch fish. Fish like to eat worms. Right now it is raining."

I'm lost again. "What does rain have to do with it?"

"Rain makes the ground wet—hard for worms to breathe. Rainy night is the best time to catch worms."

He can't really mean what I think, can he? "You want me to go outside in the rain, in the dark, and catch worms for Gōnggong to use as bait for fishing?"

"Yes, yes," Bàba says impatiently. "This is what I said already."

"But what about tornadoes? They start with thunderstorms. My teacher says that there are a lot of tornadoes in Ohio. We're even having a tornado drill at school next week."

Bàba frowns. "No thunder now. So no tornado. This is just regular rain. You will be fine."

"And I have to do this because—"

"Many pies," Bàba says, and he strides out of the room.

Ten minutes later, I find myself in the backyard, holding the blue bucket in one hand and a flashlight in the other. The rain doesn't bother me—it rains all the time in Boston—but the darkness is suffocating. Back home, there are so many lights in the city that you can always see where you're going, even at midnight. Here, the closest streetlight is so far away that its dim yellow glow doesn't reach our yard.

I shine the flashlight at the giant tree behind the Batchelder twins' house. It's so huge that half the branches hang over the fence onto our side. Trees don't care about boundaries. In the dark, the branches look like the tentacles of a giant kraken reaching out to drag me under the waves. I want to run back into the house, but I have to obey Bàba's orders.

Beaming the light down at my feet almost makes me scream. There, nearly touching my sneaker, is the longest, fattest, grossest earthworm in the world. It's so big I can see the ridges along its sides, and the pointy head looks like a snout. It just lies there, and I can't tell if it's dazed from being in the waterlogged ground, or just waiting to leap up and wind around my arm like a snake. Quickly, I grab it with my thumb and forefinger. The moment I touch it, both ends flail around, curling up and around my hand. It's wet and slimy and muddy and both ends are pointy so I can't tell which is the head and which is the tail and it won't stop wriggling so I fling its bloated body into the bucket.

The beetles in my stomach are scurrying, churning, pushing, making me gag. Twenty worms, Bàba said. Tears spring to my eyes when I realize I have to catch nineteen more of these disgusting things.

It's for Gōnggong, I tell myself. Fishing will make Gōnggong happy and that will make Bàba and Māma happy and that means I'll have been a good daughter. I spot another worm between the blades of wet grass and snatch it up, tossing it into the bucket. And then another and another, my chest heaving, rain and tears running down my face.

I'm on worm number fifteen when I hear a voice.

Chapter Twelve

I'm back in my room before I even realize that I ran. I stare out the window at the spot where the giant tree looms, hidden by the night. The blue bucket sits on the back step, five worms short of my assigned goal. I don't care. I'm not going back out there.

"Lan, what are you doing in the dark?" Māma appears beside me. She reaches up to smooth my hair and pulls her hand back. "Oh! You are still wet! You cannot go to bed with wet hair," she chides in Mandarin. "You will get sick that way."

She leaves, quickly returns with a towel, and briskly rubs my head with it. She glances out the window. "You always loved the rain, ever since you were a little girl. You even wanted to wear your rain boots to bed."

I remember. My boots were red even then, but with Hello Kitty over the toes. I used to jump off the curb and splash into the water streaming through the gutter, dodging paper chopstick wrappers, bits of limp vegetables, and toothpicks as they swirled toward the storm drains. At night, I'd lie awake, listening to the soothing plink of raindrops on the metal awning over the bakery below. In the morning, the syrupy, sweet smell of egg custard and steamed sugar cake mingled with the fresh scent of clean sidewalk cement.

Here, it smells like dirt and worms and things decaying under wet leaves. Suddenly, I hate the rain. I hate the yard and all the worms drowning in it. I hate this tiny town, and most of all, I hate myself for being the reason we're here.

I pull away from Māma and yank down the window shade. "Don't bother," I say, grabbing the towel out of her hands. "I still have to take a shower. I'm just going to get wet again."

Māma presses her lips together but doesn't say anything. She turns and leaves the room, her slippers shushing down the hall.

Why did she have to bring up the past? Since we arrived in Redbud, we've all been so careful not to talk about the bakery, my uncles and aunts, or Năinai—it's an unspoken rule. Memories and family stories are like rocks. Not the kind worn smooth by time and waves, but the heavy, sharp-edged kind that cut you when you dig them up.

Later, zipped into my sleeping bag on the floor, I let myself think about what had happened in the backyard. Someone—or something—had called my name. Not "Lan," the short, crisp version that my family now uses. It was my full Chinese name that floated between the raindrops, in a voice as haunting and sweet as the moon. Huā Měilán. Flower. Beautiful Orchid.

Was it a ghost? Liam said that the ghost of Mr. Shellhaus haunts my house. Maybe he also haunts the yard? But how would he know my real name? And in Mandarin, no less. It couldn't be Mr. Shellhaus. Did one of the twins hide in the tree to scare me? That doesn't make sense—neither of them knew I was going to be in the yard, and anyway, they think my name is Melanie. The voice had come from the giant tree in Logan and Liam's backyard. Besides me, there are only three people in Redbud who know my full name and how to pronounce it in Mandarin. All three of them were inside the house when I heard it.

I conjure up images of all the times I've looked at the tree, both at night and during the day. It doesn't look like a kraken. The tree is more like a Chinese dragon, ancient and scaly-barked, with pronged branches for horns and claws, and twisting roots for a tail.

Gōnggong once told me about shùjīng, spirits who inhabit the thick trunks of old trees; shùjīng are the reason big trees must never be cut down. I get up and raise the window shade. The half moon hangs in the sky behind a scrim of clouds. In the dim moonlight, I can just make out the tree's trunk. It's as wide as a car—a perfect home for a tree spirit. The leaves dance in the rain like hundreds of rippling dragon scales.

A tree spirit called out to me, in a woman's voice. I lie back down and ponder what this could mean. Why does she know my true name? What does she want with me? I wonder if tree spirits are good or evil. Gōnggong never said, and many creatures in the old Chinese tales can be one or the other, or a mixture, just like humans.

But Chinese dragons are like gods, revered as wise protectors. A tree spirit living in a dragon tree must be good. I cringe. Maybe she's calling my name because she knows I'm not good anymore. I'm not the graceful and rare flower that I'm named after. Beautiful Orchid doesn't exist anymore. Who am I now? I'm Lan, Destroyer of Families, the one who plucked away the petals of the Hua Family and cast them onto the wind.

I hope the tree spirit isn't angry that I ran away. I hope she greeted me because she knows I could use her protection and advice. I hope she can show me a way to get back home.

Chapter Thirteen

It's Saturday morning, bright and early. Māma would be happy—I'm such an early bird that I already caught a bunch of worms last night. My body still thinks there's school today, but, for once, I don't mind waking up early. I've been meaning to call Xing. We haven't talked at all since I left Boston, and part of me is worried that she'll be mad. Even though she hasn't called me, either. I thought she would. As we drove west, the time difference increased until Boston was an hour ahead of us, and the miles between me and Xing increased from zero to over eight hundred. I could feel the ribbon of friendship connecting us stretching thinner and thinner as we drove farther and farther away.

I reach for my cell phone, and my hand smacks the wood floor before I remember that I'm lying in a sleeping bag. My bed hasn't arrived yet. Or the little table that usually sits beside my bed. Even if I had furniture, it wouldn't help, because Bàba made me give up my cell phone before we moved. He and Māma said it cost too much and they didn't need to be able to reach me all the time anymore because the countryside was safer than the city. I had my doubts about their safety reason. Did they not watch the news? Bad things happened in rural areas, too. But I didn't say anything. The beetles had climbed into my throat, clogging up my ability to speak. Plus, I knew it was more about money.

The house is quiet, and I don't hear any movement in the kitchen. Maybe everyone is sleeping in—a luxury they never had with our bakery.

Scooting out of the sleeping bag, I pad silently to the phone in the kitchen. The room is empty except for a half-full coffee cup in the sink. Bàba must have already gone off to deliver his pies for the Saturday morning crowd at the café. Good. No one around to hear me. The dull beige phone isn't even cordless. I dial Xing's number by heart and sit cross-legged on the floor, my back against the faded wallpaper. I feel a moment of panic—what am I going to tell her about Redbud? There's nothing fun or interesting to say.

"Hello?" Her voice is so familiar that I almost break into tears. Xing sounds breathless, like she's been running up the stairs.

"It's me," I say, "how are you?"

There's a pause. Has she already forgotten my voice? "Meilan! Is that you? Oh my god, where are you?"

"Some tiny town called Redbud. In Ohio. Bàba got a job and we rented a house." I don't give her any more details. I don't want her to feel sorry for me. I just want things to be the same as they always were.

"Ohio! Whoa, I'm not even sure where that is." Xing laughs. "Hey, I'm sorry, but I can't talk—I'm on my way to dance class."

"Dance class? But it's Saturday, not Sunday. Did you stop taking Lín Lǎoshī's class after Chinese school?" We'd both taken Mrs. Lin's dance elective since we started Chinese school years ago.

"No, I'm still in her class. I started taking classes up at the Woburn Chinese Folk Arts studio. It's totally awesome—we have a bunch of performances lined up for Lunar New Year already, and the costumes are gorgeous!"

"Wow, that's fantastic," I say half-heartedly. Xing and I had begged our parents to let us take classes at the Folk Arts studio, but it was a long drive away and they had to work at the bakery all day on Saturdays. They had to work all day Sundays, too, but Chinese school was just around the corner, so we could walk there ourselves. I wonder if Tiffi started going to Chinese school this year. Did Xing walk with her now?

"Isn't it?" Xing crows. "Hey, I have so much to tell you. I wish you still had a cell phone. I didn't know how to reach you when you were on the road. I've been super busy with dance, and I started piano lessons, too. Plus, I just got back from a sleepaway camp for Chinese kids."

"Your mom let you go to sleepaway camp?"

"I know, right?" Xing laughs again. "But the camp was just outside Boston, and the fact that it was on a college campus didn't hurt. I'm sure she hoped it would make me try harder to get better grades and go to a good school."

My brain whirls. Extra dance classes, piano lessons, and now summer camp. Xing's life is a blur of happy activity, while mine is . . . What is my life? I don't know anymore. Catching worms, worrying about ghosts and demons, surviving school. Just waiting it out until someone forgives me and we can go back home.

I blurt, "I can't believe you're so busy!" I try to sound pleased for her but sound desperate and jealous instead. I change the subject. "How is the bakery?"

"I don't know," Xing says. "I mean, it's still there."

It's not the answer I expect. "Are the new owners taking care of it? Do they have a lot of customers? Do they give you the day-old stuff for Old Yang and Nàonào?" I miss the rush of people, the hustle and bustle of weekends, helping in the kitchen and the front counter, the stories and lives of our neighbors. I miss being part of a community that understands me.

"Ugh," Xing says. "No, and I don't care if I never see Old Yang's stinky mutt again. Honestly, I'm glad we sold the bakery. My mom and dad are so much happier now. Dad's taking classes to become a physician assistant, and Mom found a job at some lawyer's office. It's awesome because they have weekends free." Her voice changes abruptly, becomes harder. "I can't believe Big Uncle kept the money from us all this time. Nǎinai always said I was the graceful one. Just think how much better I'd be at dance if Big Uncle had actually shared the money with us years ago. Nǎinai would've loved watching me perform!"

Big Uncle? Her Big Uncle is my Bàba, who pinched pennies wherever he could. "What do you mean, 'kept the money?' There was never any money to spare, I keep telling you that." The kitchen is suddenly too hot. "You can't believe Third Aunt's nonsense about the hidden treasure!" There's a sound from upstairs, and I curse myself for forgetting to keep my voice down.

"Listen, my dad says that the bakery didn't sell for that much. So where's all the money coming from? It must've been some hidden stash. Your dad probably didn't want to admit that he's been stealing money for years, probably so he can pay for some fancy college for his brainy daughter." Her voice is icy.

"That's ridiculous." My voice shakes. "Bàba is . . . he is . . . an honorable man. He would never do that." Snippets of arguments between my parents and grandfather click into place. Gōnggong talking about yíchǎn, which I later discovered means inheritance.

I struggle to remember what happened to the bakery after Nǎinai died. Gōnggong wanted his children to keep running it, so he made them all equal owners. But he was still part owner of the bakery, too. He must have given his share of the money from the bakery sale to his children. It would be just like Gōnggong to give them their inheritance before he died. That's where the extra money came from. That's why my parents are even more worried about money now. Because even though Gōnggong doesn't eat very much, my parents have another person to take care of and feed. And now, Bàba is the only one with a job.

I try to explain this, but Xing doesn't want to hear it. "Whatever," she snaps. "I gotta go." And she hangs up.

The dial tone blares in my ear until I set the phone back in the cradle gently, as though it might break. But what's really broken is my heart.

I dash to my room and dive into the nook between the radiator and the wall, out of sight of the door. The fins of the radiator are warm against my side, and I close my eyes for a moment, pretending that I'm in the utility closet, the heat of the pipes blanketing me and Xing. I want that back. I want my cousin and best friend back. I want my whole family back. I want my life back the way it used to be.

Chapter Fourteen

Bàba's voice sounds like it is coming from a great distance, muffled by trees, drowned out by the rain. I half listen to his voice fading in and out, getting softer and louder and softer again, like he's going up and down the hills of the island of Gont.

"Lan? Where are you?" he calls. "Are you outside, Lan?"

A screen door slams like the sound of powerful jaws snapping shut. Startled, I look up and slip a bookmark into *A Wizard of Earthsea* and hurry to the kitchen.

"I'm here, Bàba." I stand still as my father carefully unties his shoelaces and takes off the unfashionable, sturdy brown Oxfords from L.L.Bean he splurged on ten years ago. He tucks the free ends of the laces into each shoe before placing them neatly side by side under the bench. His graying hair needs a trim, and there are new lines around the corners of his eyes, wrinkles that have nothing to do with too much laughing. He's working long hours again, and although he isn't short-tempered, his cheerfulness from the trip has evaporated.

He slides his feet into his house slippers and finally looks at me. "Where have you been, Lan? I was looking all over for you, calling the whole time! Why didn't you answer me?"

I bend my head. "I was in my room. I'm sorry, I didn't hear you."

"I looked in your room!" he says, exasperated. "You were not there!"

I don't say anything. I had been tucked in the corner behind the radiator again. Now that our furniture had arrived, my bed would have been a comfier spot to read in. But I still preferred the radiator nook. It was a perfect hiding place for an only child with overly protective parents.

Bàba's face softens. "You were lost in a book again, Lan?"

I nod. Bàba points to a small book with a worn paper cover on the kitchen table. "Why don't you read this one instead? I marked one of my favorite poems." He pulls a bag of apples out of the refrigerator and begins to wash them. Tomorrow must be apple pie day at the café. I wonder if Bàba misses baking egg tarts. I definitely miss eating them.

The title of the poetry book is in Chinese characters. I forgot that it's already Sunday. Chinese school day. Ever since we left Boston, even on the road and in other people's houses, on Sundays Bàba has homeschooled me in Chinese reading and writing. I thought it would end once we were settled, but Māma discovered after we moved to Redbud that the closest Chinese school is two hours away in Columbus. That means the home-schooling continues plus I don't get the chance to make friends with other Chinese kids.

I swallow a sigh. Bàba is a good businessman and an amazing baker, but not a teacher. His idea of teaching me Chinese is making me translate passages from ancient Chinese philosophers and poets who died millennia ago. There's no alphabet in Chinese. Every character is a word, and there are thousands of them. I'm not even allowed to use a computer. Instead, I have to look up each character in a Chinese-to-English dictionary and write it ten times in my notebook next to the definition in English and the pronunciation in Pinyin. After that, I have to write the complete translation of the text, making it sound as much like regular English as I can. The whole process can take hours. I should've stayed hidden in my nook.

I take a seat and flip the book open to the page marked with a shopping list: corn syrup, pecans, butter, flour, brown sugar, eggs, bourbon. Are these ingredients for a pie? I can't imagine putting bourbon in a dessert. Xing and I saw a bottle in Third Uncle's liquor cabinet once and took a sniff. It smelled like medicine and floor cleaner mixed together, with a dash of vanilla extract.

The poem is short, only three stanzas. Bàba must be in a good mood today. He told us last night at dinner that he got lots of compliments on the pies that he baked for the café. Samantha, the owner, was happy, too, and asked him to bake several more types. She said that if he did well with those, she'd think about putting some of his Chinese pastries on the menu, as long as they weren't "too strange." Well, if she thinks putting bourbon in pie is normal, then Bàba should have no problem getting his pastries approved. If that happens, maybe Bàba will be too busy to keep teaching me Chinese.

"Bàba, I'll be right back. I need to get my notebook and the dictionary." He looks up from peeling the apples and nods. I head down the hallway to my room, thinking about homeschooling and American pies and how quickly things can change.

In November, a few days before I told the fateful

story of the fènghuáng to Tiffi, I'd been on stage with my friends, rehearsing for the annual Lunar New Year celebration. I'd taken pride in each scissor-like snap of my fan, each twirl of my red ribbons. I didn't realize then that I was about to slice each ribbon that bound me to Boston, to Xing, to the bakery.

With one silly bedtime story, I had lost everything. Instead of foretelling good fortune, seeing the fènghuáng had spelled catastrophe for me.

Chapter Fifteen

As I pass by Gōnggong's room, I hear a strange sound through the door—like the car radio when it's between stations. There's the faint sound of singing, but it starts and stops, with a muffled breathy static over it. I didn't even know Gōnggong had a radio. He had an old-fashioned record player in his apartment in Chinatown, but he stopped playing music when Nǎinai died. When we moved, he gave the record player and his record collection to Fourth Uncle, who was happy because "vinyl is back in."

His bedroom door is open just a crack. I peek through the gap and catch a glimpse of my grandfather. He's sitting on the edge of his perfectly made bed, his slippered feet flat on the floor, and his hands, wrinkled but strong from years of kneading dough, rest on his lap. His back is as straight as a bamboo pole. Everything about him looks fine except for his face. Tears run unchecked down his cheeks, slide along the curve of his jaw, and drip noiselessly onto his faded shirt.

I guess I'm not the only one who's been crying.

I shouldn't be intruding on his privacy. But before I can turn away, Gōnggong sings a few words in Mandarin, a song I've heard before from a time and place that no longer exists. After a moment, he pauses and takes a deep, rattling breath. Underneath it, I still hear a thread of music, a woman singing. Her voice sends a jolt of electricity down my back and stirs up the beetles in my stomach.

It is Nǎinai's voice.

It has been so long since I've heard Nǎinai that it is only a memory of a memory in my mind. We must have videos of her, but I don't know where they are, and asking would break the rule about bringing up the past. My grandmother's gentle voice calls to me. I wish I could hear what she's singing. Before I can stop myself, I slip through the door and kneel at Gōnggong's feet. He doesn't even notice me. His eyes are focused on the wall behind me, where a treasured photo of him and Nǎinai hangs. It's the two of them on their wedding day.

I touch Gōnggong's hand gently. His skin is dry and feels like the soft rice paper in my Chinese-school notebooks. His other hand clasps a small black plastic box with silver buttons on one side. Nǎinai's voice springs out of it, quiet but true, young and strong.

He bends his head and looks at me, his eyes as sad as I imagine Lady Meng Jiang's to have been before she threw herself into the rushing water out of grief for her lost love. Of the four classical Chinese folktales, her story was the most heartbreaking. And my favorite.

"Gōnggong?" I whisper. "Are you okay?" He doesn't answer, but I've gotten used to that. "Here," I say, taking a tissue out of the box on his nightstand and pressing it into his free hand.

Gōnggong stares at the tissue like he's not quite sure what it is. Then he raises his hand and slowly wipes his eyes. "This song," he says. "Tīngguò méiyǒu?" His voice is ragged from crying and from not being used.

Had I heard the song before? "I think so," I reply. "I don't know the words, though." I don't want to make him start crying again, but I have to be sure. "Is that Nǎinai singing?"

He nods. "This song . . . her favorite. She sing, long time ago. I make tape."

"Tape?" What does tape have to do with singing?

Gōnggong shakes his head, but he smiles a tiny bit at

the same time. "You too young." He lifts the black box and hands it to me. "Cassette tape. Like, what you call? CDs? Except different."

"CDs are practically ancient, Gōnggong. Everything is digital now."

"Maybe, but everything not have Nǎinai's voice."

Gingerly, I turn the tape player in my hands and find the volume control. It isn't even a button, just a portion of a grooved plastic disc sticking out of the side like a coin stuck halfway into a vending machine. I spin the disc a tiny bit, and Nǎinai's voice grows louder.

"What is it about?" I ask. "Is it a love song?"

Gōnggong smiles again. This time it reaches his eyes. "You right. Song about love for cute family."

I almost laugh. "A *cute* family? Like bunny-rabbit cute?"

"Maybe I not say right. Here," Gōnggong stands up and goes over to his desk. "I write down for you. You translate, okay? You tell your Bàba that Chinese school lesson today is this song." He writes quickly, surely, only pausing once to dab at his eyes with the tissue.

Right. Chinese school day. Bàba is still waiting for me to come back. I take the paper from Gōnggong. "Wǒ de jiātíng zhēn kě'ài," I read the first line out loud, amazed that I recognize every single character. "You're right, it says, 'My family is very cute.' That's funny. Maybe 'kě'ài' has another meaning?"

Gōnggong pats my shoulder. "You find out, you tell me." He lets me borrow the tape player that holds Nǎinai's voice.

"Are you sure?" I ask, but I don't try to hand the tape player back to him. There's a part of me that is desperate to hear my grandmother's voice again, singing just to me.

"Yes," he says, tapping two fingers to his chest. "Your nǎinai forever in my heart. Only her voice on tape."

Chapter Sixteen

In my room, I tuck the tape player under my pillow and grab the notebook and dictionary before heading back to the kitchen. I show Bàba the lyrics Gōnggong wrote and explain that he wants me to translate the song. I don't mention that Gōnggong was crying, even though I haven't seen him cry since Nǎinai's death. The only cemetery that was affordable and fit Nǎinai's last wishes had been in Lowell, an hour away from Chinatown. We all knew we wouldn't be able to visit her very often. At her funeral, Gōnggong had thrown himself over her coffin just before they lowered it into the grave, like he wanted to follow her down, but he hadn't cried.

I expect Bàba to tell me that he wants me to translate the poem, too, but he doesn't. Instead, his eyes get red and watery like he's been slicing onions, not apples. What is it about this song that makes everyone cry?

Translating the song is surprisingly easy—fifteen minutes later, I'm done. Maybe Bàba's hands-off teaching method is working after all, not that I'd ever tell him that. I look down at my notebook and reread my translation. The song is about a poor but close-knit family. I'd decided to use the "lovely" definition of kě'ài instead of "cute." It makes more sense to have the first line be "My family is very lovely."

I stop suddenly at the sixth line. There it is, the word orchid. Part of my name. I had scribbled the Pinyin lán, the pronunciation in English letters, without even really thinking about it. Now I wonder if the tree spirit had been saying my name or something else. There are tons of words in Mandarin that sound the same but have different characters and meanings. My English teacher last year, Wèi Lǎoshī, called them homophones. All I know is that individual sounds can mean almost anything unless you know what the written character looks like.

Curious, I flip to the page for lán in my Pinyin-to-English dictionary, which I'd brought along to look up any other meanings of kě'ài. Instead of being sorted by Chinese characters, Pinyin dictionaries are sorted by pronunciation as translated into the English alphabet. I scan the page, focusing on the entries that are in second tone, the same rising inflection as my name. There are fourteen different characters with fourteen different definitions, but they're all pronounced exactly the same.

In addition to the character for orchid, there's a character that means mist, haze, or vapor. Another means basket, and yet another is the word for blue, which I learned my first year in Chinese school. The list goes on and on.

The beetles shiver in a line down my back. I know, of course, that my name means orchid. I've seen the character written on the birth announcement in the scrapbook Māma made. I've written it hundreds of times.

Suddenly, there's a loud sound like glass shattering that makes me jump. But when I look over, it's just Bàba tossing dirty utensils into the sink.

I stare down at the dictionary. Quickly, I tear a blank sheet out of my notebook and copy all the different characters and definitions of lán onto it. I don't know why it feels important, but it does, and I'm exhausted when I'm done. I stuff the list into my pocket.

"Bàba, I need a break. I'll be back in five minutes." Outside, the air blows crisp and clean, rustling through the first fallen leaves.

As I make my way across the yard, I stumble over something lying on the grass that looks like a lime crossed with a tennis ball. It must belong to one of the twins.

Annoyed, I kick it toward the fence. *Ow.* It's as hard as a rock, and now my toes ache. There are more green rocks under the dragon tree, and when I look up, I see dozens more hanging from the branches. What kind of dragon is this tree? I pick up one of the hard green balls and feel the rough, pebbly surface. A pungent, spicy citrus smell makes my eyes water.

Another ball falls, striking me on the shoulder. "Hey!" I look up at the dragon tree. "Well, you have my attention now. What do you want?" Would the tree spirit answer? She had spoken to me once before. I rub my shoulder and eye the hanging fruits warily.

There is a light tinkling sound. *Ting, ting, ting.* Like wind chimes, but when I look around, I don't see any. *Ting.* I'm pretty sure it's coming from the tree. The tree spirit is answering me! But what is she saying? *Ting, ting, ting.* It doesn't mean anything in English—it's just a sound. Wait. This tree spirit is a Chinese creature—she must be speaking to me in Mandarin. Ting can mean a bunch of different things, just like lán. She says it again. It sounds like first tone, flat and drawn out like *tinnggg,* in which case it means listen. The tree spirit is telling me to listen! But to what? Nǎinai's song? Or to a person? There's no one around.

After another minute, the tree spirit stops telling me to listen, and I head back to the house to show Bàba my translation. He nods and says, "Family is everything, Lan." Then he goes back to rolling pie dough.

Back in my room in the radiator nook, I take out my list and read all the different variations and meanings of lán again.

I think about *A Wizard of Earthsea.* A mage had told Ged his true name. Maybe the tree spirit is guiding me to find mine. Beautiful Orchid has never fit me. It's a name for an elegant heroine dressed in flowing silk robes, with jewels sparkling against her lustrous dark hair. My finger traces the characters on my list. Maybe I am one of these láns instead.

The tree spirit told me to listen. Bàba, Gōnggong, and the song all talk about how important family is. My finger stops on the character for basket, and suddenly it becomes clear. If I listen closely, I know that every time my parents call me Lan, they are calling me Basket. The kind that's woven from bamboo, with straps to carry it on my back. It makes perfect sense. They always tell me how they want me to have a good future with a good job so I can take care of them when they're old. I'm the carrier of their dreams and hopes and desires.

Since I'm responsible for us moving away from Boston, it's also up to me to hold their pain, worry, and sadness. The only way to put down this load is to get the family back together. But I have no idea how or where to begin.

Last week, Mr. Lewis taught our class something he called mind mapping, a way to organize information. He wanted us to use it to keep track of what happens in *The Wizard of Earthsea*, but he also said it could be used for a lot of different things, including brainstorming how to solve problems. Well, I have a huge problem and no solutions—I might as well try Mr. Lewis's method.

In the middle of a large sheet of drawing paper, I write, "Reunite Family" and draw a circle around it. That's my main goal. Then I put Xing and Tiffi's names off to one side—they're the ones I'm closest to and the ones who can help me. I frown, remembering how I already tried to reconnect with Xing and discovered that she hates me. Her parents probably hate me, too. I write their names in red ink above Xing's and do the same for Tiffi's parents. Then I draw bubbles around each of their names and lines that connect them to their daughters.

On the other side of the main goal, I add my own name as well as Bàba, Māma, and Gōnggong's, and draw lines from my name to theirs. Now the mind map looks more like a family tree—or a battlefield, with the four of us pitted against my cousins, uncles, and aunts. I don't want to actually attack them—just their belief that the family should be apart.

Xing thinks her life is better now since she got to go to sleepaway camp, started piano lessons, and takes more dance classes. I jot "camp," "piano," and "dance" next to her name, connected by three separate lines. All the aunts and uncles got money from selling the bakery, so I write "money" next to all their names. I'm still upset that they think Bàba stole money from them. Maybe I could attack that belief, too.

I draw another branch off the main goal and write "information" on it. What would help prove that Third Aunt was wrong about Bàba? I remember the first big fight, the one where she wanted to see "the books." The ledger will show that Bàba wasn't stealing money. I scribble "ledger" on a line off the information branch and make a dotted line in green that connects it to Third Aunt's "money" word. That gives me an idea for another piece of information—how much money the bakery is making now, with new owners. "Call bakery" gets its own line, too.

It would be nice to know if the aunts and uncles miss Bàba, Māma, and Gōnggong at all, or if they regret what happened. If I could tell Bàba that his siblings regret their actions, he'd take that as an apology and call them, right? I write "miss/regret," even though there's no way to find out without eavesdropping and I'm not there to hide in the utility closet.

Wait. There could be another way. I'm not there, but Tiffi is. She could spy on her parents and Xing's parents and let me know if they say anything about Bàba, Māma, and Gōnggong. I put "spy" on a line coming out of Tiffi's name and then draw a dotted line connecting it to "miss/regret." I'm not exactly sure how I'll contact her since she's too little to have her own cell phone, but I'll figure something out later. And when I do talk to her, I can tell her to drop hints to her parents about how much she misses me and wants me back. They'd do anything for Tiffi—especially if she whines enough.

In the meantime, I can try to convince Māma and Bàba that moving to Redbud was a mistake and we have to return to Boston. They'll need to think it's their own idea.

The word "spy" reminds me of another one of Bàba's Chinese school passages. It was a really complicated and boring section of *The Art of War* by an ancient philosopher named Sun Tzu. I get out my Chinese notebook and flip through it until I find what I'm looking for—a paragraph from the first chapter of Sun Tzu's book. I'd had so much trouble making my translation sound understandable that Bàba made me look up an English version by a professional translator and write it down underneath mine.

"Warfare is the art of deceit," the translation started. Bàba had explained that Sun Tzu's philosophy could be applied to many situations where two sides have different opinions, not just wars between countries. Māma and Bàba want to stay in Redbud, but I want to go home. They seem happy being separated from the rest of the family, but I believe everything would be better if we were all together again. I'm definitely on the opposite side of my parents. Deceit means to make someone believe something that isn't true. According to the philosopher, I should trick my parents.

A little farther on in the paragraph, another sentence jumps out at me. "If he is humble, encourage his arrogance." If there's one thing Māma and Bàba are proud of, it's me. Or, rather, my brain. Xing said the camp she went to was on a college campus. That could work. I'll make my parents think that moving back to Boston would give me a better chance of getting into a good college, because there are more summer programs that would look good on my applications. I write "education" on a line extending from Māma's name.

I sit back and study the map. The words "miss/regret" jump out, flooding me with sadness. I miss Năinai so much. If she were still alive, I wouldn't need a plan. The family would still be together. Slowly, I write "Năinai" in big letters at the top of the diagram, circle it, and connect her bubble to the "miss/regret" line. Then I add dotted lines radiating out from Năinai to every single member of the family. We all miss her, whether we show it or not.

I can't bring Năinai back, but now I have four steps I can take to attack this goal: finding the ledger, calling the bakery, asking Tiffi to spy, and bringing up my education with Māma. This mind map thing really does work. I should thank Mr. Lewis. I should thank Bàba, too, for making me read *The Art of War*. But I don't.

Chapter Seventeen

In Health class on Monday morning, both Batchelder twins sit down near me. Liam is on my left and Logan is just behind him. With the wall to my right, I feel a little hemmed in. It's not hard to tell who is who—Logan smiles and says "Hi," and Liam barely looks at me. I give Logan half a smile and swing my hair to the front, so it blocks Liam's view of my face. Last Friday, I overheard Liam in the hall making fun of another girl because of her braces. I don't want to give him any reason to notice me.

My hair isn't an invisibility cloak, though. Mrs. Perry announces that the principal would like to see all the seventh-grade teachers before the tornado drill starts, so she slithers off when an aide arrives, leaving the class with a warning to "Ssstay sssilent and be good." I feel something jab my thigh. Liam pokes me with the end of his pencil again, leaving a second dark-gray dot on my jeans.

"Hey. New girl. Melanie," Liam says in a low voice. He actually sounds friendly. I know better, though.

Maybe he's the real snake sprite, not Mrs. Shaughnessy.

After a couple more pencil pokes, I finally look over at him. "What?" I ask, when what I really want to do is stomp on his pencil with my boots.

"How did you get here?"

What does he mean, how did I get here? "You mean to Redbud? We drove," I say. Behind him, I notice Logan and a couple of other kids listening.

Liam makes a sound of disbelief. "That's impossible."

The beetles inside me are instantly alert, their long antennae held high and their mandibles at the ready. I've heard this tone of voice before. So many tourists in Chinatown are always surprised that my English is "so good," as if I had just arrived from China the day before instead of being born in the United States. "Why is that impossible?"

"It's impossible," says Liam with exaggerated patience, "because you can't drive over the Pacific Ocean. Everyone knows that."

The kids around us are listening, some with grins on their faces, and others who are as stone-faced as I must be. A girl with strawberry-blond hair pipes up, "Well, actually, it's technically possible if the Bering Strait is filled with ice and you have the proper vehicle and—"

"Shut up, Anita," Liam growls, and she promptly clams up, her cheeks as pink as her hair.

I feel bad for her, even though I didn't ask her to step in. She must be the class science whiz—the one who can never pass up a chance to blurt out a bit of interesting trivia. I smile at her and pay for it when Liam turns his attention back to me.

"You must have flown here. From China, right?"

I'm like a bug pinned to a board, with no escape from his attention. I force myself to straighten my back and push my shoulders down. I can feel the heat rising to my face. Rage or fear? I'm not sure. A little bit of both. "My parents are from Taiwan, but I wasn't born there. I'm from Boston," I reply. "And we drove here, like I already said."

Now Anita smiles at me. She doesn't let Liam keep her down for long. "Boston!" she says brightly. "That's so cool! Have you seen the *Mayflower*?"

"I have," I say quickly before Liam can get a word in. "We went on a tour of the inside and everything."

Liam laughs loudly. Others snicker, too, but I can't see who they are because a familiar haze has crept over my eyes and blurs their faces. Probably Big Dave and Little Dave, who always copy everything Liam does. "Your parents must have loved that," he says.

His voice is friendly again, interested. But the beetles and I are still wary. I glance around and see that more kids are watching and listening. Not answering is not an option. "They weren't there. It was a third-grade field trip."

"That's too bad. It could've reminded them of how they got here." Liam smirks. "I mean, if they didn't come by plane, then they must have come by boat."

What is taking Mrs. Shaughnessy so long? I look at Logan. I guess his buddy duties don't include calling his brother out. Anita has inched closer, and she's staring wide-eyed at Liam, pressing her lips together as if she's trying not to . . . laugh? Wait. What did Liam just say? I play his words back in my head, and then I get it. I know how to turn this around on him.

"Your parents would probably really enjoy the tour, too, then." I plaster an innocent, enthusiastic look on my face. "I mean, your family came here by boat first."

Liam's eyebrows draw together in confusion, but he recovers quickly. "Don't be dense. My family's always lived here."

Logan stifles a snort. At least I'm pretty sure it's him, but I refuse to look again since he hasn't tried to stop his jerky brother.

Beside him, Anita is practically vibrating with pent-up laughter. "Wow, really?" I say with mock fascination. "I bet Ms. Brown would love to hear all about that."

Anita bursts out laughing, and I hear muffled giggles from different parts of the room. Not everyone is under Liam's spell.

Anger flushes Liam's face. He doesn't get what just happened, and I'm not about to explain it to him. Anita can't resist, though. "Don't you remember learning about the Mound Builders in fourth grade? Or about the Original Peoples of Ohio River Valley? You know, the Shawnee, the Erie, and the Kickapoo? I suppose you could be descended from maybe a Shawnee ancestor, but I seriously doubt it since they were forced to leave in the 1800s by the Indian Removal Act. We do still have some Native communities here, though! Maybe you could reach out to them."

"What are you getting at, Anita?" Liam is clearly frustrated and not following Anita's train of thought.

"My point is that your family has *not* always lived here," she informs him. "Maybe your parents and grandparents grew up in Ohio, but sometime in the past, your ancestors came to the United States. Probably *by boat*."

That shuts Liam up, but not before he shoots Anita

a death glare fiercer than any demon or Western-style basilisk. He tries to turn it on me, too, but I see it coming and duck behind my hair again, hiding my own smirk.

That's why I don't see who murmurs, "Blockhead," but it almost sounds like Logan. Liam must think so, too, because when I look up, he's snarling at his brother. "What did you call me, *Log*?" he asks. The Daves laugh loudly, rudely. Immediately, Logan's face changes, and he blasts his twin with a matching fiery stare.

Just then, Mrs. Shaughnessy returns, and everyone rushes back to their seats and faces the front of the room as though nothing has happened. Anita gives me a tiny fist bump before she goes. None of the other kids stood up for me.

Logan insulted his brother, but it doesn't feel like he was defending me. I think about how Liam called him Log, like he was a dead tree trunk. It doesn't sound like an affectionate nickname, and judging by Logan's reaction, it's not. Aren't twins supposed to be best friends? But then I think of Xing. We used to joke that we were twins because we were so close. And look at us now. The gap between us is as wide and frozen as Anita's Bering Strait, with no signs of thawing.

As Mrs. Shaughnessy explains about tornadoes, I get more and more freaked out. Boston gets storms with high winds and lots of rain, but softball-sized hailstones? Whirling funnel-shaped clouds? A roar like a freight train? I'll pass. She goes on to explain that we "should all remember D.U.C.K.," which stands for the four things to do when there's an actual tornado, or even just a drill, like today.

D stands for "down," meaning that everyone should get to the lowest level of a building or a low place if you're outdoors. Since the Cliff doesn't have a basement or a second story, we just go into the hallway, away from the windows in the classrooms. The second letter is *U* for "under," as in getting underneath something sturdy to protect your body from falling or flying debris. I hope Mrs. Shaughnessy is right about the school's roof being strong enough, because the whole building looks old and rickety.

But then she goes and says, "*C* stands for 'cover,' so we will be protecting our heads by putting our arms over them. If you have a hoodie or jacket, you can put that over your head for additional protection." I guess she doesn't have a lot of faith in the roof, either.

Finally, the *K* apparently stands for "keep," as in keep

in your shelter until the storm passes. There are special sirens that sound when a tornado is about to hit, but no sound to tell you when the coast is clear, so we're supposed to listen to an emergency channel on the radio or check the news on our cell phones. So, really, *K* should stand for "keep your devices close to you," which I'd love to do if I still had one.

When the school's alarm goes off, it sounds like an ambulance siren right next to my head. I jump to my feet, already breathing hard. The other kids are so calm, slowly standing up and forming a line at the door. They look bored. A couple of girls sling their purses across their shoulders even though we've been told to leave everything behind.

Out in the hallway, Mrs. Shaughnessy directs us to kneel facing the lockers with our heads on the floor and our hands clasped behind our heads. I crouch there, curled uncomfortably into a little ball, the siren wailing, wondering how long this torture is going to last and if I'm going to faint before it's over. I don't see how any of this will protect us if a tornado rips through the town. Rosebud is so small that the whole town would probably lift into space. My hands feel clammy against my skull.

The person to my left shifts and bumps into my hip. I

look over into Anita's apologetic face. "Sorry," she whis-pers. "Bony knees."

That makes me smile. "Me too," I whisper back. But something in my face or voice must betray my anxiety, because Anita's eyebrows draw together.

"You okay?" she asks. When I don't respond, she nods sympathetically. "He doesn't like storms, either," she says, tilting her head to indicate the boy to her left.

I raise my head for a second to peer over Anita's. Based on the green T-shirt, it's Liam. To my surprise, he has his cheek pressed against the floor, eyes closed, and there's a sheen of sweat on his forehead.

I raise my eyebrows at Anita, but she shakes her head. "Don't know," she says under her breath. "Don't wanna ask."

We smile at each other again. As curious as I am, I would never ask, either. Everyone has secrets. And it's enough to know that there's a crack in Liam's hard shell. The beetles in my stomach settle down and let me breathe a little easier.

Chapter Eighteen

As soon as the screen door snaps closed behind me, Māma calls out, "Lan? Wait there. Don't take off shoes."

Not taking off my shoes means I'm not allowed to go any farther into the house, so I flop down on the bench beside the door and fiddle with the small charms hanging from my backpack zipper. Xing gave me the jade butterfly on a red silk cord last Christmas, and my friend Caitlin made the tiny bāozi out of polymer clay. On the last day of school, Zach Tsai surprised me with a red enamel lobster charm with a silver clasp. To remind me of Boston, he'd said. I'd had a crush on him all year and didn't think he even knew I was alive, so I was both thrilled and shattered.

The charms make me realize this is a great opportunity to start my Reunite Family plan. After Anita had been so nice to me today, I'd caught up to her just before lunch and asked her if she might know where to get what I needed. Just like I thought, she'd been really excited to help. Quietly, I unzip my backpack and take out a few brochures, sliding them into the stack of mail in a small basket at the end of the bench. Now I just have to wait.

I listen to Māma moving around in the kitchen and try to guess what she's doing. A cabinet opens and shuts. Maybe she's getting me a snack? The fridge door opens with a soft sucking sound followed by the rattle of glass bottles, and then the fridge door closes. Maybe Māma finally bought some jelly and is making me a peanut butter and jelly sandwich. But then why do I have to keep my shoes on? Just as I'm thinking that Māma has forgotten all about me, she pops out of the kitchen doorway holding a plastic container. My heart leaps; I can't wait to see what she's made for me.

I pry off the lid just as Māma says, "Give to Gōnggong. He is fishing at pond." My heart sinks back down into my chest. She didn't make anything for me. I'm just Basket, her errand girl.

The container holds small balls of what looks and smells like peanut butter cookie dough. I hold one up between my thumb and index finger and examine its coarse texture. Māma learned how to bake after marrying Bàba, so I'm not sure why she's giving Gōnggong raw cookie dough—she knows he won't eat it.

"What is it?"

"For fish," Māma says. "Gōnggong only has a few worms left, so I made different kind of bait. Old Yang told me fish like peanut butter mix with cornmeal."

"I like peanut butter, too."

"First go give this to Gōnggong—maybe if he catches big fish, he will be happy. Then you can come home and make peanut butter sandwich for yourself."

Well, okay, then. I head out again, making sure the screen door doesn't bang.

I find Gōnggong sitting on a log next to Bonnie Pond, his floppy-brimmed hat askew. I take a seat and hand him the box. "Māma made these for you."

He opens it and studies one of the peanut butter balls, puzzled.

"She said that fish like peanut butter," I explain. "For when you run out of worms."

My grandfather nods and reels his fishing line back in. There's a tiny limp thing on the end of the hook, and I look away as he pulls off the sorry drowned bit of worm and tosses it into the water. He pierces the bait ball with the hook and pinches. He stands and brings his right arm back to throw out the line, but then stops and looks at me. "Xiǎo xīn," he says, and he motions me away with his other arm.

I get up and take a few steps back, not wanting to get hit in the eye with a peanut butter ball. Especially one with a fishing hook in it.

Gōnggong swings, and the peanut butter ball sails out over the pond's surface before landing with a tiny *plop* into the water. Smiling, he sits down on the log again. I'm not sure what to do—I've completed the task Māma gave me, so maybe I'm free to go home now. Or maybe she wanted me to stay and keep Gōnggong company? I look around, trying to decide, and that's when I spot the boy.

He's a little way off, on the top of the slope that leads down to the pond. His hands curl around the handlebars of a green bike, holding it upright next to him. It's one of the Batchelder twins—Liam, I think. Did he follow me here? Is he going to get back at me for what happened in Health class? He wouldn't be mean to Gōnggong, would he? The beetles scramble around in a panic.

Then the boy slowly raises one hand off the bike in a wave and smiles tentatively. I let out the breath I was holding. Just as slowly, I wave back, realizing with relief that it's Logan, not Liam.

"Hey," he says, and I'm happy that he doesn't call me Melanie. That's just for school. "I didn't know you fished."

"I don't. I'm just keeping my grandfather company." I gesture to Gōnggong as he looks over at us. He knows the word grandfather. He knows a lot more English than he lets on.

Now, he studies Logan and says, "Tā shì nǐ de péngyǒu ma?"

I don't really know how to answer. Is Logan my friend? Liam is definitely *not* my friend, so by comparison, maybe that makes Logan a friend. A maybe friend.

"Gōnggong, this is Logan." I turn to meet Logan's eyes. They are alive with curiosity, not the venom I saw in Liam's. "Logan, this is my grandfather, uh, Mr. Hua."

Logan reaches out his hand. "Nice to meet you, Mr. Hua."

There's an awkward moment when Gōnggong switches the fishing pole to his left hand so he can shake Logan's with his right, but then he says, "Nice meet you, too," and everything is okay. "Sit, sit," Gōnggong says, patting the spot next to him. "Here, on . . . how you say?" He looks at me expectantly.

"The log," I say automatically, then immediately

wince. What are the chances that we'd be sitting on the very thing his horrible twin called him?

Logan sits on the end of the log. "So you heard that, huh?" The expression on his face is of someone who is tired. Done.

I scoot closer to Gōnggong so Logan has more room. "It doesn't seem like a nice nickname."

"Nope." He looks at me. "It's a long story," he says, and I wait for him to explain, but he doesn't.

Gōnggong asks, "How you know Lan?"

There's a brief pause before Logan answers. "From school. We have class together. I also live next door."

Gōnggong's eyebrows rise. "You are neighbor?"

"I live in the gray house?" Logan says as if it's a question. "There's a fence between our yards."

"Very big tree?" Gōnggong asks.

Logan smiles. "Yeah, that's ours. It's, like, over a hundred years old."

Gōnggong nods, and we sit in peaceful silence. I keep my eyes on the red-and-white plastic ball on Gōnggong's fishing line. The water pats gently against the shore. After a while, Gōnggong looks at his watch and starts reeling in the line. "Time go home. Fish no hungry today." He doesn't look upset about it, though.

"I should go home, too," Logan says. "Gotta start reading that book for English."

I pick up the blue bucket at Gōnggong's feet, happy and guilty to find it empty of its squirmy residents. Gōnggong strides ahead, his fishing rod in one hand and Māma's bait container in the other. Logan pushes his bike up the slope.

"So. Lan?"

I make a face. "You heard that, huh?"

He smiles, hearing his own words. "I've never heard that as a nickname for Melanie before. I like it. It sounds cool, like Topher instead of Chris."

"Definitely not. Cool, that is." I really, really, hope I'm not blushing. Nobody outside of my family has called me Lan before, but somehow, I don't mind that Logan does. "It's actually part of my Chinese name," I blurt.

"Yeah? What's it short for?"

I look back at the pond, the still surface reflecting the deepening cobalt of the afternoon sky. "It's a long story." He waits, but I don't explain.

Logan's grin suddenly turns serious. "There are just some stories that aren't so fun to tell, you know?"

If I say anything, the beetles will come pouring out, the ugly ones with their spiny legs and bulbous eyes. Instead, I dip my head in agreement and let him walk ahead. When he's a few feet away, I whisper through clenched teeth, "I know."

Chapter Nineteen

The next morning, I wake up early and peek out the window at the driveway. Bàba's car is gone. Perfect. Quietly, I change into a gray T-shirt and darker gray leggings while keeping an ear out for Māma. After I hear her come down the stairs, I count to thirty and open my door. Icy air rolls through me, and the beetles freeze into tiny balls like hail. I shudder—was that Mr. Shellhaus's ghost? Did he just come into my room? I scoot into the hall and close my bedroom door, praying the ghost doesn't follow me.

The sounds of my mother filling the tea kettle and putting the clean dishes away drift down the hall. Leaving my slippers and backpack at the bottom of the stairs, I silently climb up and enter my parents' bedroom.

Where would Bàba keep the old bakery ledger? I scan the room, which I've only been in a few times. The bed, nightstands, and dresser are to my right, at the end of the long room. A desk and chair are tucked in the corner in front of me, opposite the doorway. Unpacked boxes are stacked against the walls wherever there's space.

Quickly, I search the piles on top of the desk. Huh. There's a job advertisement for an office assistant at an acupuncture clinic in a town called Fairborn. Another stack has papers about the rental agreement and other info about the house. I keep looking but don't see the leatherbound book that used to be in the bakery office.

The boxes on the floor are all labeled in Māma's precise Chinese script. I recognize the characters that mean winter clothes and skip those. A few boxes have characters that I can't read, but when I peek under the top flap, I see manila folders and piles of papers. I shuffle through them and don't see anything that looks like the ledger, so I move on.

The last box is still sealed shut and turned to the side so the label is against the wall. Sliding it will make too much noise, so I try to lift it. It's super heavy and doesn't budge. Books! I dash back and rummage in the desk drawers for a pair of scissors, but all I find is a wooden letter opener. I hope it's sharp enough.

It is, just barely. My parents will be able to tell that the box was opened, but maybe each one will think the other one did it. I pry the flaps apart and stare down at Māma's collection of Chinese novels, arranged in two neat rows with the spines showing. One glance and I know the ledger isn't there.

"Lan! Gāi qǐchuáng le!" Māma calls from the kitchen.

I swallow my disappointment, hurry downstairs, put on my slippers, and grab my backpack before shuffling into the kitchen.

Māma's eyebrows raise. "You up early. What is wrong?"

"Nothing." *Everything*, I want to say, but I don't.

When Health starts, Mrs. Shaughnessy says, "Class, I've decided to give you all assigned seats, in alphabetical order. Stand up when I call your name and move to the next seat in the row, from front to back. We'll start with the front corner by the window."

Everyone groans. No one should have to deal with snake sprites first thing in the morning. She's even wearing a black-and-white snakeprint dress today.

"Anita Arnold," she barks. Anita is already standing— she must be used to being called first. She moves to the desk in the front corner and calmly sits down. I've noticed that she usually sits in the front, so it's probably not a big deal to her. Silently, I send a little plea to the tree spirit to make sure that I'm not in the front row.

"Liam Batchelder and then Logan Batchelder," Mrs. Shaughnessy continues. The twins take their seats behind Anita, and the teacher continues to call several more names. When she says "Melanie Hua, are you listening?" it takes me a moment to register that she means me, because she mispronounces my last name as "Hoo-ay," the same way Mr. Reynard does. That, and I still haven't gotten used to being called Melanie. I hear a few muffled giggles, but I'm not sure if it's because I wasn't paying attention or because Mrs. Shaughnessy butchered my last name.

I get up and head toward my new desk, glad to see it's in the second row from the front, behind Fiona Gillespie. From here, it'll be easier to see the board, even through the gray haze that follows me at school, and I'm not in the front row. Liam, though, is directly on my right. He flashes his teeth at me, a shark's smile. I should have made my request to the tree spirit more specific. I sit down quickly and angle my body to the left, so most of my back is turned toward Liam.

Five minutes later, everyone has their seats and Mrs. Shaughnessy has launched into the unit about heat-related health issues. I take notes on temperature, how to calculate the heat index, and the different symptoms of sun exposure, but my mind feels separate from my hand holding the pen.

I'm back in Earthsea, the wind tangling my hair as Ged fills the sail with magewind and the boat speeds across the water toward Pendor Island. The wizard looks back at me, and suddenly I'm staring into Logan's face underneath the hood of a sweatshirt and not Ged's beneath his wizard's cowl. I snap back into reality, covering my gasp with a coughing fit.

Mrs. Shaughnessy waits until I'm done. "As I was saying, people like Logan and Liam tend to get sunburned more easily. Does anyone know why?"

All heads, including mine, turn to stare at the twins. Liam smirks and flexes his pale biceps, while Logan looks slightly embarrassed. He meets my eyes for a split second, and I swear his cheeks get pinker. I look away and find that Fiona is grinning at him. That's why he's blushing.

"They have fair complexions," Fiona says, "like me." It's true—she has the whitest skin out of everyone in the class. Māma would love to have skin like that. In Māma's world, having white skin is a sign that you belong to the ranks of wealthy nobles instead of the poor, sun-browned peasants. Never mind that emperors and nobles don't exist in China anymore, or that we would all starve without farmers and field-workers. Having light skin doesn't automatically make you a better person.

The teacher nods. "That's right. People with paler skin don't have as much melanin. Melanin is the pigment in your skin. The more melanin a person has, the darker their skin color is." Mrs. Shaughnessy writes the word "melanin" on the board. When she turns around, she stares right at me. I shrink back into my chair and tip my head down so my hair hides my face. But it's too late. The other students have noticed where the teacher is staring.

"So, like, you're saying that Melanie has more melanin than we do?" Cassidy blurts.

Liam barks in delight. "Hey, all you have to do is change one letter to turn 'Melanie' into 'melanin.' It's the perfect name for her." Everyone laughs.

"Now, now," Mrs. Shaughnessy chides, but she sounds more amused than scolding. "That's true, Cassidy. Melanie does indeed have more melanin than you do. It absorbs and dissipates UV radiation. That's why the rest of us need to wear sunblock—so we don't get too dark."

"You mean so we don't get sunburned," Logan says.

"Right, of course that's what I meant," Mrs. Shaughnessy replies, but I can tell it isn't. She starts talking about heat exhaustion and heatstroke, but I can't make myself take notes anymore. My skin might be darker, but that doesn't mean I don't need sunblock at all. I can still get sunburned.

From my right, Liam whispers, "Melanie Melanin. It has a nice ring to it." He snickers.

Oh no. Not another nickname. *My name isn't even Melanie*, I want to scream at him, at Mrs. Shaughnessy, at the entire class. I want to scream it so loud that it rattles Mr. Reynard's pointed teeth down the hall.

Instead, the argument I had with Māma on the first day of school pops into my mind. After school, I'd sat down at the cheap plastic card table that had served as our temporary kitchen table, baking counter, and desk, and started on the "All About Me" writing exercise that Mr. Lewis had given us.

Māma had looked over my shoulder. "Change," she said, pointing to the top of the paper where I'd written my name. Out of habit, I'd written Meilan Hua. I stared at the two simple words that I'd been writing since kindergarten.

"But Māma, my name is not Melanie!"

She frowned at my tone. "Rù xiāng súi sú."

I glared at her. "I don't know what that means. I'm not going to the countryside. I'm already *in* the middle of nowhere."

Māma made a *tsk* sound that managed to convey both irritation with my lack of Mandarin comprehension and my bad attitude. "It means 'when you enter a village, you follow their customs.'"

"Is that like, 'When in Rome, do as the Romans do'?"

Māma nodded. "Yes, that is what I said already. We must accept the ways of the local people."

"I'm pretty sure that they don't rename every new student," I persisted. "I hate the name Melanie. People are going to call me Mel. Can't you just tell the principal that you changed your mind and everyone should call me Meilan?" My voice got louder. "I mean, that *is* my name, right? The one you and Bàba gave me."

Māma shushed me with another Chinese saying. "Sài wēng shī mǎ, yān zhī fēi fú."

"Please. Just tell me what you mean."

"This is a story about an old man who lost his horse. The horse eventually came back, bringing more horses with him."

I crossed my arms and tried not to completely lose it. Māma continued, "So what was a bad thing at the beginning turned out to be a good thing for the old man. You accept this new name even if you think it is a bad thing; it may become a good thing later."

And that had been the end of the argument. I had erased Meilan and written Melanie on my paper. I'd been defeated by a story about an old man and his runaway horse.

Now my fear has come true, only the other kids aren't going to call me Mel. If Liam has his way, they're going to call me Melanin, which is infinitely worse. If my real name was a horse that ran away and then returned, it had come back with a mutant, not another horse. Definitely not a good thing.

Chapter Twenty

"Hey, Lan! Wait up!"

Logan hurries over, pushing his green bike. "Wow," he says. "You can walk and read at the same time?"

I shut *A Wizard of Earthsea* quickly. "Do you ever ride that thing, or do you just push it around?"

He grins. "Do you want a ride home? You can sit on the rack."

The metal rack over the rear wheel looks really uncomfortable. Plus, what would I hang on to? Logan? There's no way I would do that, never mind risk Māma seeing me pull up to the house with my arms around a nánháizi. There would be *days* of lectures and embarrassing ancient sayings about the dangers of love. *Not* that I feel anything like that for Logan. I barely know him. We chatted for all of five minutes at the pond.

"Thanks, but I'd rather walk." I wave the book a little. "And read." I head down the sidewalk again.

Logan doesn't take the hint. He doesn't jump on his

bike and ride away. He just starts walking next to me. I'm not sure if I'm annoyed or glad. Maybe both. His eyes widen. "Wow," he says again. "You're, like, halfway through the book!"

"I guess I read fast." I was right at the part where Ged changed himself into a dragon when Logan interrupted me. "Plus, it's really good."

"Yeah? What do you like about it?"

I don't really know how to answer him. I love the magic in it, of course. The shadow thing that Ged accidentally summoned is scary and exciting. Then there's the part about how everyone and everything, even a rock, has a true name. But that all probably sounds silly. I stuff the book into my backpack. "I don't know. There's a lot that . . . calls my name, I guess."

To my surprise, Logan looks worried. "Um, speaking of names," he says, "I hope it's okay that I called you Lan just now. I tried using Melanie, but you didn't respond."

I didn't even realize that Logan had called me Lan. And like yesterday, I find that I don't mind. "Sure, that's okay." I wrinkle my nose. "It's better than Melanie."

Now he looks both anxious and puzzled. "Also, I heard what Liam called you during Health class."

Oh.

"I'm sorry," he continues. "Liam can be a pain. He thinks he's being funny, but . . ."

"I think he's a pain, too," I say.

Logan looks startled, then laughs. I laugh, too, pleased to be having a normal conversation. It feels like it's been a long time since I've laughed with a friend. A friend. I guess that is what Logan is now. No maybes about it.

"Do you always apologize to the kids he makes fun of?"

My question seems to throw Logan. He's silent for a moment. "No, I don't. I just . . . don't want you to think that he and I are alike. We're not. At least, not our personalities. We don't think the same about everything. Heck, Liam and I don't even hang out anymore."

For some reason, that last part makes me sad. "I didn't think you were the same," I tell him, and it's true. Even though I've seen the thread of meanness that runs through Logan, it's different from his brother's. In fact, his anger seems to be pointed only at Liam. Liam, on the other hand, is mean to everybody.

We walk another minute in silence. "You don't seem to have a problem telling us apart," Logan says.

It sounds like a question, another one that I don't know how to answer. What would I say? That his hair curls differently over his collar? That he smiles instead

142

of smirks? That his niceness radiates off him like the heat from a fresh almond cookie?

"People can't tell you guys apart? I mean, haven't you lived here your whole life?"

Logan makes a face. "You'd be surprised by how many people call me Liam. They just can't be bothered. Liam is louder and more outgoing, so that's who they remember. Even Foxman does it, and he's, like, my dad's best friend."

I feel a flash of something hot and bright, like the sun tearing through clouds. "Foxman?" Could he possibly mean . . . ?

"Mr. Reynard," Logan confirms. "The principal? My dad says reynard means fox in French. Liam told everyone last year, so we all started calling him Foxman." Logan snorts. "The weird thing is, I think Mr. Reynard likes it. He thinks it makes him our *pal* or something."

It sounds just like how a fox demon would behave. Thinking it was funny that he named himself what he is, just in another language. And then believing the kids were calling him an affectionate nickname, when all along it marked him as a trickster and a liar. Exactly like how the Evil Queen named herself Regina in my favorite TV show, *Once Upon a Time*.

"You don't like him?"

Logan shakes his head. "He's super annoying. Even my dad thinks so, but they've been friends for so long that he says it's just easier to not say anything than to try and change things." Logan stops suddenly, so I stop walking and turn back to look at him. "I'm sorry," he says.

I don't understand. "For not liking your dad's friend?"

"No. For what happened the first day of school." Logan looks down and fiddles with the gear shifter on his bike. "I'm guessing you didn't want to be called Melanie."

For the second time, I feel dazzled by a flash of light. But it's warm and liquid, like sunlight rippling across water. "You're right. It wasn't my idea. It was . . . Fox-man's." Saying the principal's nickname feels strangely like saying his true name. In Earthsea, there was magic in knowing someone's true name. Maybe knowing Fox-man's will give me more power over him.

"Why didn't you tell him no?"

I turn away and keep walking, forcing Logan to catch up to me. "My mom didn't want me to. She'd already agreed that it was okay."

"That's messed up," Logan says. "Letting someone else rename your own kid."

I suddenly feel guilty for blaming Māma. It isn't her fault that we're here in Redbud. "I guess it's like your dad said. Sometimes it's easier to not to say anything."

I think of all the things that I've left unsaid, all the times I didn't speak, the beetles that would swarm out if I opened my mouth. I don't want to go home right now. The thought of becoming Basket, of slinging that burden across my shoulders again, feels impossibly heavy. I don't think I can carry one more thing.

I look over at Logan. "Want to go to the pond?"

Chapter Twenty-One

I point to the log where we sat yesterday with Gōnggong. "Look," I tell Logan. "They named a bench after you."

"Ha ha, very funny." But he drops his bike in the grass next to the log and takes a seat. "You really want to know why Liam calls me Log?"

"I do," I say.

Logan plucks a weed and shreds it, tossing the bits into the pond where they float on the surface. "It's totally embarrassing. But I'll tell you if you tell me what Lan is short for and what it means."

My shoulders stiffen. This is how Ged must have felt when Vetch told him his true name, Estarriol. Even if Logan is only telling me the story of his nickname, he is trusting me with it. Do I trust Logan enough to tell him my real name? I only met him last week. What if he tells Liam and Liam makes up some other, even worse nickname for me? Even as I think it, I know that Logan would never do that. He understands what it's like to be called a name that isn't your own. I let out my breath and relax my shoulders. "Okay. Deal."

Logan slumps a little, too. "Well, there's this camp that Liam and I go to for a few weeks every summer. Camp Carson. It's not far away, so lots of kids from the Cliff go there. We've all been going since we were, like, six or something. It's awesome—I love the woods. Liam and I always have the best time. We hike, have campfires, and hang out with all the guys. Except this year, it was like he had it out for me. I don't know what happened, but just before school ended in May, it was like Liam turned into a different person."

I think about Xing and how she was my best friend . . . until suddenly she wasn't. She had turned into a different person, too. "Yeah," I tell Logan. "I get that."

He gives me a sympathetic look. "He kept playing pranks on me—putting ketchup packets under the toilet seat or throwing my shoes onto the cabin roof. Annoying stuff like that."

"That doesn't sound like a prank. That just sounds mean."

"It was kind of funny at first. But it got old. One night, I wake up to this horrible smell. And it was coming from my sleeping bag. So I jump out of bed and shine my flashlight on it, and it's this enormous turd, just sitting there." Logan flings another handful of weed bits into the pond.

"Eww! That's disgusting!"

"Tell me about it," Logan says. "I thought it was an animal at first, because it looked like it was moving. And then I realized that it was Liam—he was in the bunk above me, trying so hard not to laugh out loud that he was making the whole bunk bed shake. I didn't know how he did it or why, but I knew he was responsible."

"What happened? What did you do?"

"Liam noticed me looking at him, so he pretended that he just woke up. He started freaking out about the smell and woke everyone else up, too. Then he accused me of, uh, making it myself." Logan's cheeks turn pink. "He said I must have 'sleepcrapped.' Of course that wasn't possible—I was still wearing my shorts—but nobody cared. They made me take my sleeping bag outside, and Liam locked me out of the cabin for the rest of the night. The next morning, everyone called me Log. Because, you know . . . it was *massive*."

Logan's whole face is dark red, and I regret asking him to tell this story. "I can't believe your own brother did that to you!"

"Right? Or that he took the time to find it in the woods. I just don't get it. All that stuff they say about twins? It was true for me and Liam. We were best friends. We always had each other's backs. But then—wham! The Turd Incident comes out of nowhere. It was like a declaration of war."

Everything he described could have been about me and Xing, except we aren't real twins. Plus, I know why she stopped being my friend—she couldn't believe her parents were lying about Bàba. It was much easier to believe that my dad—and I—had been lying to her. But even understanding why she felt that way didn't make me feel any less betrayed. Logan had to be feeling all that and the pain of not knowing what had made Liam turn against him.

"You really don't have any idea why Liam started targeting you?"

Logan tears another weed out by its roots and crushes it in his hand. "I've been over it a million times. It's like he woke up one morning and decided his mission was to make my life miserable." He looks over at me. "That's why I was in the office the first day. I was trying to get my schedule changed."

Bits of his conversation with Mrs. Perry come back

to me. "You didn't want to be in all the same classes as Liam."

"Right. But Mrs. Perry nixed that idea. Said it 'wouldn't be fair' to the other kids." He makes an aggravated sound. "So now I'm stuck with Liam literally twenty-four seven. All day at school, all night at home. And the other guys won't hang out with me unless Liam's there, because they're afraid to make him mad."

No wonder he always seems to be alone. Logan didn't just lose his best friend; he lost his whole friend group. Just like me. He didn't move away, but it still happened to him. He made a plan to change things, but it didn't work. That's where I am. I struck out trying to find the ledger this morning and don't know where else to look.

"Sounds like we both had a *wonderful* first day of school!" I say, mimicking Foxman's fake cheerfulness. I try to re-create his pointy sneer, too.

Logan laughs—a real, authentic laugh. "Okay," he says, finally stopping. "Your turn. My nickname story for your nickname story."

Chapter Twenty-Two

Nicknames. I'm already regretting that I agreed to tell Logan anything. "It's not nearly as interesting as your story."

He elbows me. "I wouldn't call mine interesting. Humiliating, maybe. Or enlightening."

"Enlightening?" My eyebrows raise. I've never heard a kid my age use that word. Honestly, I'm not sure most of them know what it means.

"Yeah," Logan's voice sours. "Enlightening as to the levels of suckitude my brother can reach." He elbows me again. "So, come on. Spill. You said Lan was part of your Chinese name. What's the other part?"

I stare at the bugs skating around on the surface of the water. It shouldn't be this hard to tell someone your name. "It's Mei. Měilán is my full Chinese name. Actually, it's my English name, too."

There, I said it. But it doesn't feel like my name anymore. It belongs to someone else, someone who lived in another place and time. A girl who had a big complicated family and lived above a bakery full of delicious treats. A girl who didn't know what she had until she had to leave it all behind. A girl who didn't destroy a family. I look over to see Logan's reaction.

"Měilán," he says slowly, careful to copy the falling and rising tones. "What does it mean?"

There's a rock half-buried near my foot. I try to dig it out with my heel, but it won't budge. "It's silly. Mei means beautiful and Lan means orchid."

"Beautiful Orchid?" Logan laughs, and a wave of shame washes over me. Even he, a boy I barely know at all, can see how much the name doesn't fit me. Then he says, "That's not silly. Try Little Hollow—that's what Logan means. So basically, I'm a hole in the ground. Not even a big hole. A small hole." He laughs again. At himself. "Does that make you feel better?"

It does, actually. "Hollows are nice," I tell him. "Lots of animals take shelter in hollows." Warmth floods my cheeks. I keep digging at the rock, this time with the toe of my boot.

Thankfully, Logan doesn't seem to notice me blushing. "Thanks. Orchids are nice, too. They're, you know, exotic."

Without thinking, I shove Logan. He loses his balance and falls off the log with an *oof.* "Hey!" he says as he gets to his feet and brushes himself off. "What was that for?!"

I scowl. "Do *not* call me that!"

Still standing, Logan looks at the space between us, as if he's trying to measure the distance with his eyes. He's making sure he's out of reach, and I feel a bit guilty for pushing him. Not guilty enough to apologize, though. After a pause, he says, "Aren't exotic things nice?"

I take a deep breath. "For starters, I am not a thing." I snort. "I guess I'm not that nice, either." I reach out and pat the log next to me, silently promising that I won't shove him again. He sits, still looking confused.

Part of me is annoyed that Logan doesn't already understand. Why should I have to explain this to him? I sigh. Xing and my friends and I used to talk about this stuff a lot, but I've never discussed it with someone who isn't Asian. Remembering my Asian friends gives me an idea. "So, think about it this way. What do you, Liam, Cassidy, Fiona, Anita, and practically everyone else in our class have in common?"

He mulls it over and finally shrugs. "Except for all being in the same class at the Cliff, nothing. We're all really different people."

"You're all white," I point out.

Logan shifts his feet. "Well, yeah." He looks at me warily. "But you're not."

"That's my point. I'm not. I'm the only one who isn't."

"You're just the only one on the Chalk Team. There are others at the Cliff." His eyebrows pull together, and I know he still doesn't get it.

Even though Logan isn't being mean to me on purpose like Liam was that day in Health class, this conversation makes me feel the same way. Tired. I take a deep breath and try again. "You know how we were just talking about meanings? Do you know what exotic means?"

Now he looks offended. "Of course I do. It means special and unique."

He would think that. The worst thing he's probably ever had to deal with is sibling issues. Try having people question your culture, your family, your existence. Even in Chinatown, with all the tourists gawking at us. And here, in Redbud. Every. Single. Day.

"Okay, you're right. But 'special' and 'unique' in the sense of being strange and unusual."

"What's so wrong with that? I like strange and unusual people. They're more interesting."

"Have there ever been any other Asians at the Cliff?" I ask.

"Of course," he says again. "There's Emerson Park. He graduated last year."

I blink. "He graduated from *high school* last year? So I'm the first Asian to come along in *six years*?" That would explain a lot.

"Hey, I can't help who moves here and who doesn't," Logan protests.

I kick the rock, the pain in my toes giving me a jolt, a little more energy to deal with this discussion. The silence drags on as I worry the rock with my toes, back and forth, back and forth, like working a loose tooth. Logan should be putting in work, too.

"Try something with me," I finally say. "Name the first thing that pops into your head when I give you a category."

He looks suspicious. "What is this, a test?"

"No, it's more like a game. Like Ms. Brown says, there aren't any wrong answers."

Logan agrees to play along even though I can tell he doesn't want to. That's okay—I don't really want to, either. But if we're going to be friends, he has to understand.

"Exotic food," I say.

His right eyebrow arches. "Sushi."

I fight the urge to laugh. *Sushi!* Sushi is not strange or unusual—they sell it in every grocery store in Boston, near the deli meat and the rotisserie chicken.

"Okay. Next one: exotic car."

Logan smiles. "Easy. Ferrari."

Hmm. I think Ferraris are from Italy. I can work with that. "Last one. Exotic pet."

"Tigers. Chinchillas. Pythons." He grins. "Want me to keep going? Do I get bonus points?"

"No! Stop!" I laugh. "I want you to tell me what all those things you named have in common."

"This again?" He pauses. "Let's see. Sushi, Ferraris, tigers, chinchillas, pythons . . . Umm, they're all things I want."

"No," I say again. "Wrong answer! Plus, you want a python?!"

"Hey!" Logan protests. "You said there were no wrong answers."

"Ms. Brown said that, not me. *I* say people are full of wrong answers."

"Fine." He crosses his arms against his chest. "What is it?"

"All the things you came up with are from another

country, another culture." The rock under my toes finally begins to shift in the ground.

"So?"

The last of my energy drains, and my shoulders slump. "So when you call people like me exotic, you're basically saying that we're foreigners and that we don't belong. It's like Liam insisting that I'm from China. Or Foxman telling me that my name isn't American enough. Even though I was born here and I'm as American as they are."

Logan doesn't say anything. "I get it," he finally says. "I won't call anybody exotic anymore. I'm nothing like Liam or Foxman."

I want to tell him that it's not that simple. Not just a rule about not calling people a specific adjective. It's about how you see and treat other people. And you have to constantly be aware of what you're doing and how it affects others, so your adjustments don't stop. Ever.

The silence stretches out. "I'm sorry," Logan says quietly. "I've never really been anywhere. We visited Nashville once, but that's about it." His eyes home in on mine, like he's trying to see my thoughts. "I'm sure I'll say more unintelligent things. But I'm going to try harder to recognize when I do." Then, even more softly, he says, "I think you can be special and unique *and* American all at the same time."

There's a fluttering in my chest, and I don't know if it's the beetles or some other winged creatures brushing against my heart. All I can do is smile with my mouth closed so they don't fly away.

It's nice sitting here with Logan, on the edge of the blue water reflecting the blue sky. The list of Chinese characters for lán pops into my mind, and I think especially about the third one, which means blue. Here, away from home and school, I feel more myself than I have in months.

And then Logan says, "Blue."

"What?" How could he possibly know that I was just thinking about being the lán that means blue?

Logan's face reddens. "Your hair. It's so black it looks blue in the sunlight, like . . ." his voice trails off.

I've heard this before. "Like an ugly crow in a comic book."

"No," he says, shocked. "I was going to say, like . . . a starling."

A starling. That sounds much better than a crow. I admit to Logan that I don't know what a starling looks like, so he pulls up a photo on his phone and shows it to me. I've seen them in Boston before, a bird with dark-teal, indigo, and brown feathers. There are white speckles all over it, like fairy lights against a deepening night sky.

"Maybe that should be your nickname," Logan says. "Starling."

I think about it for a moment but then shake my head. I don't have a great relationship with birds right now, especially the fènghuáng.

"But your name isn't really Melanie. So what do I call you? Meilan?"

I surprise myself by saying, "No." Logan looks surprised, too. "I guess I don't want to go against Foxman," I explain. "My mom wouldn't be happy if she found out."

"I don't want to call you Melanie. I can tell you hate it. Besides, you never answer to it."

Even though only my family uses it, I tell Logan to call me Lan at school. I can pretend that it's short for Melanie while also knowing that it refers to the me that is Basket or Blue.

Blue. Now I have a name for who I am outside of family and school. Out from under the gaze and expectations of Māma, Bàba, and Gōnggong. Out here, where I can be sadness and sky and the iridescent sheen of a starling.

Chapter Twenty-Three

Every day, I eat lunch in the courtyard. The peapods, tiny only just last week, are growing longer and fatter. Today, Māma has packed thick slices of pork belly cooked in soy sauce on a bed of white rice. When the pork was served hot at dinner last night, it was melt-in-your-mouth tender. Cold, it's a lot tougher and greasier, so I push it aside and just eat the rice.

When I'm finished, there's still about fifteen minutes of lunch period left. I decide to explore behind the maple tree even though the path doesn't extend back there. Yesterday, I saw a flash of red from that corner and wondered what kind of flowers could bloom in the deep shade. I push my way past a shrub and duckwalk under the low branches of the tree. When I get there, my stomach sinks. They're not flowers at all. Instead, a sad, deflated red balloon hangs from a tree branch by its ribbon. I tug at the balloon, trying to untangle it from the branch. Suddenly, it comes free and I stumble backward into a window.

Whirling around, I come face-to-face with a scowling Foxman. I can't keep the gasp from leaving my throat. Something small and brown tumbles to the ground near my foot. Maybe it's a bit of twig. Or maybe it's a beetle.

The principal raps on the glass and says something. I can't hear his voice, but his lips are perfectly clear: *Leave. Now.* He points toward the direction of the courtyard door.

Clutching the limp red balloon in my hand, I scramble back to the path, gather up my lunch and backpack, and dash back into the school hallway. The courtyard door is warm against my back as I put my hands on my knees and try to catch my breath. When I finally straighten up, I spot Liam.

He looks at the door behind me. "Don't you know you're not allowed out there, Melanie Melanin?"

There isn't a sign on the door telling students to keep out or anything. I manage a small shrug, which seems to make Liam angry. His eyes narrow, and he takes another step toward me. "Whatcha got?"

Confused, I follow his eyes to my hand, which is

clenched tight around the dead balloon. I uncurl my fingers and show him. "God, you're pathetic," he snarls. Shame rises up in me, greasy and nauseating like the pork in my lunch.

Anita appears in the hallway behind Liam. She hesitates for a moment, then waves at me. I wave back, noticing too late that I'm waving the balloon at her, too. Smiling, she comes over and stands next to Liam. "Did you find that in the courtyard?" She sounds intrigued instead of grossed out. I nod, wondering what could be so fascinating about a deflated balloon.

"Cool!" she says. "I bet that's from Mrs. Robinson's going away party. They had it in the courtyard after school one day. She was my guidance counselor in elementary school. She was awesome." Anita holds out her hand. "Do you mind if I take a look?"

Immediately, I toss her the balloon like we're little kids in a game of Hot Potato. Anita examines it closely, then stretches it between her hands. Liam looks at her like she's completely bonkers and shakes his head in disbelief. Anita looks up at me, her eyes sparkling. "Did you know that Mrs. Robinson's party was over a year ago? And this balloon still looks brand new. Well, it would if you washed the dirt off. And it's still incredibly elastic—no signs of material disintegration at all. Do you know what that means?"

Blinking, I shake my head. I understood all her words but not what she's trying to get at. Liam is suspiciously quiet, too. Thankfully, she's happy to explain and doesn't press us. "It shows that latex—that's what this balloon is made of—takes an incredibly long time to break down in the environment. Which proves how dangerous latex balloons are to wildlife." She thinks for a minute. "This would be an amazing science fair topic!" Anita stuffs the balloon in her pocket and grins at me. "Thanks for the idea, Melanie! Come on, we better get to Math class." I slide away from the courtyard door and walk with her, happy to get away from Liam, who's still scowling. I want to tell him that Anita doesn't think I'm pathetic. But I don't.

In Math, Anita plops down in her usual front row seat while I head to the back. I can feel Logan's eyes following me, but I ignore him. Why couldn't that have been him in the hallway and not his twin? There's a seat in the third row by the window, and I slip into it grate-fully, swinging my hair across my face. Looking outside always makes me feel better.

Someone sprawls in the seat directly behind me and sticks their feet into the aisle. I just fled those steel-toed construction boots two minutes ago. Prickles crawl down my neck and along my arms. I wish that I could change my schedule, but now I know from Logan that it's impossible. I wish that I could change schools and go back to An Wang Middle School. I wish that I were anywhere but here.

Mr. Becker starts explaining proportional relationships and drawing graphs on the board. I squint through the gray hazy mist in my eyes and try to copy everything down, stopping to rub my eyes every few minutes. Maybe I'm allergic to this school.

Mist. Yet another meaning of lán. I hate to sound like Bàba, but this is a sign. Here, I am Mist. I need to move lightly, almost invisibly, through the Cliff. Keep my head down, do my work, get good grades, and above all, not be noticed.

As Mist, I can be formless, shapeless, as unnoticeable as air. All the pointed comments and barbed looks will sail right through me and land somewhere else, far off in the cornfields. Not even Liam can get to me.

Chapter Twenty-Four

Before I know it, another week has gone by, and it's September. I've fully embraced Mist. This meaning of Lan, this other version of myself, has really worked—almost no one looks at me in class or in the hallways anymore. Teachers rarely call on me, their eyes sliding over my seat like it's empty. I sail in and out of the nurse's office looking for—but not finding—an old-fashioned pay phone. I slip out of classes and school so stealthily that even Logan doesn't see me. Best of all, I can sneak out to eat lunch in the courtyard again without being caught.

In Social Studies, Ms. Brown hands out small postcards with the school logo of a sun rising over a cornfield on the front. On the other side is a printed invitation.

Dear Students, Staff, and Community Members:

On behalf of Clifton Middle School, I would like to invite students to bring family members, neighbors, and friends to a special Veterans Day ceremony on Friday, November 11th. A program honoring our community's veterans will begin at 9:00 a.m. in the auditorium, followed by refreshments in the cafeteria.

Please RSVP to the Main Office by Tuesday, November 8th if you or a family member will be attending. I am excited to welcome our veterans to Clifton Middle School in celebration of their service.

Sincerely,

Casimir Reynard
Principal

The lower left corner of the card has words printed in color and a larger font. CLIFTON M.S. VETERANS WEEK, it reads, HONOR, SUPPORT, EDUCATE.

More handouts are passed back from the front-row kids. The top sheet has a paragraph of instructions, a rubric, and a list of questions. "Veterans Day Project: Biography of a Veteran" is written across the top in bold letters.

"Everyone have the handouts?" Ms. Brown asks. "We're going to be doing an exciting project leading up to and for the Veterans Day ceremony here at Clifton. Redbud has a long history of military service, and we want to honor our veterans. You'll each choose a veteran, interview them, and write a three-page biography. I know some of you have family members who are currently deployed. Although they're not technically veterans until they're discharged, if you want to, you can still do your project on them."

"My uncle served in the Iraq War," Frankie says.

Lily Summers looks sad. "My dad is still in Afghanistan."

"Well, then, Frankie, you're all set. And Lily, I bet your father would still like to participate, even if he can't make it to the ceremony." Ms. Brown smiles at her sympathetically. Her gaze sweeps over the rest of the class. "If none of your relatives are veterans, think about your neighbors and your parents' friends. Maybe someone in the community that you see often is a veteran and you just don't know it. For example, Mr. Parker who runs the post office is a veteran of the Gulf War. Now, who knows why it's important for us to document veterans' experiences?"

"Veterans can teach us how to fight," Liam says.

"Actually," Ms. Brown says, "We need to understand the impact of war and the honor of serving our country so we can all learn from history and not repeat the mistakes of our past."

I think she's trying to say that we could prevent another world war by interviewing veterans and telling their stories, but I have my doubts. Stories, even if they're not real, can be dangerous. I should know. Besides, the list of wars, interventions, and invasions included in the handouts is really long. It seems like our government is doing a lot of repeating and not a lot of learning.

"Do you have a question, Dylan?" the teacher asks.

A shaggy-haired boy looks at me while he replies. "Aren't we in a war with China right now? My dad says he's been fighting them. Some group called the 'Tariffs.'"

Ms. Brown's forehead creases. "I believe your father is talking about the trade war with China. Tariffs are a type of tax, not people. We aren't in an armed conflict with China—our government disagrees with the way trade is conducted between our countries. That's a job for the president and Congress, not the military.

"Okay, I'm glad we cleared that up. Take a look at the rubric. I've given you plenty of time for this project, and there'll be an assignment each week to help you get it done. It concludes with a celebration on Veterans Day. Each of you will present the veteran you interviewed to the audience on stage and share a bit of their story."

Dylan isn't finished. "So I can't interview my dad? Even though the president called China the enemy?"

"No, Dylan," Ms. Brown says firmly. "You'll have to find someone else."

Now everyone is staring at me. After days of being unseen, it feels like being jabbed with multiple sharp blue and green pencils. My hair covers part of my face, but still, I feel their gazes judging me. I keep my mouth shut and stare down at the list of suggested interview questions.

Question 1: What is your name?

Right now, I am the Lan who is Mist. Mist is invincible because everything flows right through her. Mist cannot be hurt. Mist reshapes herself after any attack. My name is Mist. I am Mist. It's good to be Mist. I feel light and free again.

Ms. Brown's voice brings me back to the classroom. "I want you all to get started thinking about which veteran you will be interviewing. Let me know who it is next Monday."

A chill crawls across the back of my neck and makes the beetles shiver. I think Gōnggong was a soldier. I've seen an old photo of him in a uniform that looks like it might be military. But not here in the United States—in Taiwan, where he was born. Does that make him a veteran?

And then I remember the sounds that Gōnggong sometimes makes at night. Sounds I'd never heard until he started living with us. At first, I'd thought it was Mr. Shellhaus's ghost and burrowed deeper into my sleeping bag, afraid to peek. Then I heard bits of Mandarin mixed in with the terrible sounds and realized it was my grandfather. That was frightening in a completely different way, and I'd run to get Māma. She went into his room, murmured soothing words, and soon the noises stopped. I waited in the hall for her to come out, and all she said was, "Bad dreams."

What could Gōnggong be having nightmares about? Maybe being in a war? I won't ask about Gōnggong's bad dreams, but maybe I can ask if he or anyone else in our family is a veteran. I hope it counts if they weren't soldiers in the US military. Ms. Brown didn't say anything about that.

Chapter Twenty-Five

There are so many things I want to ask my parents. I decide to start with the Veterans Day project. "Bàba, did you ever want to join the military?"

Bàba laughs. "Me? No, no, I do not like to fight. I would make a bad soldier." He sneaks a look at Gōnggong, who doesn't look back at him. I can't tell if Gōnggong is listening to the conversation or not.

"So we don't have any veterans in our family?"

There's a pause while Māma and Bàba look at each other. "Well," Bàba says a little too carefully. "We do not have any veterans of the United States military in our family."

Both my parents are trying too hard not to look at Gōnggong, who is concentrating on eating his dinner. "Are you saying that we have veterans of the Chinese military in our family? Do I know any of them?"

Abruptly, Gōnggong scoots his chair back, the rubber pads on the legs squawking against the tile. He picks up his bowl and chopsticks and leaves the table without a word. He puts his dirty dishes in the sink and disappears down the hallway. There's a soft click as his bedroom door closes. Then all is silent. I guess he did understand what we were talking about. And I guess his actions answered my questions.

I search my parents' faces. First one, then the other. They're both shuttered, closed. They won't look back at me. After a moment, they both start eating again, as though nothing happened. Another thing they won't talk about.

I know I should leave it alone, but I have a school project to complete. Doing well in school is practically mandatory—ever since I started first grade, Māma and Bàba have been very clear that good grades are super important so I can go to a good college. Like Princeton. I'd been the youngest kid on the tour this summer, which was incredibly embarrassing. After college I'm supposed to get a good job to help my parents support Gōnggong and then take care of my parents when they're old. Even though that's all way in the future, I know that's what my parents expect. All of that means that I not only have to complete the Veterans Day project, but I have to get a good grade—the best grade. At home, I am Basket, after all.

But how am I going to do that?

I try again. "So Gōnggong was in the Chinese military? What happened to him?"

Bàba shakes his head. He looks sad and a little bit angry. Is he angry with me? "This is a long story; very difficult to tell. Many things I do not know. Also, it is not my story to tell. Gōnggong suffered many hardships in the Vietnam War. He does not like to talk about it." Bàba waves one hand, as if pushing away a small animal. His English gets more abrupt, more clipped. "Long time ago. Much water under bridge." Suddenly, he stares straight at me. "Why you keep asking? This not good conversation topic."

"No reason," I say quickly. "Just curious. There was a kid in school talking about his uncle being in the war in Iraq. Sorry." Both my parents nod and go back to eating in silence.

I can't explain to them about the Veterans Day project now. Bàba already said that it isn't his story to tell. If he knows it's a school assignment, he'll be forced to either answer my questions or ask Gōnggong to do the interview. Both options would cause them pain. And even if Gōnggong did the interview, there's no way he would want to participate in the celebration at school when he doesn't even want to admit to me that he was in the military.

I'll have to make something up to tell Ms. Brown. Some relative who doesn't live in Ohio, can only be interviewed by phone, and can't come to the celebration. Of course, I'll have to make up the interview answers, but I can do that by looking information up on the internet. I'll pick a war—maybe the Vietnam War since Bàba let slip that Gōnggong was part of it—and do some research. Good stories have details that make the story sound authentic and true. I'm great at making up stories that people think are real.

I feel guilty for planning to lie, but relieved, too. This way, Basket won't disturb the peace at home, and Mist won't have to get up on stage and be noticed, either. We can still be ourselves. The only one who isn't happy is Blue, who made a vow not to tell stories anymore. But being Blue means being unhappy, so in a weird, ironic way, my plan still holds true to all the versions of me.

Now that I've got the Veterans Day project all figured out, it's time to switch to my other duty besides being a good student—being a good daughter and bringing my family back together. But I've been talking a lot tonight, and my questions have upset Gōnggong and Bàba. The beetles clog my throat like a lump of rice. I swallow hard. Casually, I turn to Māma. "How was your day?"

She looks at me like I've grown antlers. "So much fun," she says in Mandarin. "I found a magic ring, made me so happy. It did all the cooking and cleaning. I just relaxed and watched dramas on TV."

I ignore her sarcasm. "That sounds great. Did you get any interesting mail recently?"

"What do you mean, interesting?" Māma looks suspicious. "Who's writing to you?"

"I was hoping Xing would write to me since she can't text me anymore." Maybe if I seem pitiful enough, my plan will work *and* Māma will get me a new cell phone.

Her face brightens, which I don't expect. "Good— letters are better than text anyway. I'll keep watch for a letter for you."

Hmm. New approach needed. "There might be stuff from my school counselor, too."

"What kind of stuff? Why did you see the counselor? Are you in trouble?"

"No, Māma, I'm not in trouble." Why does she always

think the worst of me? "The counselor said she would send some brochures for summer camps. The educational kind."

Māma waves her hand dismissively. "I threw those away."

That takes me by surprise. "What? You threw them away? Why did you do that?"

"Summer is over. Next summer is a long time away. There's no need to think about this now."

I resist the urge to smile. She just gave me the perfect opening. "But there aren't too many good opportunities for educational summer camps around here. You know, the kind that focus on math and science and other academic stuff that colleges like. So you have to apply early and write a great essay to get a spot." I hurry to add, "At least that's what the counselor says."

I hold my breath as Māma and Bàba look at each other. Finally, Bàba says, "We can't apply now. I've been working at my new job for only a few weeks. We can apply later—if they still have spots, then maybe you can go. If there's no space, then it's not meant to be."

Even though I was expecting his answer, a needle of disappointment jabs me. And even though I know we don't have the money for me to attend camp, anger burns in the hole left by the disappointment. Carrying their hopes and dreams is never about me and what I actually want. Telling them I'd like to become a librarian would never get them to agree to camp, never mind moving back to Boston for my education. I tamp the feelings down—this is all part of the plan. Can't let the beetles get the better of me.

I take a breath. "You know, Xing said she went to a camp at a college campus this summer." As soon as the words leave my mouth, I feel slightly nauseous. I'm manipulating my parents, just like Third Aunt, just like Foxman. Who is the evil trickster creature here?

Māma whirls to stare at me. "How do you know this? You talked to Xing? I thought you were waiting for her letter."

"Oh, umm," I cast about for a logical answer. "I called Xing. To give her my new address. That's when she told me." The beetles squirm inside. It's only partially a lie—I did call Xing, she did tell me about camp during the conversation, but I didn't give her my address. She hung up on me before I got the chance. "She probably didn't apply until after school ended. There are lots of programs like that in Boston, so it probably isn't as difficult to get in. They might even have scholarships." I shrug, deliberately casual. "If we still lived there, I bet they'd take me. I mean, if Xing can get a spot . . ." I let my voice trail off.

Māma and Second Aunt have always been in competition about who has the smarter daughter. Using that against them feels like karma. Especially after what Xing said to me on the phone. She must have heard all that stuff about me from her mom.

My own mother nods slowly, her fingernails clicking against the tabletop. "Yìng jī lì duàn?" she asks Bàba, who shrugs. To me, she says, "Bàba and I will consider this opportunity."

It's not a promise, but it feels like one. My arrow found its mark. Now to launch the attacks on the aunts and uncles. A tiny bit of brick crumbles and lightens the basket on my back.

Chapter Twenty-Six

Even though it's not due for a while, I'm taking notes on the Vietnam War for the Veterans Day project. Writing a fake interview is a lot harder than just interviewing a real person and writing down their answers. It feels like I'm writing a history paper. But to have any chance of getting the best grade, I'm going to have to put in the work. I finally found a person I can use as the veteran I'm supposedly interviewing, and I'll only have to change his name a tiny bit. He did a lot of stuff, so the interview will hopefully be really interesting and impress Ms. Brown.

A breeze carries the sound of voices through my open window. Bàba put my desk under the window so I have a view. I look up from my notebook and spot two figures standing in the yard underneath the dragon tree. One of them is Gōnggong, gripping a shovel in his hand. The other is one of the twins. He's turned slightly sideways, so I can't tell who it is. It's not until he runs a hand through his hair that I realize it's Logan. I feel a little bad that I haven't talked to him in over a week, but those are Mist's rules. Plus, if my plan works, I'll be moving back home soon, so maybe it's better this way. But what is he doing talking to Gōnggong?

I strain to hear their conversation, but the wind has shifted, taking their voices away. Logan points to the tree, then down to the ground. Gōnggong tilts his head, and Logan makes a circular motion with his hand, holding it palm-down. Then he picks up a fallen branch and snaps it in half, showing it to my grandfather, who shakes his head. I'm mystified, too. Then Logan gestures over to the other side of our yard, near the fence with our other neighbors, whom I haven't met yet. Gōnggong nods and they both walk over there. With the tip of the shovel, Gōnggong draws a line through the grass and dirt, sketching out a large rectangle. Then he starts digging and weeding inside the rectangle. Logan climbs back over the fence and heads toward his house.

It's a garden, I realize. My grandfather, who refused to leave his apartment after Nǎinai died, is making something where he'll have to spend a lot of time outdoors.

I'm just about to go out and help Gōnggong when there's movement on the street to my left. Logan reappears, pushing some sort of machine across our yard. It's not a lawnmower like the old one our landlord left us. Instead, it looks like the snowblowers that people use to clear their driveways and sidewalks back home. But there's no snow.

Logan leans over the machine and yanks a long cord. The engine sputters and dies. He tries again, and this time I hear the loud chug of a motor. Motioning for Gōnggong to stand back, Logan slowly pushes the machine across the rectangle, leaving a trail of churned-up dirt and weeds behind him. Ten minutes later, the entire patch of ground has been dug up, ready for what-ever Gōnggong wants to plant. I'm amazed; that would have taken Gōnggong all afternoon to dig up by himself. Still staring, I watch Logan turn off the digging machine and raise his hand. Even more amazingly, Gōnggong's face lights up with a grin as he gives Logan a high five.

Part of me wants to go outside and join them, but I don't know if I'd be Basket since I'm at home, or Blue because I'd be in the yard with Logan. It's better if I keep my different selves separate. Plus, it looks like they're getting along fine, even without me there to help trans-late. There's a sharp twinge under my ribs as a beetle nips me. I turn back to my research.

When I raise my head again, there's a pile of weeds

next to the new garden, and Logan and Gōnggong are raking the yard. At one point, Logan looks up at my window, and I instinctively duck to the side. I hope he didn't see me watching him. I wonder if he asked Gōnggong about me. Why is he even helping my grandfather? He said he's lived here all his life—he must have other relatives that he can do yardwork for.

After a minute, I sit up and am relieved to find the yard empty. Gōnggong must've gotten tired and Logan must've gone home. But then I hear voices from the direction of the back door, and my heart beats as fast as a beetle's wings. What is Logan doing here?

"Bǎobèi. Bāng wǒ kāi mén." Gōnggong's voice travels through the house. I drop my pencil and scurry to the back door. He's standing on the stoop, holding the bottom of his shirt out with gloved hands to make a kind of pouch. A pile of the hard green fruits from the dragon tree rest inside. Behind him, Logan has a T-shirt full of them, too.

Quickly, I hold open the screen door so they can come in. The tiny mudroom feels claustrophobic with the three of us crowded together, and I can't catch my breath or meet Logan's eyes. He's in my house. What do I do? What do I say? The beetles are twirling, jumping, prancing . . . Oh, god. I'm wearing my old house slippers, blue plastic ones with Mickey Mouse's face across the top, which Māma found for super cheap in Chinatown. The beetles come to a screeching halt.

"Zhǎo yī gè sùojiāo dàizi," Gōnggong says.

I squish myself against the wall so I don't accidentally touch Logan as I slide past and retrieve a plastic bag from the cabinet where Māma keeps them. I stand in the doorway and hold it open while Gōnggong carefully pours the contents of his shirt into the bag. When he's done, he changes out of his shoes and into his slippers, nice brown leather ones, then comes into the kitchen.

Logan steps forward, and I keep my eyes lowered as the green fruits roll from his shirt into the bag. He adjusts his grip on his shirt, revealing a narrow strip of skin just above the waistband of his shorts. It's not as pale as I thought it would be, which means he must have spent time outside this summer without his shirt on. I swallow and look away, accidentally meeting his eyes.

"Hey," he says, and he lets his shirt drop. "I didn't know you were home."

The bag in my hands is heavy. "What kind of fruit is this?" I ask.

He laughs, and the beetles whirl with embarrassment. "Fruit? They're not fruits, they're nuts."

"Nuts?" Of course they're nuts. I should've known because of how hard they are. Still, they don't look like any nut I've ever seen.

"Walnuts," he says at the same time that Gōnggong calls, "Lái kàn!" from behind me. My grandfather reaches for the bag and beckons to both of us before walking over to the kitchen counter.

I look at Logan. "Um, would you like to come in? He wants us to see something."

"Sure." He takes off his gloves and puts them on the bench. Without prompting, he kicks off his sneakers, too. His feet are bare. The beetles race wildly around my insides. Those bugs are getting a ton of exercise today.

Gōnggong gets out a cutting board and the meat cleaver. The board has a narrow trough carved around the edge—Bàba said it was to catch the juices from roast chicken. But Gōnggong is clever. He sets a walnut in the trough, so it doesn't roll. Then he takes the cleaver and, in one powerful stroke, chops through the walnut with a loud *thwock*.

"Nice!" Logan exclaims.

The green part of the walnut, the husk, has fallen away in large wedges, revealing the wrinkled brown nutshell inside. Bits of actual walnut are scattered across the cutting board. Gōnggong picks up a piece and hands it to me to try. "Shì shì kàn," he urges. He hands a piece to Logan, too, who promptly tosses it into his mouth.

"They taste different than regular walnuts," Logan cautions.

I put the piece in my mouth and chew. It's like grass and earth and black tea that has been left to brew too long. It's not bad, though. And for once, looking from Logan to Gōnggong, I don't mind the bitterness.

Chapter Twenty-Seven

"Your great-uncle fought in the Vietnam War?" Ms. Brown looks doubtful. "And his name is Hua Chi Minh?"

I nod nervously. In the research I was able to do yesterday, I found a man named Ho Chi Minh who played a large part in the Vietnam War. His nickname was "Uncle Ho," so I got the idea to make him my great-uncle and change his last name to Hua to match mine. Since most white people can't tell Asians from different countries apart, I figure that all Asian names sound alike to them, too. And I'm counting on the fact that the Vietnam War was so long ago that Ms. Brown won't know everything about the real Ho Chi Minh, who I'm planning to use in my fake interview.

"And you're going to interview him for the Veterans Day project?" she continues.

"Yes, but over the phone," I respond. "He doesn't live near us." I hasten to add, "He won't be able to come to the ceremony, either."

"That's too bad," Ms. Brown says. I can't decipher her expression. She doesn't look displeased, but she doesn't seem pleased, either. More like confused. When she makes a note on her chart and moves on to the kid sitting behind me, I let out a little sigh of relief.

Once she has written down the names of the veterans everyone will be interviewing, she continues the lesson on the Revolutionary War. I already studied it last year, so my mind wanders to my own battle. Could there be a pay phone in the Redbud Café? Or somewhere else in town? Did a tiny town like this ever even need a pay phone?

"Melanie. Melanie!" Ms. Brown calls. I snap back to attention. Social Studies is the hardest class to be Mist in—the teacher always seems to notice me. She's my favorite teacher, but still . . .

"Yes?" I look away from the window to find the other kids smirking. Great.

"I was saying, Melanie, that you must have a deeper appreciation of the Revolutionary War since you lived in Boston."

"I guess so." Growing up in Boston, we started walking the Freedom Trail in third grade.

"Do you have any stories or photos about the historic sites that you can share with the class?"

I shake my head.

The teacher's face dims. "Let's talk about it after class. It would be wonderful to hear from someone who's actually been to these places."

I nod and wrap Mist's cloak around myself more tightly.

When class is over, I wait until everyone has left before approaching Ms. Brown's desk. Logan gives me a sympathetic smile on his way out, but I ignore him.

"Have a seat, Melanie."

I sit on the edge of the chair and decide to nip this conversation in the bud. "I'm sorry, but I really can't bring in any photos of stuff in Boston. Most of that is still packed and . . ." I drift off, hoping she'll get the hint. I'm not in charge of unpacking—Māma is. She has enough to do without looking for photos of me at boring historical sites. Like finding a job. I'm supposed to help carry her load, not add to it.

"Oh, of course. I didn't think of that," Ms. Brown says sympathetically. "Never mind, then. I'll pull photos off the internet." She looks at me a little more sharply. "What I really wanted to talk to you about is the Veterans Day project. What's going on with that?"

I feel like my stomach is clenched in a dragon's fierce

grip. The beetles are crushed together and panicking. "Um, what do you mean? I told you that I'm interviewing my great-uncle."

"Melanie, Ho Chi Minh is the name of the North Vietnamese prime minister during the Vietnam War. The name you gave me sounds suspiciously close to his. I'm not saying your great-uncle doesn't exist, but . . . Is there anything you want to tell me?"

My face heats up, the talons around my stomach squeeze tighter, and the beetles squirm harder. I can't lie to her face. On paper, maybe, but not when she's staring at me. Slowly, I shake my head. That's not a lie. I don't want to tell her anything.

She studies my face. "I know a lot about Ho Chi Minh. Including that he died in 1969. Therefore, he can't possibly be interviewed anymore."

The dragon's talons now feel like fishhooks. I'm caught. So much for impressing her with my fake interview. I look down at the floor, searching for inspiration, for a way out. Will she tell my parents?

Ms. Brown scoots her chair closer and looks at me with kind eyes. "Melanie, I want to help. Please tell me what's going on with you."

Mist can't shield or cover me from this one. But maybe

if I tell the truth about why I can't complete the assignment, she'll excuse me from doing it.

"My grandfather is a veteran," I say, "and I think he did fight in the Vietnam War. But . . ."

"Yes?" Ms. Brown says gently.

I stare at a map on the wall behind her. "But he wasn't in the US military. He's Chinese, so he was probably in the Chinese military. And I know China and the US aren't exactly friendly, so doesn't that make him—" I take a deep breath "—the enemy?"

Her voice is warm. "Not necessarily. There were a lot of different countries involved in that war," she says. "You won't know what his role was unless you ask. That will be a fascinating oral history project."

Wait, what? I stare at her.

"I'd like you to interview your grandfather, even though he didn't fight for the US Armed Forces. I bet he has some interesting stories to tell." She must see the horror on my face, because she asks, "Doesn't that help? You'll get to know your grandfather better, and you won't be turning in an unacceptable interview for the assignment."

That is a relief, but it still doesn't solve my problem. "The thing is, he doesn't like to talk about his time in the war." I don't tell her that my parents practically forbade me from asking him about it.

She looks thoughtful. "I understand it may be hard for him to talk about it, but it's so important for us to preserve his memories. Maybe you can think of other ways to get him to open up about his past? Instead of sitting him down for a formal interview, try asking him a question or two when he's doing something he enjoys. Or when he seems open to it." She pats my hand. "And it would be great if you could persuade him to come to the ceremony. We should honor all those who fought for freedom."

I can only nod. This is even worse than trying to find photos of me on the Freedom Trail. Now I have a direct order from a teacher to interview Gōnggong on what is probably one of the most painful parts of his life. As if he needs more things to be sad about. He was just starting to be happier again, too.

What am I going to do? If I go against Ms. Brown's wishes, she'll give me a failing grade and Mist will be a bad student. Basket has to prevent bad feelings from hurting my family further. I'm pretty sure asking Gōnggong about his war experience is going to bring up a lot of terrible memories. Either way, the shame of an underachieving, misbehaving daughter could keep Māma and Bàba from ever showing their faces in Boston. I might never see Xing and Tiffi again.

Blue's only rule is that I be my true self, to acknowledge my thoughts and emotions. But if I were her right now, all I would feel is the never-ending midnight blue of despair.

Chapter Twenty-Eight

Being Mist helps me survive the next two classes. Neither Mr. Lewis nor Mrs. Florence, the art teacher, call on me. My head and stomach spin endlessly. I need to escape to the courtyard and figure out what I'm going to do about the Veterans Day project. I'm keeping my head down on the way to get my lunch bag, when someone rudely bangs into my shoulder, pushing me into the lockers against the wall.

"What was that?" Liam sneers.

"Must've been a bug," Big Dave offers.

Little Dave shrugs. "I didn't see anyone."

The three of them swagger down the hall, bulldozing several other kids. I'm not sure if I should be upset that they think I'm insignificant or happy that Mist is keeping me mostly under their radar.

Up ahead, Logan stands next to my locker. I pause for a moment, hidden by the crush of kids on their way to lunch. What is he doing there? What does he want? We haven't really hung out, except for the few minutes he was in my kitchen the other day.

I feel awkward around Logan now, after we shared about our names and nicknames. He knows too much about me. I still can't believe I invited him to go to the pond. Basket would be horrified at breaking Māma's rules. I have no idea how to be friends with a boy. The only ones I know are the boys in fairy tales, thieves with flying carpets and greedy, selfish ones who are cursed and become beasts. Not boys who help dig gardens for random elderly neighbors. Logan is just as confusing as the tree spirit in the dragon tree. *Walnut tree,* I correct myself.

Suddenly, I know exactly what to call the tree spirit. Tao. It's both the second character in the Mandarin word for walnut and an old, non-Pinyin spelling of the word for way or path. I smile. Tao, the tree spirit, has helped me find my way so far. Maybe she can help with my Veterans Day project, too.

"You look happy today."

I glance up to find the hallway has cleared and I'm standing alone awkwardly in the middle. Great. Logan's eyes meet mine, and even from here I can see that today, they're green and blue and gray, like the lichen on the trees by the pond. Every Disney prince has light-colored eyes, so we're practically brainwashed into thinking they're better. But Liam's are the same color as Logan's, and I think Liam's eyes are evil.

Growing up in a large family that either doesn't talk about a lot of things or doesn't say exactly what they mean, I've had to learn to read people's expressions. The way his eyes are focused on mine and his head is tilted a little forward means interest, I think. The thought makes me blush, but I step forward, relieved that he's not mad at me for avoiding him. As I get closer, I notice a slight furrow between his eyebrows—worry—but about what? And then I'm standing in front of him, and there's no mistaking the meaning behind his smile.

"Hey," he says. I feel a shiver run through me, like a small golden carp darting through a cold clear stream. I open and shut my mouth soundlessly, just like that little fish. "Where are you off to?"

I blink. Where was I going? Right—the courtyard. To figure out my dilemma with the Veterans Day project. The one I'm probably going to fail. My eyes fill with tears before I can stop them.

Logan's forehead wrinkles with confusion and concern. "Are you okay?"

Silently, I curse my face, which never hides what I

want to keep hidden. Logan might see me, but I can still follow Mist's rule about not talking in school if I don't have to. I shake my head the tiniest bit. Logan taps my locker, the metallic plink startling me. "Come on, get your lunch. Let's go to wherever you normally go. The caf is too crowded for me today."

Logan doesn't seem to care about my silence. He steps aside so I can get my lunch.

I lead the way to the courtyard. "This is where you eat lunch?" Logan looks around at the colorful jumble of flowers and plants. "I don't think we're supposed to be out here." I shrug, and he laughs. "That's what I like about you. You're full of surprises."

Blushing, I turn away to show him the sunflowers and the peas. "I think this is an eighth-grade science project," he says, touching a pea pod. "Anita was saying something about peas and genes and families. I didn't know what she was talking about. I kind of just want to eat one. Fresh peas are awesome. Maybe your grandfather will plant some."

The mention of Gōnggong makes me even sadder, but I force a smile anyway. We make our way to the dragonfly bench and take out our lunches—a ham and cheese sandwich for Logan, and leftover mápó dòufu on rice for me. He looks over at my food. "Do you want to heat that up? You could do it in the teacher's lounge. I don't think Mrs. Perry would care."

In my mind, I see Foxman's snarling face at the window, ordering me to leave the courtyard. I frown and shake my head.

"Okay," Logan says. We eat in silence for a minute. "You don't talk much in school, do you?" he asks. I freeze and stare straight ahead. Sunlight dapples the leaves, and flowers sway in the breeze. The gray haze begins to lift from my eyes again. I'm Blue out here. I'm only Mist inside the school.

"I guess not," I say, my voice croaky because I haven't talked since second period. "I don't have anything interesting to say."

"That's not true. You probably have lots of great stories since you lived in a big city." Logan leans back on his elbows. "I can't wait to get out of Redbud and move to a city where there's more to do."

Even though I want to move out of Redbud, too, I'm surprised by Logan's comment. "But I thought all your family lived around here? Your grandparents and aunts and uncles?"

"I'll come back and visit," he says airily. "I want to

travel, see the world. I didn't want to go to Camp Carson this past summer. I wanted to go to this camp in North Carolina where they study the ocean." He sits up and runs a hand through his hair. "I've never seen the ocean." His voice is full of longing.

I can't imagine never having seen an ocean. I could walk to Boston Harbor from our old apartment. "What happened? Why didn't you go?"

"Mom and Dad wanted me and Liam to stick together." Logan makes a face. "Of course, he thought the camp sounded uncool, so that was the end of that idea." He sighs and flops back onto his elbows.

"That's a bummer." I shouldn't have asked him about it—now he's annoyed. "Um, I've been meaning to thank you."

That gets his attention. He looks over at me. "For what?"

The beetles are doing backflips and making me squirm. "You know, for helping Gōnggong. I haven't seen him smile like that in a really long time."

"No problem. I like your grandfather. Couldn't let him plant a garden where it was never going to grow."

"What do you mean?"

"He was going to put it under the tree." When I don't

say anything, Logan explains, "It's a black walnut tree. My mom says that its roots give off some sort of chemical that prevents other plants from growing in the same spot. They like to be alone so that they don't have to compete for nutrients and water."

"I'm glad you told Gōnggong. That's really interesting." It is, but not the way Logan probably thinks. Tao tries to keep other plants away from her tree, so she's alone, in the center. The first character in the Mandarin word for walnut is hé, which means core or nucleus. Could this be another message from Tao? Her first one helped me see that I am Basket at home and reminded me of my responsibility to my family. Maybe this message is about family, too.

The center of my family has always been Nǎinai. But instead of wanting to be alone like Tao, she kept us all close, living in the same apartment building and working in the bakery.

The bakery. Tao must be reminding me, prodding me, to get on with the next step in my Family Reunion plan. And she's channeling the message through Logan, because he has what I need. But will he still help me if he knows what it's for? He'll think I'm a terrible person for breaking my family apart.

"I need a favor," I blurt, startling Logan. "And I need you to not ask me any questions about it."

His eyebrows raise. "That sounds like two favors," he says, the corner of his mouth lifting a little.

I don't laugh. I just stare at him, trying to channel my own desperate message. It works, because he stops smirking and looks nervous instead.

"Um, yeah, sure," he says. "What do you need?" He winces. "Sorry, that was a question."

"Can I borrow your phone? Right now?"

Logan's relief is so obvious that it's almost funny. Did he think I was going to ask him to do something illegal? He unzips the front pocket of his backpack and takes out his phone, entering the password before handing it to me without a word.

I cradle the device in my hand for a moment, debating whether to walk to a different part of the courtyard before calling. But that might seem rude. I decide to stay on the bench—I can speak Mandarin to whoever answers so Logan won't understand what I'm saying. Quickly, I dial the phone number I know by heart.

"Wéi? Golden Phoenix Bakery. How may I help you?" a voice asks, so familiar that I have to blink back tears.

"Chén Shūshu! This is Lán," I tell him in Mandarin.

"Lánlán!" he says in surprise. "Where are you? Is everything all right?"

I hurry to reassure him. "We're all fine. I just called to, uh, talk to Xīng." I probably should've thought out what I was going to say, but when a tree spirit nudges you to do something, you don't dawdle.

"Xīngxīng?" my not-uncle asks, puzzled. "She is at school, isn't she? I haven't seen her for a long time."

"Oh, right. I forgot that she doesn't get out early on Wednesdays anymore. I thought she might be getting a snack," I babble. "How is business? Are the new owners making lots of money?"

Chén Shūshu laughs. "I am just the baker—they don't tell me things like that. Though I did hear them talking about expanding."

"Expanding?" I repeat the unknown Mandarin word.

"Yes, they want to rent the old jewelry store next door, knock down the wall, and add tables and chairs. The bakery will become a coffee shop."

I gasp. My not-uncle chuckles. "It is a bold idea, but I'm sure it will be a big success. Everybody loves coffee with their breakfast!" There's a pause as Chén Shūshu listens to someone in the background. "Lánlán, I must go now. There are a lot of customers and we are running out of roast pork buns. I was happy to talk to you. Goodbye!"

"Bye, Chén Shūshu." I hand the phone back to Logan, my heart sinking. "Thanks."

"Anytime," he says, putting it away. "I don't have to ask to know that didn't go the way you wanted. I'm sorry."

I shrug. "It's, um, disappointing." The bakery must be making a lot of money if the new owners can afford to take over the space next door and turn it into a café. I can't tell Tiffi to pass that kind of information along to her mom. That would just make Third Aunt even more convinced that Bàba stole money from her and the uncles. Out of everything I've tried so far, I've only made a tiny bit of progress with the camp idea. It planted a seed in my parents' brains about moving back to Boston for my education—but it could take forever to sprout.

Chapter Twenty-Nine

Logan and I are just rounding the corner to Math class when I hear a voice call out, "Melanie." I stop and turn. It's the principal. Ugh. I can't believe I just responded to the name he forced me to take. It gives him too much power.

In my mind, I say, *Yes, Foxman?* and feel a bit of power trickle back to me.

"Let's find a quiet place to talk," he says. He nods at Logan. "You're excused from your buddy duties, Liam." He turns without waiting for a response and strides away.

Logan rolls his eyes. "Told you he thinks I'm Liam."

I make a sympathetic face and follow the principal. He goes into the empty music room and motions for me to sit on the risers. Then he sits on the level above me, so I have to twist around and look up at him.

Foxman strokes his goatee and studies me. "Melanie, I'm concerned about you," he says in a soft, compassionate voice that raises the hairs on the back of my neck. "I feel like you're having a hard time adjusting, and I'd like for us to talk about that."

I look down. Talking about it is the last thing I want to do.

"All of us here at Clifton Middle School take pride in our community, in how welcoming and accepting we are of others. Therefore, it wounds me to hear that you are not participating in class, not even math or science, which surprises me. Furthermore, you are refusing to eat lunch with all the other seventh graders. Do you deny it?"

I shake my head. I wouldn't say that I'm refusing to do anything. More like I'm following Mist's rules. But what Foxman says is essentially true. I don't talk in school, and I eat alone.

The principal sighs. "By your own admission, you are rejecting becoming part of Clifton's community. Can you understand how that makes the other students feel?" He leans forward, his face hovering above mine. "They feel confused and uncomfortable around you. That's right," he continues, seeing the dismay on my face. "Some have even said that they feel like you are betraying their values."

I lean back in shock. Some kids actually believe that? I shake my head again, trying to tell Foxman that it was never my intent to make others feel bad. I've only been doing what I felt I had to do to protect myself.

"So perhaps you can see why inviting your grandfather to be part of the Veterans Day ceremony isn't a good idea. We don't want to make the other veterans feel uncomfortable in any way." His amber eyes are piercing.

Wait, what? Mist prefers silence, but I let a tendril of fog form and arch my eyebrow in question.

"It's come to my attention that your grandfather wasn't in the American military. He's not a member of the patriot community. Our flag is not his flag. Our national anthem is not his anthem. As I'm sure Ms. Brown has taught you, Veterans Day was created to honor the soldiers of the United States military. Not only is it inappropriate for him to participate in the celebration, but he would probably feel uncomfortable as well, surrounded by people he didn't serve with. Of course," Foxman says in an oily voice, "he and your parents may come and sit in the audience. The public is welcome to attend."

His demon eyes drill into mine, and his words rise over me like shadows. *Inappropriate*, they whisper. *Not white enough, not American enough*, they cackle. *Understand?* they hoot.

Foxman isn't done. "Since he's the only veteran you know," he says, his tone implying how disgraceful he thinks that is, "of course you may still interview him for your homework. I will let Ms. Brown know what we agreed upon today." The principal descends from the risers and lopes away, the word shadows trailing behind him like dog-headed demons.

My grandfather is the most honorable man I know. How can Foxman say that Gōnggong isn't worthy of attending a silly school event? I want to scream, but I can't. Mist binds my mouth and the beetles eat my voice. All I can do is stand there, humiliated and angry.

"That jerk!" Logan appears in the doorway, making me jump. "I can't believe he just did that! And made it sound like it's your fault! Just because Gōnggong wasn't a soldier in the US military doesn't mean he isn't a veteran. I mean, he served his country, right? And he was in the Vietnam War."

I stare at Logan. Did he just call my grandfather Gōnggong? How does he know all that about him? I tilt my head and point at him accusingly. When he doesn't answer right away, I get up and poke him in the chest. Mist doesn't use words, but she can still be felt.

"Okay, okay." Logan winces. "I *may* have overheard

you and Ms. Brown talking this morning. And Foxman giving you the guilt trip just now."

I cross my arms and narrow my eyes at him.

"I wasn't spying on you, I swear!" Logan says. "I was waiting to walk with you to English." He flushes defiantly. "Fine, I have a bad habit of listening at doorways. But I'm not sorry I did it. Gōnggong—I mean your grandfather—is a good person. He deserves to be honored just like every other veteran."

That makes me smile, and relief floods Logan's face. He looks at me curiously. "You feel the same way. So why didn't you say something to Foxman?"

I raise both hands and shrug in a *what good would that have done?* gesture.

"You're right. He probably wouldn't have changed his mind." The bell rings and kids stream down the hall past the music room. Logan leans toward me. "You should do it anyway," he says in a low voice.

Do what? I turn my head to look at him quizzically, and we almost bump noses. I catch a whiff of something green and spicy—his shampoo? A black walnut? We jump apart, my face flaming.

He clears his throat. "Invite your grandfather anyway. As a veteran, not to just sit in the audience. My friend

Debbi's on stage crew. She's super nice, and she can't stand Foxman, either. I'll ask her to put an extra chair on the stage for your grandfather. Go up with everyone else and introduce him. No one will even know he wasn't invited. And by then, it'll be too late for Foxman to do anything. He won't risk causing a scene by making you and Gōnggong leave."

It's a tempting plan. Māma always talks about honoring our elders. What better way to do that than have the whole community give their respect to Gōnggong? And tricking a fox demon like Mr. Reynard would be so satisfying.

But I know I can't. It's too risky. What if the principal found out ahead of time and refused to let Gōnggong up on stage? That would be humiliating for both of us. Participating in the ceremony is also against the rules. Not just Foxman's rules. My rules. Mist isn't allowed to talk in front of everyone. Basket can't expose Gōnggong's pain. Blue can't tell stories anymore, not even true stories. Thinking about breaking all those rules makes me feel sick.

Quickly, I shake my head.

Logan makes a frustrated noise and runs his hand through his hair. "Fine. Want to talk about it at the pond after school?"

Reluctantly, I nod. Maybe Blue will be able to explain everything.

With a sigh, he says, "Okay, good."

I don't know if that sounds like a good thing or a bad thing.

The last bell finally rings, and I see Logan is at the bike rack, unlocking his bike. I head toward him so we can walk to the pond together, but then Liam shows up to get his own bike. Swiftly, I change direction and cross the street instead of walking right past them. When I glance across, Logan is talking to a girl I don't know. Her long blond hair floats around her like a glowing aura around the Norse Goddess Sif, wife of Thor. Logan smiles widely, and they take out their cell phones. It looks like they exchange numbers. After she walks away, Liam punches his twin on the arm and gives him a thumbs-up sign.

Does Logan like that girl? The beetles start pinching under my ribs again. *So what?* I tell myself. Of course he has other friends. Just because he compared my hair to a starling's feathers and wanted to give me a new nickname doesn't mean anything. He probably smiles at everyone the way he smiled at me in the hall. No matter what I tell myself, the beetles won't stop. They bite me all the way back to the house.

The radiator nook is quiet and warm. Ms. Brown suggested that I ask Gōnggong about his war experience when he's doing something he enjoys. That still feels too direct to me. I need to be more like Bàba, hinting at but not actually asking about what I want to know. But even if I manage to get answers to the interview questions, Logan would definitely want me to sneak Gōnggong into the celebration, which would be a total disaster. He's only helping me to annoy Foxman, whom he doesn't like. And probably to impress glowing-aura girl. I feel like the dead balloon in Anita's hands—pulled in all different directions.

Maybe what Tao is telling me is that I should stick to the core. In the big picture—Redbud, Logan, the girl—none of them are important. I tell myself they're temporary. *Melanie* is temporary. I stay behind the radiator all afternoon. I don't go to the pond.

Chapter Thirty

For the next two weeks, I avoid Logan. He'd come up to me the day after he told me about his great plan and asked me why I didn't show at the pond. I could tell he was upset, but Mist doesn't have eyes or ears or a mouth, so I glided soundlessly past Logan as if he wasn't there. After that, he didn't try to talk to me.

It's so easy to be Mist. Cloaked in gray, I am invisible. Even Liam has mostly stopped harassing me, although every now and then he gives me an evil glare.

This morning on my way to Health, I see Liam chatting with Foxman through the open door of the teacher's lounge. *They belong together,* I think as I weave unnoticed through the morning rush of kids. Halfway through class, Mrs. Perry's voice crackles through the intercom "Mrs. Shaughnessy? Please send Melanie Hua to the office immediately."

All eyes turn to me. Mrs. Shaughnessy nods, and I get up and collect my things. Across the aisle, Liam brays like a donkey while Logan quickly turns away to study the wall. None of it matters. I gather the tatters of my cloak around me and slip out of the room.

Mrs. Perry frowns and ushers me into Foxman's cramped office. He leans forward across his desk, the red hairs in his goatee glinting in the harsh fluorescent light. "Did you think you could get away with it?" he snarls. Gone is the soft, concerned voice from our last chat.

I stare at the principal's orangey-yellow eyes. Old Chinese tales say that human eyes contain a tiny human shape. I search for a miniature fox shape and raise my eyebrows. I've been getting away with being Mist for weeks. I see no reason to stop now.

"Oh, you know what I'm talking about. Don't pretend you didn't do it." He grimaces. "Of course Ms. Brown defended you because she's a very trusting person. But all the other teachers are horrified. I see you for who you really are. A devious, crafty girl with no respect for others."

Funny, that's exactly what I think of you, I want to say. But I don't. I look back at him emotionlessly, but inside, the beetles are getting agitated. I swallow them down, waiting this out until Foxman reveals whatever trick he's trying to play on me.

My not talking only seems to enrage him further. After yelling at me for a few more minutes, he finally leaps up and circles around his desk, knocking off a pile of folders in the process. Papers spill out all over the floor. Growling, he jerks open his office door. "Come with me."

I follow him to the one place in the school where I feel like I belong—the courtyard garden. But it isn't a garden anymore. As the haze clears from my eyes, I see destruction everywhere. The sunflowers have been pulled up by their roots, their bright faces crushed by the boots of trolls. Broken branches litter the walkway, and the pea vines have been torn off the trellis to lie in wilted heaps on the ground. Even the dragonfly bench has been knocked over onto its side, one corner chipped.

I can't help it. I gasp. Out here, I am Blue, only now I'm frozen blue with shock and despair. Some evil creature has shattered this little jeweled garden, this perfect haven from the smog of school. I survey the damage with tearful eyes.

Mr. Reynard snorts. "You can't fool me. I bet you're thrilled to see the ruin you've made of this courtyard. All the hard work the teachers and students put into it over the years is gone—just because you had to show everyone how different you are. I knew the moment you stepped into my office that you were going to make trouble. You people have no regard for the feelings of others or the sanctity of life."

He's wrong—I do care about people, plants, and animals. I'd be lost without Tao and her dragon tree. I feel bad about the worms I caught for Gōnggong. But the really sneaky thing about Foxman's words is he's right, too. I am trouble. I leave everything in ruins behind me.

His nostrils flare as he watches me, a fox ready to come in for the kill. "What do you have to say for yourself?"

Summoning Blue's voice, I whisper, "I didn't do it."

"Oh, please," he laughs, and his sharp canines glisten. "I've personally seen you in here when you weren't supposed to be. We have eyewitnesses that saw you in the courtyard numerous times, even after you knew it was off-limits. Apart from the eighth-grade science classes, which are supervised, you are the only person who comes in here." His lip curls in contempt.

Kids point and whisper as Foxman marches me back into the school and parades me through the hallways. Formless as Mist, I can't respond. He steers me into a chair in his den and grabs the phone. "Mrs. Perry! Get me the Hoo-ays number," he shouts through the open door. "I need to inform them that their daughter is suspended!"

What? No. This can't be happening. Bàba and Māma will never confront the principal and tell him he's wrong, even if they believe that I didn't destroy the garden. Being suspended will mark me as a bad, misbehaving daughter. It's the kind of shame that the rest of the family must never know about, which means all hope of going back home to Boston may be lost.

Foxman dials. The beetles are going bonkers, scurrying and pushing and biting. I lean over, hoping to keep them in, hoping I don't throw up. I focus on the papers on the floor, trying to calm my breathing. There are photos of men and women in uniform with descriptions of who they are. The veterans, I realize. The ones who will be included in the Veterans Day ceremony.

An old black-and-white photo catches my eye. A young man with a pointed chin and narrow eyes. Below his name are the words, "Vietnam War. POW-MIA," followed by a logo. It shows the silhouette of a man inside a circle. His head is bent forward toward a string of barbed wire. A guard tower rises behind him, and a length of chain with arrows on both ends curves around the bottom of the circle. The same abbreviation, POW-

MIA, runs across the top of the circle. Below the circle and chain, it says, "You are not forgotten."

Mr. Reynard snaps, "Your parents don't seem to want to be located. Wait on the bench behind Mrs. Perry until they come to retrieve you." He points to his door.

I bypass the bench and approach Mrs. Perry. She looks at me with only the tiniest shred of sympathy, but at least it's there. I clutch my stomach. She nods curtly and writes me a hall pass. When she isn't looking, I slip a piece of scrap paper out of the recycling bin and a pencil from the front counter into my pocket. In the bathroom, I shut myself into a stall and quickly scribble a note.

> L—
> I need your help. Pond this afternoon?
> Please. And I'm sorry.

I don't know how to sign the note. I'm not Melanie. I'm not Meilan. No one knows I'm Mist. Finally, I jot a word. *Starling.* I fold up the note and jam it into the vents in Logan's locker.

Chapter Thirty-One

Bàba finally hurries in after lunch, his clothes and hair dusted with flour. He shoots me an exasperated glance before Mrs. Perry ushers him into the principal's office. The door does nothing to block Foxman's loud voice. Stiffly, the principal tells Bàba that I have destroyed school property and am suspended for the rest of the week. Three days total. The school will hire someone to repair and replant the garden, and he expects my family to pay for the cost. My heart sinks. I have added to Bàba and Māma's burden.

The conversation is short and mostly one-sided. Bàba's muffled voice says something that I'm pretty sure is an apology, and they come out into the main office. I pick up my backpack and walk over to stand behind my father.

Foxman narrows his eyes at me. "I hope you take this time to think about your behavior. You need to realize there are consequences for your actions." His voice is gloating.

As Bàba and I leave, a dog-headed, word-shadow demon growls, *Behave, you people* and bites at my heels.

Bàba and I don't speak all the way back to the house. He comes inside for a moment to tell Māma what happened and that he has to go back to the café to bake the desserts for dinner. I know I shouldn't interrupt him, but I can't help it. "Bàba, I didn't do it."

A shadow crosses his face before it smooths out into that perfect mask of white jade. He has the same unreadable expression as the night he told me that we were moving. "Méiyǒu bànfǎ," he says and walks out the door.

I am Basket now, already so full of everyone else's expectations that adding my own fear and anger threatens to tip the whole thing. Māma reaches out to touch my hair, but I pull away. "What does he mean, there's no way? Why won't you or Bàba stand up for me?" I manage to whisper.

I've seen that look on my mother's face before. It's the one she made when Third Aunt or one of Bàba's brothers did or said something to upset her. She isn't their real sister—she only married into the family. She told me once that to argue with them would be to lose face. Sometimes she would complain to Bàba later, in private, but she didn't often do that, either. She told me her job was to keep the peace, not to put Bàba in the middle of a disagreement between her and his siblings. It was a balancing act, one that she'd been good at up until that last big blowout argument. Everyone has a role to play, I guess. "Mù yǐ chéng zhōu," she simply says and goes back to the kitchen.

I repeat the four words all the way back to my room, grabbing Bàba's laptop on the way. After a quick internet search, I find the translation: "Tree cease make boat," which means that the tree has been made into a boat—it's not a tree anymore and will never be again. Basically, what Māma told me was that it was too late to change anything.

Across the yard, the dragon tree beckons with waving branches. Tao the tree spirit has been a good guide. She told me to listen to my heart, which led to Basket, Mist, and Blue helping me get through the past month. She encouraged me to work on my plan to reunite my family. And her tree is still a tree—it hasn't been made into a boat. Māma is wrong. There's still time to change things.

For once, I'm glad we live in a house so big that we can't hear each other and that my room is on the first floor. I leave Basket in my room, holding my family's love for me, and crawl out the window.

Logan shows up fifteen minutes after school lets out. He coasts down the hill, jams on the brakes, and leaps off his bike, letting it fall to the ground. The beetles flutter wildly and then drop to the pit of my stomach.

Logan paces back and forth and runs his hand through his hair. Finally, he stops, and we stare at each other for a long moment. "I'm sorry," I say, the words dropping into the long grass.

"You said that already." His voice is low and tight.

I try again. "I need your help."

Logan exhales sharply. "You said that already, too."

I feel a sudden urge to laugh wildly. All my life, I've been surrounded by family members who tell me that they've already said things while at the same time leaving so much unsaid. And now I've become one of them.

The dragon tree is still a tree. There's still time to change things.

"Okay," I say, then take a deep breath. "I didn't come that day because . . ." Ugh. I really should've planned out what I was going to say. I can't tell him about the messages from the tree spirit—he won't understand. "Because," I begin again, stumbling over my words.

"Your plan . . . I couldn't . . . and then . . . the girl . . . core . . . family . . ."

This is not going well at all.

Logan's mouth is compressed into a thin line, and his eyes are stormy. "Girl? What girl?"

That's what he picked up on from my babbling? Heat floods my face and incinerates a few beetles clogging my throat, making room for more words. "The girl! With all the hair? At the bike rack?" He still looks confused. "You exchanged phone numbers!"

Sudden recognition blooms across his face. "Seriously? That's Debbi! Remember I told you about her? She's on stage crew. I got her number so I could ask her about putting a chair on the stage for your grandfather. Jeez! I was just trying to help you!" Red creeps up his neck and colors his ears. "I waited here for hours! And then at school you acted like I didn't exist!"

The hurt in Logan's voice makes me want to hide. If this log were hollow, I would totally crawl into it. But there's nowhere to go, and all I have left are my words. "How was I supposed to know? I never said to go ahead and ask her to do that. And I had to pretend I didn't see you because every time I look at you . . ." I catch myself just in time. Maybe he won't notice.

222

But Logan immediately picks up on it. He glares at me. "Every time you look at me what?"

I owe him the truth. I can't leave it unsaid. My voice trembles. "I see Liam."

The devastation and rage on his face makes me feel like a monster.

"I can't help my face!" He kicks his bike. "You think I want to look like him?"

"I can't help my face, either! You think it's easy to look different from everyone else? Why do you think I work so hard to be invisible?!"

That stops him cold. He stares at me. "Wait. Is that why you don't talk in school? You're trying to be invisible? Why?"

I sigh. "Simple. If no one notices me, then no one can pick on me. Not Foxman, not Mrs. Shaughnessy, not . . . Liam." I stare at the pond, hoping its still waters will calm the churning beetles. "Being invisible has been working, too. Except now someone's destroyed the courtyard and blamed me for it. I've been suspended for the rest of the week."

Logan finally comes over and sits down on the log. He's so close that the sleeve of his shirt brushes my arm. "Liam."

"I think so. I saw him talking to the principal this morning."

"It was him. I'm sure of it. He snuck out last night and came back covered in dirt. I thought he and The Daves were just out pranking people again." He grips the rough bark of the log. "I'm going to kill him."

"No, don't do that. Mù yǐ chéng zhōu," I say without thinking. Oops. Wrong language.

"What does that mean?" Logan doesn't sound snarky, though. Just curious.

"Um. Something my mom said to me. Literally, it means a tree ceases to be when you make it a boat. You can't change it back."

"That's kind of like what my mom says, 'What's done is done.'"

We smile tentatively at each other. Moms have the same language even if they don't speak the same language.

"Yeah. I guess I'm starting to see what she meant. I can't change the fact that the garden has been destroyed or that I'm suspended."

"Maybe I can do something about your suspension. I'll tell my dad that Liam was responsible and get him to talk to Foxman."

"No," I say quickly. "Don't do that. Liam will take it out on you."

Logan protests, "You can't let Liam get away with it."

"I won't. That's one of the things I want to change. I'll figure something out."

There's a pause as we both think.

"Hey," Logan says. "If you don't want me to do anything about Liam, then what *do* you need me to help with? Your note said you wanted my help."

Right. All the talk about Debbi and Liam had distracted me. "I saw something in Foxman's office today." I fill Logan in on the black-and-white photo of the veteran and the strange logo under his name. "Do you know who he was? Or what the logo means?"

He shakes his head slowly.

"Would your dad know? Do you mind asking him? Or maybe he can ask Foxman?"

A strange look passes over Logan's face. He seems reluctant. "What's wrong?" I ask. "Isn't it the same as asking him to help with my suspension?"

Logan shifts on the log, obviously uncomfortable. "I was only going to tell him that Liam trashed the courtyard and framed an innocent person for it. I actually wasn't going to mention you or your suspension."

I'm so confused. "Why not?"

"You have to understand," Logan begins and then stops. He rakes a hand through his hair. "My dad is a good guy, but . . ." After a long pause, he finally says, "He used to work for a place that made washing machines. He really liked his job, but a couple of years ago, he got laid off because the company wasn't doing well." He gives me a pointed glance, but I'm still lost.

"I'm sorry . . . ?"

Logan sighs. "Remember what Dylan was talking about in Social Studies? When Ms. Brown handed out the Veterans Day assignment?"

My mouth opens in a silent "Oh" as I understand what he's trying to say. "Your father lost his job because of the trade war, and he blames Chinese people. You think he might not help me if he knows I'm Chinese." Logan hangs his head. How can a grown-up who's never even met me decide that he doesn't like me? It makes me sad and angry at the same time. I take a deep breath. "I'll figure it out another way."

"What are you planning to do with this info? Is it going to help get your grandfather invited to the ceremony?" He seems relieved that I didn't ask more questions about his father.

I snort. "I don't know, really. I haven't thought that far ahead. But I doubt anything will get Gōnggong invited to the celebration."

Logan looks hurt. "Wait. Why not? What was wrong with my plan?"

"Nothing," I say quickly. "Your plan was great."

He looks at me sideways. "But . . ."

"But I can't interview Gōnggong."

"Yes, you can. Even Foxman said you could."

"It's not that. Talking about his time in the war really upsets him. I barely mentioned it at dinner, and he got up and left the room without a word. My dad was mad at me for bringing it up and basically told me not to talk about it anymore. How am I going to interview my grandfather when my parents forbade me from asking him about it?" My eyes sting just remembering how upset Gōnggong and Bàba had been with me.

"Oh. Did you tell Ms. Brown that?"

"I tried. She wants me to get his story anyway." The rock I'd been kicking at the other day stares up at me darkly, like Fei, the one-eyed bull with a serpent's tail. Seeing Fei is a sign of impending misfortune. "I don't know any other veterans, and it's too late to switch even if I did. I guess I'll just have to get an F on this project.

My parents will still be mad, but at least it'll be better than going against them and upsetting Gōnggong." I hope that's true. I hope they won't be so mad that they stop talking to me. They're the only family I have left.

"That's not going to happen," Logan says.

"How do you know?"

"Because I'm going to help you."

Tucking my hair behind my ear, I study Logan. He sounds so confident, so matter-of-fact. "And why, exactly, are you helping me with this? There's nothing in it for you. Except maybe getting suspended if Foxman finds out you arranged to have an extra chair on the stage."

The tips of his ears turn pink. "I don't know. I just, you know, think you're . . ." He stops, and for a horrible half second I think he's going to say "exotic" again. But he doesn't. ". . . Interesting," he continues. "I never know what you're thinking. You're really smart. That day in Health you got Anita to make Liam look like a fool without either of them realizing you were behind it. Also, you read really fast." He grins and bumps his knee against mine.

I feel a jolt inside, as if the pinching beetles have all transformed into fireflies and they've lit up all at once.

I grin back. "Oh, I see. You're trying to get me to write your English essay."

"Yeah, that's it. You caught me." Logan laughs. "All I have to do is get your grandfather to talk, and you'll write three pages about the symbolism in a book about wizards."

His words remind me about the task ahead, and the light inside me fades. "Seriously, though. How *are* you going to get my grandfather to talk? He barely knows you."

"Hey, I tilled his garden, remember? He likes me. I figure that whenever I see him outside, I can help him plant stuff and ask him questions at the same time. You know, all casual, like I'm just trying to get to know him. And then I'll tell you what I learned so you can write it down."

I think it over. This plan might actually work. It fits with my earlier idea about not asking Gōnggong directly. What's more indirect than getting a friend to ask for you? Plus, it keeps Basket in the clear. Basket won't be disobeying Bàba and Māma. Mist won't fail Social Studies class. We all still have a chance of moving back to Boston. "That's actually kind of brilliant," I admit. "If it works, I won't write your essay for you, but we could, um, talk about all the different symbols. Like a book club. If you want."

Logan's eyes gleam like the scales of a carp. "Deal. Especially since I'm only on page twenty-four."

We laugh together, and I feel my shoulders relax. This is going to work.

Leaning over, I pry Fei's eye out of the ground and heave it into the pond. Take that, impending misfortune.

Chapter Thirty-Two

Wednesday morning, I wake up to the sound of Bàba's car leaving for the café. He gave me the silent treatment all through dinner last night, and it looks like he's going to keep it up. Fine by me, since I'm still annoyed at him for not defending me against Foxman's accusations.

At breakfast, Māma and Gōnggong eat zhōu with salty peanuts and wedges of pídàn. Some say that the gray-green gelatinous eggs were created by accident. A young duck farmer from Hunan named Shuǐgē left a gift of duck eggs in the garden of the girl he had a crush on. She didn't find them until two weeks later when she was cleaning out the ash pit, and by then they had been preserved by the chemicals in the ashes. It's kind of a romantic story, because the farmer called the eggs "pine eggs" after the girl, whose name was Sōngmèi, or Pine Sister, and also because the preservation process left delicate patterns on the surface of the eggs that looked like pine branches.

I have problems with this story because who leaves a gift in an ash pit? And who eats food that has been left in an ash pit for two weeks? Maybe they're a good match after all, Shuǐgē and Sōngmèi. And pine eggs are a much better name than pídàn, which literally translates to skin egg. But no matter what they're called, I won't eat them. Eggs should only be green in stories.

I sample slices of leftover pie from the café instead. The nuts in the pecan pie stick to my teeth. The cherry pie filling is gloopy. I like the lemon meringue pie best, but all the pies are too sweet and leave a coating in my mouth like I've been drinking maple syrup. The only way to get it off is to swish mouthfuls of hot jasmine tea, which earns me a disapproving glance from Māma.

Even though I'm suspended, the Cliff expects me to keep up with my schoolwork. I try to work on math after breakfast, but it's hard to concentrate. Seeing the twins' house from my window reminds me of Liam's destruction of the courtyard and my unfair suspension. Thinking about the school garden makes me nervous about Logan's plan to get Gōnggong to talk. Worrying about the Veterans Day assignment makes me angry at Foxman all over again. Around and around, my thoughts and the beetles spin.

Finally, after a couple of wasted hours, I gather up all my notebooks and papers and sling my backpack over my shoulder. My desire to dodge Māma is greater than my fear of Mr. Shellhaus's ghost, so I cross the living room on my way to the front door, making sure to avoid the chilly spot by the coffee table. If I had to guess, that's where he . . . No, better not to think about it.

"Māma," I call out from the front hall. "I'm going to the library to do my homework."

"Wait a minute, Lan." Her voice commands from the kitchen. "I have job for you."

Great. This is exactly what I was trying to avoid. I slump down onto the bench and drop my backpack on the floor, prepared for a long wait. Surprisingly, Māma trots right out of the kitchen, carrying my old insulated lunch bag. The purple one with prancing unicorns on it that I adored until I decided qílíns were cooler.

"Here," she says, holding out the bag. Automatically, I grab it and then wish I hadn't. "Take this to Bàba. He forgot his lunch this morning. Enough in there for both of you."

"Wait. Bàba works in a café."

Māma raises an eyebrow at me. "Yes, this you already know."

"So why does he need to bring lunch? Can't he just eat the food that the café serves?"

"Āiyā," Māma says in exasperation. "How you not know American expression, 'no such thing as free lunch'?" Her lips pinch together, and I suddenly realize that she's trying not to smile.

"Māma! You just made a joke in English." I grin at her. "And it was funny!"

"I always funny," she says. She tries to look offended, but I can tell she's pleased. "Cook at café puts cheese in everything. Your Bàba cannot stand the smell of cheese. My job is to make Bàba lunch."

"Your English is fine, Māma. You could get work anywhere. You just need to be more confident." Uh-oh. Now she really does look insulted. I went too far, was too direct. "I mean—"

"Go," she says, and pushes me toward the door. "You do your job."

Bàba is arranging pie in the pastry case when I walk into the café. Quickly, I scan the back wall, but there's no pay phone. How am I ever going to get in touch with Tiffi?

"Hi, Bàba." I force a small smile, which my father doesn't return. "You forgot your lunch this morning, so Māma asked me to bring it to you. She said there's enough for both of us."

Bàba looks at the big clock on the wall behind the counter. "Chīfànle méiyǒu?"

"No, Bàba." I swallow my irritation, but some escapes. "I just said that Māma packed enough so we could eat together."

My father frowns and sighs. Great. I've managed to annoy both my parents in less than fifteen minutes. "Lan, 'chīfànle méiyǒu' does not always mean 'have you eaten.' It is also just a casual greeting between friends, like saying 'How are you doing?'"

"Oh," I say, taken aback. "I'm sorry." How did I never learn this fact in all my years of Chinese school? I always took it literally when my parents asked me if I'd eaten yet, because, well, Māma was always cooking something. And also, Bàba thinks we're friends?

Maybe he isn't mad at me for getting suspended after all. Maybe he believes me.

"Sit down." Bàba gestures to an empty booth near the door to the kitchen. "I can take lunch break after I finish this."

I curl up in a corner of the booth and watch while my father cuts a pie into perfectly equal triangles and slides them onto plates. He puts all the slices into the case except one, which he brings over to our table. I haven't seen anything like it before. There's a layer of light brown on the bottom, a darker brown layer on top of that, and then a thick fluffy layer of whipped cream sprinkled with chocolate chips and chopped peanuts.

"I learn to make this morning," Bàba says. "Chocolate peanut butter pie. In Ohio they call it buckeye pie." He shrugs and takes off his apron. "Do not know why."

I don't know, either, but the pie looks amazing. I wish I hadn't eaten all those other kinds of pie for breakfast.

Bàba takes the lunch bag and moves toward the kitchen. "I will heat this up for us."

While I wait, my eyes fall on his apron hanging over the back of the bench across from me. The edge of his cell phone peeks out from one of the pockets. My heart leaps. This is my chance to call Tiffi. Quickly, I lean over the table and snatch the phone.

Bàba's passcode is easy—Māma's birthday. I scroll through his contacts, finally finding Third Aunt under J for Jiāyù. I've never needed to call her, so I have no idea what her phone number is. There are two numbers listed, her cell phone and the landline for her apartment. Tiffi would never answer her mom's cell phone, but she might answer the landline. Plus, it's on the hall table, right outside her bedroom. It's early afternoon in Boston, so my cousin will be back from half-day kindergarten.

I breathe a little prayer to Tao and press the call button. *Please, please, let Tiffi pick up.* After a few rings, someone answers but doesn't say anything. "Tiffi? Is that you?" I have to be quick—Bàba will be back with our food soon. "This is Meilan."

"Hi, Meilan. You're not a stranger, so I can talk to you!" Tiffi's cute little voice gets me choked up.

"Hi, Tiffi. Where's your mom?"

"She's in the kitchen making me a snack. Do you want to talk to her?"

"No, no," I say quickly. "I want to talk to you. I miss you."

"I miss you, too, Biǎojiě. Xing doesn't tell me stories when she babysits. When are you coming home?"

I can't cry. Not now. "Actually, I need your help to do that."

"My help?" Tiffi asks. "What do you want me to do?"

"Can you tell me if you've heard your parents say anything about my parents or Gōnggong? Stuff about money or regrets?"

"What's 'regrets'?" Tiffi asks.

I bite back a sigh. This would be so much easier if Xing were still on my side. "It's like being sad about a choice you made," I explain. "And wishing you had made a different decision."

"Māma said she wishes your bàba didn't give Năinai's pin to your māma," Tiffi exclaims. "Is that a regret?"

"Yeah, it sure is. Good job!" It's not exactly helpful, but it's a start. "Did they say anything about missing us or wanting us back?"

"No, that's me! I said that!"

"You're right, you did," I reply. "Hey Tiffi, can you keep listening to what your parents and the other uncles and aunts say? Especially if it's about my parents or money. I want to figure out if they still blame my bàba for everything. And tell your mom that you want only me, and no one else, to babysit for you. I'll try to call you back in a few days, okay?"

"Okay," she says cheerfully. "I'm a good listener!"

"Great. Thanks, Tiffi." I see Bàba's head approaching the window in the kitchen door. "I gotta go. Don't tell anyone I called, okay?"

"O—" Her voice cuts off abruptly.

"Who is this? Why you talking to my daughter?"

I've been caught! I mash my thumb against the button to end the call and practically toss the phone back into Bàba's apron pocket just as he pushes through the door, carrying two plates of noodles. He sets them on the table, sits down, and looks at me. "Everything okay, Lan?"

"Um, yeah, everything's fine. Why?" Can he tell how dry my mouth is? Can he hear my heart pounding from across the table?

"You didn't touch pie," he says, and his mouth quirks up a little.

I smile back tentatively and am about to say something about waiting for dessert when the buzz of his phone interrupts me. My heart beats even faster. Tiffi must have tattled on me. I want to tell Bàba not to answer his phone. I want to say we should just enjoy our lunch together. I want to tell him I hope we can be friends, too. But I don't.

Instead, I watch with growing dread as Bàba pulls out his phone and looks at the screen. His eyes widen before his whole face closes down, erasing any expression or emotion. He pushes the talk button and holds the phone up to his ear. "Jiāyù," he says without any greeting.

A torrent of Mandarin bursts out of the speaker, and both Bàba and I wince. "Dà Gē?! Why did you call my daughter? How dare you talk to her without my permission!" Third Aunt's voice is laced with suspicion.

Bàba grits his teeth. "I did not call your daughter, Jiāyù. I have not spoken to her since we left, and only then to say goodbye."

If Third Aunt thinks Bàba spoke to Tiffi, then she must not have tattled on me, after all. And if that's true, then how did Third Aunt trace the call back to Bàba? I called her landline, not her cell phone.

"Lying again!" Third Aunt accuses "I know you called her. I star-six-nine you!"

Bàba's eyes catch mine, and a flicker of disappointment crosses his face. "My phone was in my pocket—must have accidentally dialed your number. Will not happen again." He hangs up on Third Aunt while she's still talking, puts the phone back in his apron pocket, and calmly takes a bite of noodles. After a moment, he swallows and looks up at me. "Eat," he tells me. "Before it gets cold."

There's no way I can force food past the beetles clogging my throat, but I take my fork and twirl it into the noodles. The minutes stretch like thorny vines, twisting and tightening around me. When I can't stand it anymore, I put down my fork and take a sip of water, clearing the way for words.

"Bàba, I'm sorry." It feels like I've been apologizing all day. "I called Tiffi."

"I know."

Maybe it's the half smile he gave me earlier or the way he just keeps eating as though nothing happened, but I open up, just a little. I'm not at home, after all. Which means I'm not Basket and I don't have to hold on to everything.

"I miss her. Xing, too."

"I know this, too," he says.

"So you're not mad?"

This makes him sit up and look at me. "No reason to be mad at you. They are your cousins." He leans forward and pats the back of my hand. "But maybe do not call Tiffi again soon. And ask before borrowing phone."

I look down at my plate and nod. This will make it even more impossible to get my family back together. "Do you think Third Aunt will ever stop being mad?"

Bàba's laugh is short and bitter. "This I do not know. She is like a snake swallowing an elephant—never satisfied, always wanting more. She has been mad at me ever since Gōnggong and Nǎinai asked me to run the bakery. Now Nǎinai is gone, Gōnggong is here, and she can never prove to them that she is capable. She knows it's too late."

This makes me sad for Third Aunt. "Do you ever miss them?" I whisper to my plate. "The family?"

My father lets out a long sigh. "We have all made our choices," he answers, which is no answer at all.

He must see my confusion, because he continues, "Do you know what Māma said to me before the family decided to sell the bakery?"

I groan. "Don't tell me . . . Another saying?"

Bàba smiles. "Yes, she said we are 'yī tiáo shéng shàng de mà zha.' Like grasshoppers tied to one rope."

I still don't get it. How do you tie insects to a rope? And why?

He explains, "The bakery is the rope. Family members are the grasshoppers." He thinks for a moment. "In English, people say 'we sink or swim together.' But we are all tied together and cannot get free, cannot swim back to land. I finally realized we must cut the rope—sell bakery so no one will drown." His lips pinch together as he stares down at his plate. "For long time, I think bakery and Nǎinai are same thing, that I must keep bakery alive to keep Nǎinai . . ." His voice trails off. Bàba clears his throat and says more brightly, "That is also why I decided to move away. If grasshoppers are free, can all jump in different directions. That is what people in Měi Gúo do, right?"

My thoughts are hopping every which way, too. I'm glad Bàba doesn't feel like he's drowning anymore. I wish I could say the same about myself.

Chapter Thirty-Three

I have even less of an appetite after the spectacular failure of my call with Tiffi and my conversation with Bàba, but to make him happy, I eat the buckeye pie. It tastes like dust and disappointment, which I don't tell him, of course. I force the last forkful down and say, "That was delicious, Bàba!"

He gives me a genuine, full-face smile. "Everybody loves dessert. Nice to see them enjoy it. Not like before, when everybody just buy pastries and leave, take away to eat somewhere else. Good to learn new recipes here. I have also been thinking about experimenting, combining Chinese and American pastries. Samantha tells me this is called 'fusion.'"

His enthusiasm reminds me of how excited he was on the journey here. How he entered each new city with wide and eager eyes. How chatty he was with his friends. Bàba actually likes Redbud, I realize, and the pie in my stomach sours. All my planning and scheming is never going to trick him into moving back to Boston.

I grab my backpack and drag myself the three blocks to the town library. It's a one-story red brick building that crouches low among evergreen bushes, with narrow rectangular windows running around the tops of the walls. When Māma and I saw it for the first time, I laughed. It was like a dollhouse compared to the Boston Public Library. But it's filled with books, there's a computer room, and anything they don't own, the librarian will request for me from the big library in Columbus, so that's all that matters.

The children's librarian gives me an odd look, but she doesn't ask me any questions. Maybe she's heard about my suspension. In a town this small, any news is big news. Or maybe she thinks I switched to being homeschooled. Part of me doesn't think that's such a bad idea, even if Bàba makes me translate the entire book of Chinese poetry.

Without any distractions, I breeze through my homework and even finish reading *A Wizard of Earthsea*. The ending shocks me so much that I read the last chapter over again, trying to figure out what it all means. I look around and realize that there is no one here I can talk to about it. That's when an icy wave of loneliness crashes down on me, colder than Mr. Shellhaus's ghost.

Desperate, I stumble over to the computers and check my email. Nothing from my old friends in Boston. Nothing from Xing. She made it crystal clear that she doesn't want to talk to me, so I don't write to her, either. I spend the rest of the afternoon huddled in a corner of the play area, pretending to read a book while really watching the toddlers build and knock down block towers.

At home, Gōnggong and Māma talk about their trip to the garden center. The plants they bought are American versions of Chinese vegetables that aren't sold here. Savoy cabbage instead of napa. Broccoli instead of jiēlán. Kale instead of báicài. They are variations, just like Basket, Mist, and Blue are variations of me. Even plants have to adapt to different environments. I hope Gōnggong's vegetables are as successful as my variations.

Thursday, I follow the same routine of eating lunch at the café with Bàba, then going to the library and doing homework until dinnertime. I feel guilty for not helping Gōnggong plant his vegetables, but that's part of Logan's plan. If I'm there, Gōnggong won't open up about his experiences as a soldier.

Instead, I do a different kind of research about soldiers. The kind that involves a symbol of a person behind barbed wire with a guard tower looming over him. And far down on a list put together by the US military, I find the name Raymond Reynard. The same name on the photo in Foxman's office. Combined with everything Foxman said about "my people," I come up with a theory about why the principal dislikes me and Gōnggong so much. Whatever his reasons, what he's doing isn't right.

If everything felt lonely yesterday, today life feels unfair. The walls of the small library close in, making it hard to breathe, making my legs restless. I pack up and take a different way home, looping around the elementary school and approaching home from the opposite direction.

It's not until I hear their voices that I realize I'm approaching the Batchelder twins' house. I've never seen it from the front, which has a large porch with white pillars and a stone path leading to the sidewalk. There are white wicker chairs on the porch. Both are empty, which means the twins must be in the backyard. It would be nice to talk to Logan and find out how the plan is going, but there's no way I want to see Liam right now. Or their father.

There is a narrow strip of grass between the sidewalk and the street, with a few small trees dotted along it. I slip behind the first tree, which is near the back corner of the Batchelders' house.

"Why do you care so much?" Liam's voice sounds like he's right there, at the top of his yard, but when I peer around the tree trunk, I don't spot him.

I don't see Logan, either. But his reply is loud and angry. "Because you just messed everything up."

Where are they? I take a step away from the tree and scan their yard. They aren't there. They're not in my yard, either. It's like they took a cue from Mist and made themselves invisible.

Now Liam is mad. "No, I didn't. I was *helping.* I was being friendly. Except I'm not being friendly with a freak."

There's a muffled curse, and a walnut in its green shell lands with a thump near the fence. For a moment, I think the twins have been swallowed by the dragon tree, or by Tao, before I realize that they've climbed up onto some of the higher branches. They're well hidden; a sneaker and a bit of baseball cap are all I can spot. That's good—that means that they probably can't see me, either. But I'm not Mist here, I remind myself. I'm visible. To be safe, I dart behind the small tree again. Maybe I can sprint to the next one and get home without them seeing me.

"Dude, I can't believe you just threw that at my head!" Liam snarls.

"She is not a freak!" Logan spits back.

Wait. Logan said "she." Does he mean me? Does Liam think I'm a freak? Well, that does sound like something he'd call me. Why are they talking about me? I linger in my hiding spot.

"What if I'd lost my balance and fallen out of the tree?"

"That works for me," Logan says.

There's a slight pause. "Some brother you are." Liam's voice is wounded.

"Oh, don't give me that," Logan snaps. "I'm not the one who put animal crap in your bed at camp. I'm not the one who turned into a bully and a jerk. And I'm definitely not the one who wrecked the courtyard at school."

Liam sucks his breath in loudly before shouting, "Well, I'm not the one who doesn't want to be a twin!" There's a shower of leaves and twigs and a few walnuts as he starts climbing back down the tree.

"I never said that!" Logan protests.

"Yeah, you did. But don't worry, I'm not going to embarrass you anymore. You can go hang out with your freaky girlfriend who doesn't talk and doesn't know her own name. Sounds like a blast." Liam jumps down from the last branch and stomps off, slamming the back door.

They were definitely talking about me. My face heats up as I sneak from tree to tree back to the house, the words *freak* and *girlfriend* bouncing around in my brain.

⤚

I skip lunch at the café with Bàba and spend all day Friday at the library. It's the only place I'm guaranteed not to run into Liam. Logan doesn't show up, either, which is a relief. It means our plan must be going well, plus it gives me time to think about what his argument with Liam meant. I don't know if Logan really said that he wished he wasn't a twin—it doesn't sound like him. What I do know is that Logan accused his brother of destroying the school garden, and Liam didn't deny it. Honestly, I wouldn't blame Logan if he didn't want to be related to Liam anymore.

At dinner on Friday, the last day of my suspension, Gōnggong actually talks. He's happy that the garden is finished. He describes the flowers that were planted. He says, "Neighbor boy very nice, very helpful."

He means Logan. From Basket's load, a brick of grief and loneliness disintegrates, and the weight on my shoulders lightens a tiny bit. The interview must have gone well. I smile at Gōnggong and put another serving of steamed ginger-scallion fish on his plate.

———

Saturday morning, the sky is a cloudless pale blue above me, shimmery as a pearl. I make my way down to the dragon tree and rake the fallen walnuts into a pile. Logan appears ten minutes later, looking worried. He won't meet my eyes.

"What's wrong?" I ask. "The garden looks amazing. I can't believe you even helped plant tulip bulbs for next spring."

Logan shakes his head. "That's just it. It wasn't me."

"What? Gōnggong said you helped him."

"He did?" Logan looks confused. "Are you sure?"

I try to remember my grandfather's exact words. "Well, he didn't say your name. He said that the neighbor boy helped him. You're the closest neighbor boy, and he knows you."

Logan slumps against the fence and shakes his head again. "It was Liam. Your grandfather can't tell us apart."

I still don't get it. "Weren't you supposed to? Or did I not understand your plan?"

Logan scowls. "That *was* my plan, until Mom made

me run errands all Wednesday afternoon, then on Thursday she dropped me off at the senior center to hand out desserts at their tea party. Of course, Liam weaseled his way out of everything like he always does, with his *charm*." Logan practically gags on the last word. "When I got home on Thursday, I found out that Liam and Gōnggong had finished the garden. I was going to offer to help water it with him yesterday, but Mom made me go mow some old sick lady's lawn."

He doesn't mention the fight he and Liam had up in the dragon tree. But that must have been what they were yelling about when Logan said his brother had messed everything up. And the person Liam was helping was Gōnggong. I don't understand. Why would Liam help my grandfather? He hates me. And he crushes gardens—he doesn't create them.

Logan looks away when I catch his eye. He runs a hand through his hair. "I'm sorry, Lan. I didn't get a chance to see your grandfather at all, never mind talk to him."

His words snap me back to reality. The plan wasn't really about the garden. It was about the Veterans Day project. "But . . ." My legs feel wobbly, and I sink down onto the grass. "Ms. Brown wants the rough draft of the interview on Wednesday! And Gōnggong's garden is already finished. I'm never going to be able to get this assignment done." Tears spring to my eyes, and I turn away so Logan can't see. It's always like this, I think. Everything seems like it's going great until the sky falls in.

As if on cue, something hard strikes my head. "Ow!" I look up to find an angry squirrel chattering at me, most of a walnut clutched in its tiny paws.

Logan picks up the husk of the walnut from where it fell. "Wow. Good thing it didn't decide to chuck the whole nut on your head. You'd probably have a concussion. Hey, maybe Ms. Brown would give you an extension for a squirrel-related brain injury."

I know he's trying to cheer me up, but something else distracts me. "Do you hear that?"

He's silent for a moment, listening. "You mean the squirrel? Or the wind chimes?"

"Never mind." I stand up straight and square my shoulders. "You said you served dessert at the senior center?" Logan nods, perplexed. "Can you come over later?"

Logan's face lights up. "You got an idea!"

I look up at the squirrel, who is still scolding us. "You could say inspiration struck me."

He groans and tries not to laugh at my horrible pun. Then I give him the basic details and arrange for him to come over in the afternoon. I pray that I can find everything I need. I pray that I have enough time to get it done. I pray that Tao grants me success. It is, after all, her plan.

Chapter Thirty-Four

I rush back to the house and ransack the kitchen, piling ingredients and equipment on the table. "Māma!" I call. "Māma!"

She emerges from the basement door, wiping her hands on a dish towel. She must be making tofu again. A few weeks ago, she'd declared, "All the dòufu in grocery store here is so old, turn sour and yellow. More like cheese than dòufu." Next thing I know, she'd turned a corner of the basement into a bean curd factory. Sometimes I wonder if she's going to make it into a job and sell it. Her eyes widen at the mess I've made. "Āiyā." She sighs. "Luàn qī bā zāo!"

It's far from a total mess, but Basket doesn't argue. "Māma, I want to make jiālí jiǎo for Gōnggong, but I can't find the curry powder."

Her face softens. She goes over to the cabinet by the stove and plucks out a bottle of the yellow powder that

I swear wasn't there two minutes ago. "Gōnggong ask you to make?"

"No, I just thought it would be nice to surprise him."

Māma pats my arm. "You are a good girl, always taking care of Gōnggong. Hěn xiàoshùn." She disappears back into the basement.

Wow. That's, like, the highest compliment, being told that I'm taking good care of my elders. She wouldn't be so approving if she knew that it was Tao's idea. That the yǐn I'd heard was not the sound of wind chimes, and the chá was not the scolding of a squirrel. That it was the tree spirit telling me to serve snacks and tea, yǐn chá, to Gōnggong. Jiālí jiǎo are small, half-moon-shaped pastries filled with a savory mixture of curried beef, onion, and potato. Gōnggong's favorite savory pastry. This is how I'm going to get Gōnggong in a good mood—good enough to talk about his past.

The next few hours are filled with boiling, sautéing, rolling, filling, and baking. The traditional pastry dough for the curry pockets is actually made from two kinds of dough—a water dough and an oil dough—kneaded together. I don't have time for that, so I use one of the balls of Bàba's homemade pie dough that he keeps in the fridge. It still takes forever.

Finally, the pastries are done and cooling on the counter. Māma leaves to go grocery shopping at the Asian market thirty minutes away. It's now or never. I hurry to hang a red dance ribbon on my windowsill and wait anxiously by the back door.

Logan appears soon after, wearing a blue polo shirt and khakis. I thought his being here would make me less nervous. I was wrong. I'm still in my Defy Gravity T-shirt that a friend gave me after seeing *Wicked* and jeans that are ripped because they're old, not trendy. My arms are dotted with curry powder, and I'm pretty sure I reek of onions. He looks nice—really nice. I hope he thinks my cheeks are red from the heat of the oven, not from blushing.

He steps inside in his socks. "It smells amazing in here," he says, his eyes bright, and there's no way for me to back out of this interview now.

"Um, thanks . . . yeah . . . I hope you like curry . . . and tea . . . I mean, not mixed together," I babble. I take a deep breath. "You can sit over there. I'll go get Gōnggong."

I tap on my grandfather's door and poke my head in. He's sitting on his chair and reading a Chinese newspaper. "Gōnggong? Would you like some tea and jiālí jiǎo? I made them for you."

"Hǎo!" he says enthusiastically and follows me down the hall. So far, so good.

If Gōnggong is surprised to see Logan, he doesn't show it—he just says hi and sits down at the kitchen table opposite him. I set out a platter of the curry pockets, three small plates, and three handle-less teacups. Then I carry over the matching porcelain teapot with the hare's fur glaze, place it on the table, and take my seat.

Ready? Logan mouths silently. I nod, the beetles in my throat clicking.

Lifting the lid of the teapot, I check on the tea. Gōnggong doesn't like it too strong, but he doesn't like it too weak, either. It has to have the exact right color and be at the right temperature. I pour tea into Gōnggong's cup first, and he taps the table with his fingers in thanks. Then I pour Logan's and mine. The silence draws out, as thin and fragile as rice paper.

Gōnggong looks at the pastries, at me, and then at Logan. Is it my imagination or does he study Logan a little bit longer? When neither of us speak, he finally says, "Lan, nice have tea with you and friend. Is special day?"

I say, "Not really," at the same time that Logan says, "Yeah, kind of." We glance at each other, and I can see that Logan is trying not to smile. Well, at least someone is feeling relaxed.

I start again. "It's about school."

"Yes? You make jiālí jiǎo for teacher?"

"No, Gōnggong, it's not about the jiālí jiǎo." I nudge Logan's foot under the table.

He clears his throat. "What Lan's trying to say is, there's a project we have to do in school, and we need your help."

Well, there goes trying to be subtle. Gōnggong's eyebrows wrinkle as he thinks about this. "Project? What project?"

"We have to interview a veteran for my Social Studies class." I beg him with my eyes. "You're the only veteran I know." I clench my hands in my lap, holding on to Basket's straps, trying not to let anything spill.

Gōnggong's eyebrows draw closer together, and his lips press into a line. He sighs. "This why you ask Bàba before? Teacher want me talk about my time as soldier?"

"Yes." It's hard to breathe. He's all that stands in the way of my passing this project or getting a zero. If I fail the project, I'll get a bad grade for the semester and Māma and Bàba will be angry with me. Angry enough to see that moving to Redbud was a bad idea and we should move back to Boston? Probably not. They'll just think I didn't try hard enough. But what if Gōnggong agrees to do the interview and it makes him unhappy? Then Māma and Bàba will be mad at me for that, too. It's a no-win situation. I try to grab for a silver lining, a bright spot, a gleam of gold. "The project is for Veterans Day, Gōnggong. There's going to be a celebration at school. All the veterans are invited." I don't tell him that Foxman has specifically not invited him.

His frown deepens. Oh no, what did I say that was wrong?

"War not something to celebrate, Lan." His eyes lose focus, as though they're looking inward, at memories of a faraway place and time.

I shoot a panicked glance at Logan. "No, no, I didn't mean that," I say hastily. "The, um, gathering is to honor everybody who served. To, um—"

"To thank you," Logan finishes for me. "For doing your duty for your country."

Gōnggong stares at Logan. "Why thank me for doing duty? Duty mean no choice. I no have choice—everybody must join military when finish high school, like or not."

"Everybody? In China?" This is news to me. I thought

Gōnggong had wanted to be a soldier. Things were turning out to be way more complicated than I thought.

"Not mainland China," Gōnggong says. "Taiwan. Different country."

Logan taps on his phone, then says, "Whoa. Wikipedia says Taiwan has mandatory military service. All guys have to enlist when they're nineteen. It's been that way since, like, 1949."

Gōnggong nods. "Nineteen forty-nine—Gúomíndǎng escape communist China and set up new capital in Taipei. They make new law. I just a baby then. Join military in 1966." He looks at us in turn. "You really want know?"

"Yes," Logan and I say simultaneously. My heart is pounding. Is it possible that Basket can do this?

Gōnggong picks up the plate of curry pockets and offers it to Logan, who seizes one and takes a huge bite. Flakes of pastry rain down on his plate and the table. He looks sheepish but thrilled.

"That was awesome," he says when he finally manages to swallow.

I roll my eyes. Gōnggong looks amused, too. He slowly eats a pastry, savoring it, and finishes with a sip of tea. "Okay," he says. "You ask. I talk."

Chapter Thirty-Five

"So you joined when you were only nineteen?" That seems so young to me. Only seven years older than I am right now. Even though seven years is a lot, I don't think I'd be ready to go to war then. Or ever.

Yesterday, when Gōnggong was out fishing, I snuck into his room and looked in his closet. In the way back, a uniform hung, encased in a plastic garment bag. The same uniform that he's wearing in the old photo. The jacket has a patch on the sleeve near the shoulder, with an embroidered shape like a stretched-out star. It looks a little like a bird, or a plane. "Were you in the air force, or whatever they call it in Mandarin?"

Gōnggong looks surprised for a moment, then almost smiles. "Yes, I assign to Zhōnghuá Mínguó Kōngjūn. Hard to get in but eyes good then, so they take me."

"Cool! You were a pilot? What was that like?" Logan's excitement is clear. What is it with boys and planes?

"I not pilot. I helper on plane—" He turns to me. "How

you say? Other people on plane, do other job?"

I think for a moment. "Do you mean the crew?"

"Yes, yes, I part of crew on board. Communication engineer," he adds, sitting up straighter.

Wow. An engineer. No wonder my grandfather had been so good at fixing machines. He'd even repaired one of the bakery's ovens when it stopped working. "That sounds important. Were you ever in combat? Like, fighting against an enemy?"

Gōnggong's proud face immediately turns somber again. "Vietnam War. Bad time."

Logan looks confused. "I didn't know Taiwan was in the Vietnam War. Were you, uh, I mean, which side . . . ?"

Gōnggong hesitates. I'm not sure if he understands what Logan is getting at or if I should translate, or if he just needs some time to process. I stay quiet. I remember parts of the articles I read about the Vietnam War and Ho Chi Minh. Basically, the two parts of Vietnam, the north and the south, were fighting against each other for control of the entire country. The North Vietnamese ruler, Ho Chi Minh, believed in communism and was supported by Russia and China. The leaders of South Vietnam were backed by the United States, which wanted Vietnam to become a democratic country.

Logan and I glance at each other, and I know we're thinking the same thing. If Taiwan had supported the North Vietnamese, and Gōnggong had been in the Taiwanese Air Force, then he would have fought against the South Vietnamese. Against the United States. That would not go over well at school. Not with the students and teachers, and definitely not with Foxman. The principal would probably kick me and Gōnggong off the stage as soon as he heard.

But was that fair? Gōnggong hadn't chosen to join the military. He'd been forced to sign up. He didn't get to choose who the Taiwanese government decided to support in the Vietnam War, either. Poor Gōnggong. He hadn't had any control over his life then—he was doing his duty. He had to obey orders, just like I have to obey Māma and Bàba without question. He fought for his country like he was supposed to. Didn't that make him a patriot, just like the other veterans that would be at the celebration?

Gōnggong places his hands on the table, startling me out of my thoughts. He takes a deep breath, and I steel myself to hear the words that would confirm he had fought against US soldiers. "I no tell anyone this, not even your Bàba. But Vietnam War long time ago. I think okay to tell now." He pauses again, and the beetles in my stomach flutter wildly.

"Hēi biānfú zhōngduì," Gōnggong murmurs.

"What did he say?" Logan leans forward, the curry pastry in his hand forgotten.

I shake my head. "I didn't catch all of it. Something about a black bat? That can't be right."

Gōnggong nods and repeats the phrase. "Name of my group. Black Bat—how you say?—Squant? Squat?"

"Squad?" Logan offers. "Or maybe squadron?"

"Squadron. Black Bat Squadron." Is it my imagination or does a small gleam enter my grandfather's eyes? "We top-secret group," he says with a trace of smugness. "Work with CIA."

Top secret? The CIA? But the Central Intelligence Agency is part of the US government. That means—

"Taiwan was an ally of the United States?" Logan finishes my thought.

"Yes, yes," Gōnggong says. "Taiwan a republic, like here. US help Taiwan, Taiwan help US. Our countries are friends."

I let out a breath I didn't realize I'd been holding. The beetles in my stomach settle and still. Gōnggong's story is more incredible than I ever imagined.

Logan is wide-eyed, too. "Top secret, huh?" he says. "Like covert ops? What kind of missions did you do, or are you not allowed to tell us?"

I have no idea what covert ops means, but it sounds like something from a video game the kids at my old school used to play. From Gōnggong's expression, he doesn't understand most of what Logan says, either, but he gets the gist. The part about top secret for sure. His face goes through a complicated dance of emotions, not all of which I can figure out. We wait for him to gather his thoughts.

"Black Bats take US soldiers to places in Vietnam. In the south and in the north." Gōnggong looks at us intently.

"You flew into enemy territory," I say softly.

"Yes. We fly big plane, drop combat team. Deliver supplies and equipment, too. Sometimes, we deliver CIA spies. They try to persuade communist soldiers to come over our side." He shakes his head. "Spies no return to Taiwan." From his tone, it's clear what happened to them.

We have to be careful. I don't want to remind him of people who died. Like the spies. Like Nǎinai. If he gets too upset, he might stop talking or retreat into his room like he did before. I try another topic. "Why were

266

you called the Black Bats?" I ask. The name sounds like something out of a fairy tale.

"Yeah," Logan says. "It's cool, but creepy."

"It's not creepy!" I protest. "Bats are considered good luck in Chinese culture."

"Really? That's weird." At my frown, he backs off. "Okay, okay. Not weird. Just cool."

Gōnggong smiles. "We call Black Bats because planes painted black. We fly very low, at night. That way enemy cannot see us."

"But couldn't they hear you coming if you're flying that low?" Logan clearly knows more about planes and war than I do, but I worry that his questions focus too much on the actual fighting.

Gōnggong nods grimly. "Very dangerous. Often, other plane shoot at us. We almost crash many times. One time, we get away only because other plane use up all their bullets. Other time, bullet came through side of plane, almost hit me in head!"

I suck in my breath, and Logan murmurs, "Whoa."

Gōnggong's gaze turns distant again. "Sìshíjiǔ," he says to himself.

"Forty-nine what?" I ask, thinking he's talking about 1949 again.

My grandfather's eyes, dark and brimming with unshed tears, meet mine. Oh no. This is what I was afraid of. "Forty-nine Black Bats. Ten plane shot down, everybody die. Many my friends. We get medal, but for what? We not heroes. No winners in war—everybody lose something. Zhēn xīnkǔ." He stands suddenly, bumping the table and making the tea in his cup slosh over the side. "I tired, must rest." And then he's gone, leaving me and Logan staring at each other.

That's it. The source of my grandfather's nightmares. And we just made him relive it.

Chapter Thirty-Six

"Lan, you go pond today?" Māma rushes to meet me when I walk in the door Sunday afternoon. "You see Gōnggong there?" Her English is more clipped than usual—she must be anxious about something.

Guilt washes over me. "No," I mumble. I haven't seen Gōnggong since yesterday afternoon when he abruptly left me and Logan sitting open-mouthed at the kitchen table. His words still haunt me. *Zhēn xīnkǔ*. So much suffering that it makes your heart bitter.

He'd been so upset that he didn't even come out to get more curry pastries that afternoon. I'd thought about going in and apologizing, but I was afraid I'd make him feel worse. When Māma went to get him for dinner, he'd said he wasn't hungry and stayed in his room. She came back, looking worried, but brushed off Bàba's questions.

And then, in the middle of the night, I'd heard the sounds again. Gōnggong's nightmare sounds, but worse this time. Garbled words. Hoarse shouts. But I hadn't woken Māma up to comfort him. Instead, I had been selfish and pulled my blankets over my head to muffle the awful noises. I was too afraid of being blamed for Gōnggong's pain.

The weight of my shame makes my knees buckle, and I sit down heavily on the bench. As Basket, I am not just failing to hold my family together, I'm breaking it further apart. I look up at Māma, who is wringing a corner of her apron.

"Which is it?" Māma switches to Mandarin. "You went to the pond and didn't see Gōnggong there, or you did not go to the pond?" Her voice is sharp with worry.

"I didn't go to the pond. I was at the library." It had been easier to write my Veterans Day assignment there. The house is too full of memories and ghosts. Forty-nine Black Bat ghosts, plus Mr. Shellhaus. I feel a tiny glimmer of hope. "Maybe he's still at the pond? Fishing can take a long time."

"I do not think so." Māma turns and walks off, still talking. "I checked the garage, and his fishing pole is still there. When I woke up this morning, he was gone. I went out to run errands and when I came back, he was still gone."

Quickly, I shuck off my boots and follow her into the

kitchen. She picks up a bowl and puts it down again in the same spot. She frowns at a colander full of leafy greens, still wet from rinsing.

"I'm sure he'll be home in time for dinner," I say. "He never misses it when you're making hóng shāo niú ròu miàn." The aroma of the beef and spices that have been simmering in a pot all day is unmistakable. My stomach growls. Even though it's a simple recipe for beef noodle soup, it takes time. It cannot be rushed, Māma often says. Which is why she usually only makes Gōnggong's favorite dish when it's a special occasion.

I take a closer look around the kitchen. Little bowls of dried fruits and nuts clutter the counter. The faintly sweet scent of sticky rice wafts out of the rice cooker. A pretty tablecloth covers the worn surface of the kitchen table. Māma has already set the table, with the ceramic chopstick rests in the shape of arched carp and the dark wood chopsticks with the silver caps.

"Wait a minute. What's going on? Is today a special day? It's not Gōnggong's birthday, or yours, or Bàba's. What are we celebrating?" For a moment, my heart leaps—maybe we're moving back to Boston, maybe Bàba and Māma will finally admit that moving here was a mistake.

"It is a special day, but not a happy day." Māma lifts the cover of the large bamboo steamer and checks the leaf-wrapped bundles inside. "Today is the first anniversary of Nǎinai's passing."

Nǎinai. It all comes together. The beef noodle soup, the steamed zòngzi, the ingredients for Eight Treasure Rice Pudding. I glance at the small altar set up on a shelf above the television. Sure enough, there are new offerings in front of the small photo of Nǎinai—a bowl of oranges, a bowl of rice, and new incense sticks.

It's not a celebration. It's a ritual feast to honor my grandmother, to pay her our respects and show that we are still devoted to her, even though she is gone.

I can't believe a year has flown by already. Nǎinai's death is still so fresh in my mind, like it happened just a few days ago. I can still hear the chanting of the monks at her funeral and smell the incense clogging my lungs. I can still feel the roughness of the tissues against my swollen, crying eyes. I can still see Gōnggong clutching the coffin, trying to hold her one last time.

Gōnggong would never forget this day. Where could he be?

"Maybe Gōnggong lost track of time," I say even

though we both know it isn't true. "He probably went for a walk. Maybe he stopped to talk to Bàba at the café."

"I called Bàba," my mother says. "He said Gōnggong is not there, did not show up today at all." She sinks into a chair and rubs her eyes. Is she crying? Māma almost never cries. She almost never sits down, either. She must be really worried.

"I'll find him," I promise. "I'll check the pond first. I bet he's there. You stay here in case he comes home." A spattering sound draws my attention to the window. The sky has turned a strange greenish gray, and raindrops pelt the glass. "Look, it started to rain. He wouldn't stay at the pond in the rain. He's probably on his way home, or maybe he went into a store to get out of the storm."

"Storm?" Her voice raises. "Bad storm? Lightning thunderstorm?"

I try to downplay it even though I think I just saw a flash of lightning. "No, no, I'm sure it's just a quick shower. I'll pack a jacket and umbrella for him." I head toward the coat closet.

"Bù yí yú lì," Māma calls after me in a strained voice. This one I know. I've heard her say it often enough when she's trying to get me to do better in school. It's basically the Mandarin version of "Do your best" except with an added dash of "Even if it kills you." Today, though, I don't roll my eyes at her. I'm going to do whatever it takes to find Gōnggong and bring him home.

Chapter Thirty-Seven

It's raining steadily by the time I finish searching the Redbud Market and the stores on the north side of Main Street, and the wind has picked up. I cross the street at the one stoplight in town. The carved wooden sign for the Redbud Café swings creakily above the door. Maybe I just missed Gōnggong at another store and he stepped into the café to see Bàba and wait out the storm. I should check.

Inside the café, I push back my hood and take a look around. Mary, the waitress, nods and smiles at me as she carries plates of sandwiches to a couple by the window. There are a few elderly people sitting in mismatched chairs at small wooden tables, sipping coffee from thick white mugs. None of them are Gōnggong. A beetle pinches at my heart, hard.

At a table in the back corner, three boys are laughing and blowing straw wrappers at each other. Another boy sits quietly at the table next to them, concentrating on eating a slice of pie. He looks up, and with a start, I realize it's Logan. He smiles at me, but all I can do is stare. If Logan hadn't pushed Gōnggong to talk about the dangers he faced as a pilot, maybe Gōnggong wouldn't be missing right now. But he was only trying to help me, so I can't be angry with him. The boy diagonally across from him notices Logan's expression and turns to look at me. It's Liam. He frowns as Logan waves me over. I shake my head, which makes Logan frown, too.

Logan and Liam aren't sharing a table. It definitely seems like Liam and The Daves are excluding Logan on purpose, and I can't help but feel that it's partly my fault. There's no way I'm going over to Logan's table with all of them watching. Besides, I have to keep looking for Gōnggong. I catch Mary on her way back to the front counter and ask if she can go get Bàba for me. *Please let Gōnggong be in the kitchen*, I pray to Tao.

I must not be worthy, because Bàba comes out alone. "Lan!" He reaches across the counter and clutches my hands. "Did you find Gōnggong?" His forehead is creased with worry.

"No, Bàba," I say around the lump in my throat. "I checked all the stores on the other side of the street already. I'm going to look in the stores on this side now."

276

I squeeze my father's hands, stained purple from making blueberry pies. "I'll find him, I promise."

Bàba's eyes flicker to the windows behind me and his mouth thins. "Storm getting worse. Radio say there is thunderstorm warning. Too dangerous. I will go with you." He starts to take off his apron.

"No, Bàba! You can't leave work." What if Samantha gets mad and fires him? Then it will be my fault that Gōnggong is missing *and* that Bàba lost his job. I have to fix this problem on my own, like Ged the wizard confronting the shadow creature by himself.

Bàba starts to argue with me, but Samantha steps in. She must have come out of the kitchen while we were talking. "I'm sorry, I couldn't help overhearing. Your daughter's right, Jiarong. None of us can leave. Since we have a generator, when there's a storm we stay open to take in people who have lost electricity. We give them shelter and food. I can't manage without you and Mary." She gestures to the back corner and says to me, "Why don't you ask one of those boys to help you find your grandfather? They all know Redbud like the back of their hands. I'm sure they'll find him in no time."

I follow her hand to where it leads—straight to Logan. I grimace as he sees Samantha pointing to him and raises his eyebrows. Then he gets up and comes over. "Hi, Samantha," he says. "Hi, Lan, Mr. Hua. Did you need something?"

I want to tell him that I do not need his help. But I don't, because it's not true. I do need his help. Again.

Before I can say anything, Bàba turns to me. "Lan, you know this boy?"

Logan glances at me, in a *I can't believe you didn't tell your dad we're friends* kind of way. He sticks out his hand and says, "Hi, I'm Logan," at the same time that I say, "This is Logan." I hurry to add, "He helped Gōnggong make the garden. He lives in the house behind us . . . next to us . . . he's our neighbor . . . we're, uh, in the same classes." I'm babbling again. My face flushes.

Thankfully, Bàba doesn't seem to notice I'm flustered. His expression softens, and he returns Logan's handshake. "We are new here, so it is good to have someone familiar with the town. Thank you for helping my father with his garden. He is right, you are a good boy."

Oh my god. Quickly, I explain the situation to Logan before Bàba can say anything else embarrassing. His grin disappears when he realizes how serious it is that my grandfather is missing in the thunderstorm and immediately agrees to help. I can hear The Daves ask him what's going on when he goes back to his table to get his coat, but he just ignores them. He also ignores Liam, who stares at me as we say goodbye to Bàba and Samantha and plunge into the rain. It's pouring now, so we dash into the next store, which is full of sewing supplies and fabric. I zip through the aisles while Logan goes to ask the shopkeeper if she's seen anyone who looks like Gōnggong. No luck.

I run smack into Liam in my hurry to get to the next shop. Quickly, I step back and swipe the water out of my eyes. He's standing on the sidewalk outside the fabric store. Surprisingly, he doesn't say anything snarky—just gives me a strange look. If I had to guess, I'd say that Liam looks nervous, but that can't be right.

"What do you want?" Logan asks, moving around me to face his brother. "Bugging me all day wasn't enough?"

"Dude, we were just keeping you company." Liam's voice is defensive. "You looked lonely."

Logan rolls his eyes. "Right. So you made me buy pie for all of you. And then sat at a different table where you were incredibly annoying and made a mess. Some company. What happened to not embarrassing me any-more?"

Before Liam can retort, I clear my throat, loudly.

Both boys turn and look at me. I clear my throat again, swallowing the beetles back down. "I don't have time for this. You"—I stare at Logan—"can keep arguing with *him*." I jerk my thumb toward Liam. "But I'm going to look for Gōnggong." Without waiting for a reply, I spin around and head to the next store.

"Wait."

Sighing, I turn back to see what Logan wants, but he's glaring at his twin. It was Liam who asked me to wait. I cross my arms. "Fine. You have thirty seconds."

The rain pours down while we wait for Liam to reply. He's not wearing a jacket, and his hair and clothes are soaked. Anger crosses his face, replaced by resignation. He walks past us to stand under the awning of the next store and beckons us over. We join him, and for a moment, there is just the drumming of the rain on the awning, a sound so familiar and so heartbreaking. If I close my eyes, I could be back in my old room, listening to the rain thrum against the bakery awning below.

Liam shifts from foot to foot and mumbles something.

"What?"

"I said . . . " Liam repeats in a louder voice, "I want to help, too."

The beetles must have gotten into my ears somehow

and clogged up my hearing. "You want to help us find my grandfather?"

Liam nods. I glance at Logan, who looks angrier by the second. "Your *help* is the reason he's missing!" he accuses his brother. "I was supposed to help plant the garden, not you. If you'd stayed out of the way and I'd interviewed him, he wouldn't have gotten upset and run away!"

"What are you talking about?" Liam asks. "I didn't do anything to him. What interview?"

"Logan was helping me with the Veterans Day project," I say. "We had a plan to make it a casual talk in the garden so he wouldn't get upset. But since you took Logan's place, we had to go ahead and sit down with him yesterday. And it looks like something triggered him."

Liam shakes his head. "So how is any of this my fault?" His voice is defensive. "It sounds like you guys are the ones that made him take off."

I don't say anything, because he's right. It's my fault. I should've just failed the assignment instead of trying to do it all.

"Fine," Logan says. "We're all to blame. Now stop wasting our time and go home. Lan and I will find him."

"Let me help." Liam's voice is belligerent, but his eyes are pleading.

"Why? What's in it for you?" Logan peers into his brother's face. "Tell me the truth. Are you just trying to get Lan in trouble again?"

The surprise on Liam's face mirrors my own. It didn't occur to me that Liam could be using my own grandfather to make my life even more miserable. Would he really sink that low?

"No!" Liam insists. "It's not like that at all. He was . . . nice to me. He made me see that I might've gotten some stuff, uh, wrong."

"Yeah?" Logan's voice is incredulous. "How'd he do that? I've been telling you the same thing for months!"

Liam's laugh is a bit sour. "He called me Logan. Can you believe that? No one ever mistakes me for you."

"So he thought you were me. That was all it took?"

"Yeah, I guess. He was so happy to see me . . . I mean you. He waved me over and showed me all the plants he bought. I actually enjoyed it. That's why I thought I'd pretend to be you for a little while." Liam looks thoughtful. "I didn't expect it to feel so different. People like you," he tells Logan with a tinge of jealousy. "They *respect* you. And it bugs me that they don't see me that way. All this time I've been so mad at you because I thought you didn't want to be around me, to be my brother. But really, when you said you didn't want to be my twin, you meant—"

"—That I wanted to be seen for myself," Logan finishes. He stares at his twin for a moment, a mix of emotions playing across his face. "It's not hard to get people to like you for you," he says. "Just treat people the way you want to be treated. Stop being such a jerk."

Liam winces. "Okay, I guess I deserved that," he says. "I might not have been the nicest guy to you lately." He pauses for a moment and catches my eye. "Or to you, either." Another pause. "I'm sorry."

For once, I'm speechless without the beetles blocking my throat.

Logan takes a deep breath. "Well, that's a start." He looks at me, but I'm not ready to accept Liam's apology. Not yet. Not until I'm sure that he means it. Not until Gōnggong is back home safely.

"Come on, then," I say. "Enough talking." I turn and head into the store.

Chapter Thirty-Eight

"What is this place?" I ask Logan. In the front of the store, metal bins filled with random items cover long wooden tables. Small plastic animals, bouncy balls, packages of white socks. There's no order to the items—decks of cards are next to toothbrushes—and the effect is dizzying. In the back, tall shelves crammed with stuff form a dim and dusty maze.

"It's technically Mr. Evans' Emporium, but everybody just calls it 'the variety store.' Because . . ." Logan waves his hand at the piles of objects. "Why don't you two search the back while I talk to Mr. Evans?"

I glance at Liam, who simply shrugs and struts off. After a moment, I head for the opposite back corner. Logan *is* better at talking to people.

The first aisle has all kinds of kitchenware, spatulas, and other utensils hanging on hooks sticking out of the wall. On the other side, pots, pans, and cupcake tins clutter the shelves. Bàba would love this place. No sign of Gōnggong, though. He's not in the next three aisles, either. Liam almost runs into me as we turn a corner. He didn't find Gōnggong, either.

There's a short hallway at the back of the store, and I'm about to ask Liam to check the men's bathroom when Logan calls to us from the front. I hurry back up the aisle and skirt around the bins, spotting Logan at a counter by the front window.

"You found him?" I gasp, my breath catching on a few beetles.

Logan says, "No, but I think we have a lead. Mr. Evans says your grandfather was in here earlier today."

"Really?!" I turn to the tall man standing behind the messy counter. "What did he say? Was he okay? Did he buy anything? Did he mention where he was going?" The words tumble out of me like grains of rice. It's the most I've spoken to any adult outside of my family in weeks.

Mr. Evans's voice is low and soothing. The same voice I used to hear Gōnggong use in the bakery to calm impatient customers. "Like I was just telling Logan, your grandfather didn't say where he was going. But I did talk to him. He asked me if I carried certain things and bought a few of them. He seemed fine, if a bit driven."

"Driven?"

"Like he had a purpose—something he really wanted to accomplish today," Mr. Evans replies. "Logan and I have been racking our brains trying to figure out what it could be."

Logan jumps in. "But you know him better than we do. I bet you can figure out what he's doing."

"I'll try," I say, sending a quick silent plea to Tao for guidance. "What did he want to buy?"

"Well, first he asked for a broom, so I showed him where I keep the cleaning supplies." The shopkeeper looks thoughtful. "He didn't want a long-handled broom, though. Ended up picking out a dustpan with one of those short-handled brushes."

A brush and dustpan? What did Gōnggong want with those? We already had a broom at home. "Is that all he bought?"

"No, he also asked for incense and paper money. I haven't carried incense for years, but he seemed happy with a scented candle. The paper money stumped me, though. Took me a while to figure out that he wanted toy money and not cash. Told him that the only toy money I have is in the Monopoly games." Mr. Evans gestures to the top of the counter. What I thought was just random clutter is actually the guts of the board game, without the fake money. "I had to charge him the full price of the game, though." At this, the man looks slightly apologetic. "I mean, you can't play Monopoly without money, right?"

"Right," I say absently, my mind trying to make sense of the items. A dustpan, brush, candle, and fake money. What was Gōnggong going to do with them? Were they gifts for Māma and Bàba? That didn't explain the toy money, unless it was for me? Why wouldn't he just give me the whole game? "He didn't buy anything else? Say anything else?"

Mr. Evans's kind face droops. "No. Not unless you count the matches. I pick those up from restaurants, so I don't charge for them." He points to a glass fishbowl filled with matchbooks printed with the names and logos of different restaurants.

I stare at the fishbowl, not really seeing it. I ignore the three pairs of eyes focusing on me. The list of things Gōnggong bought run through my head like song lyrics on an endless loop. Like listening to Nǎinai sing about the family over and over again on Gōnggong's cassette tape. *Nǎinai*. Images flicker through my mind—all the food that Māma had made for tonight, the framed photograph of my grandmother on the family altar, the offerings in front of it.

"Incense!" I exclaim, making the others jump. "You said he asked for incense?"

"That's right," Mr. Evans says, looking at me curiously.

Logan prods, "Did you figure it out?" at the same time that Liam says, "Spit it out already!"

I whirl to face them. "I think he wants to pay his respects to my grandmother."

Logan looks confused. "I thought your grandmother was, um, dead?"

"She is!" I hurry to explain. "Today is the anniversary of her death. My mom put out some things to honor her. Including incense sticks. But it's also near the end of Ghost Month. I remember my Third Aunt making a big deal of Nǎinai passing away during Ghost Month." I turn to Logan. "Can you look up what day it is on the lunar calendar for me?"

Logan takes out his cell phone. "Looks like today is . . ." He squints at the screen. "July twenty-ninth on the lunar calendar. Does that mean anything?"

I gasp. "It's the last day of Ghost Month! What if Gōnggong is trying to communicate with Nǎinai?"

Logan and Liam's eyes go wide. "What do you mean, 'communicate' with your grandmother?" Liam says, a tiny thread of worry in his voice. He doesn't sound so brash and brave anymore.

"There's a Chinese holiday called Tomb Sweeping Day, where people go and clean the graves of their ancestors. Don't you see? The brush and dustpan?" The other items make perfect sense now. "The incense is an offering and so is the paper money. Burning the money will send it into the afterlife, where Nǎinai can use it to buy things."

"Buy things? What kinds of things? I mean, are there, like, stores—" Liam pauses awkwardly "—where she is?"

I hold up my hand in a stop gesture. I don't have the time or energy to give him a presentation on how Chinese people pay their respects to their dead ancestors. "Later. Mr. Evans, where's the town cemetery? My grandmother is buried in Massachusetts, but I think my grandfather got confused and went to try to find her grave."

"There are actually three cemeteries in town," Mr. Evans replies. "And I'm sorry, but your grandfather didn't give any clues about which one he was planning to visit."

We thank him for his help and are halfway out the door when he adds, "You kids be safe, now. Find him quick." Something in his voice makes me turn back. He looks surprised. "You didn't hear? They just upgraded the thunderstorm warning to a tornado watch."

Chapter Thirty-Nine

I stop for a moment outside the store, my mind whirling. What direction should I go in? Which cemetery would Gōnggong know about? He walks around while I'm at school, so he's had a lot more time to scope out the town. All I know are home, school, the pond, the library, and the little downtown area.

"Where are each of these cemeteries?" I ask Logan.

"The Grove is that way," he says, pointing down the street past the café and the library. East, then. "Let's see—St. Dorothy's is at the other edge of town." Logan sweeps his arm to point in a northwesterly direction. He looks at Liam. "What's the name of the one that's on the way to Grandma and Grandpa's house?"

"Woodlawn, I think," Liam says, gesturing to the south. "It's, like, a couple miles away, though. You really think your grandfather could've walked out there?"

I shrug, frustrated. "I don't know what's running through his mind. He could be at any of the cemeteries, and they're all in different directions. I don't have time to search them all!"

"We could split up," Liam suggests. "My bike's at the café. I can ride out to Woodlawn and check it out."

"No," Logan says. "We're not splitting up. Didn't you hear Mr. Evans? There's a tornado watch in effect."

Liam's face pales. He swallows hard. "I'll be fine. It's just a watch, not a warning. It's probably not going to turn into anything, right? Isn't that what you always tell me?" He glares at his brother, as if challenging him to say something.

I'm puzzled until I remember the tornado drill we had during the first week of school and how frightened Liam was at even the thought of a tornado. I can't believe he's willing to go to the farthest cemetery by himself when there's any chance of a tornado hitting the town. He must be telling the truth when he says he cares about Gōnggong.

Logan grimaces. "Look, I'm sorry for teasing you about having tornado phobia. You've just always been the braver one, you know? I had to have something I could give you a hard time about. But there's an actual tornado watch on, and I'm not letting you go out there alone."

"Besides," I say. "If Gōnggong isn't thinking straight, he might not listen to either of you. I have to be there when we find him. So we're all sticking together." I think for a minute. "It's Ghost Month. What if he's trying to get help from one to find Năinai?"

"What ghost?" the twins ask simultaneously.

"The one in my house, of course."

Māma is anxiously assembling the bābǎofàn when we get home. "Āiyā," she says when she sees us. "I want you find Gōnggong, not two boys."

I introduce her to the twins and tell her what we learned from Mr. Evans. That I think Gōnggong has been triggered by the anniversary and has gone to a cemetery to try to find Năinai. This makes sense to Māma, but she doesn't have any idea which cemetery he could've gone to. She never took him to visit any of them, because we didn't know anybody in Redbud who had passed away.

"We do, Māma. Mr. Shellhaus, the man who lived in this house before us," I remind her. "Did you or Bàba ever mention him to Gōnggong?"

She shakes her head. "We not want to upset him."

There goes my idea. If Gōnggong never knew about Mr. Shellhaus, then he wouldn't try to talk to his ghost or visit his grave. Unless . . . "Māma, what about the landlord? The papers you signed—did Gōnggong see those?"

Her eyebrows draw together. "Maybe, but what does that matter?"

Instead of answering, I dash out of the room and upstairs. When I return, all three of them are still gaping at me in confusion. "He might've seen this!" I shake the paper that I grabbed off my parents' desk. "It's Mr. Shellhaus's obituary. The landlord gave you a copy."

Thankfully, Māma is too worried to ask how I know where the rental documents are. She looks down at the printout. "You think this will help find Gōnggong?" she says hopefully.

"Yes. Look—they listed the name of the cemetery where Mr. Shellhaus is buried. The Grove. If Gōnggong read the obituary, then it's probably the only cemetery he knows about here."

Logan's eyes widen as he remembers. "There's a sign for the road to the Grove on the way to the pond."

"That has to be it, then!" My heart hammers as loud as the rain pelting the window. "Let's go!"

Liam makes a face. "The Grove? Are you sure?"

Just then, there's a loud crackle that makes us jump.

All the lights go out, plunging us into darkness except for the glowing tips of the incense sticks on Nǎinai's altar. I know it's the storm, that the winds have probably brought down a power line somewhere, but I can't help shivering. Tao is giving me a sign.

"Yeah," I reply. "I am."

Chapter Forty

I realize that Māma doesn't know about the tornado watch, and I'm not about to tell her. Instead, I explain that Logan and Liam know how to get to the cemetery, and she needs to stay home in case my grandfather returns on his own.

"I'll make it right," I promise her, and the three of us sprint into the storm.

I head toward the pond, but after a block, Logan grabs my arm. "This way! I know a shortcut!" He swerves down a driveway between two houses. Liam and I follow, my boots skidding on the loose, wet gravel. We run down the lane, through backyards, and across several streets before popping out in front of a set of heavy black iron gates. I stop to catch my breath, but Liam doesn't slow, barreling into the right-hand gate and pushing it open.

Logan turns to me, water streaming off his hood and face. "You okay?" He reaches out as if to steady me.

"Yes," I say, even though my lungs and legs are burning. "Let's do this." His hand clasps mine, and we chase after Liam.

We race through the cemetery, zigzagging around the headstones and looping around the small stone houses of the dead. We find Mr. Shellhaus's grave, but there's no sign that anyone's been there, not even his ghost. The Grove is deserted. Gōnggong is nowhere to be seen. Clouds block the sun, and the light in the sky turns an eerie green, like the great liquid eye of a sea dragon. The trees shelter us a little from the downpour, but they're starting to flutter and creak in the wind.

Liam glances up, and the color drains out of his face. "Mrs. Shaughnessy said that a green sky is one of the signs of a tornado! It must be coming faster than they thought!" He grabs Logan's shoulder and pulls him to a stop. "We have to get home! It's not safe to be out when it's like this."

"It's still just a tornado watch, bro." Logan holds up his phone. "They haven't called it a warning yet!" He turns to me. "We watched *The Wizard of Oz* when we were three. Ever since then—"

"Shut up," Liam growls, and he pushes Logan away. He looks embarrassed and angry. I'm reminded again of the power of stories. *The Wizard of Oz* created an irrational fear of tornadoes in Liam. My phoenix tale convinced Third Aunt that Bàba was stealing money. And now, stories about ghosts crossing back into the world of the living during Ghost Month have placed Gōnggong in danger. Placed all of us in danger.

As if to drive home the point, a streak of white lightning sizzles across the murky sky. The dragon is breathing fire—except Chinese dragons don't breathe fire, they breathe steam and mist. Sea dragons in the sky breathing fire instead of water; it's all wrong. Everything has gone wrong since we first moved here. Gōnggong is missing, and once again, it's my fault. I asked too many questions, brought my grandfather's old demons to the surface, and now the whole world is upside down.

I yank my hand out of Logan's. "I can't leave Gōnggong here! He doesn't know about tornadoes! He'll get hurt!"

"We'll all get hurt if we stay!" Liam flinches as a leaf hits his face, kicked up by the rising wind.

Logan puts his hand on his brother's shoulder. "She's right. We can't leave the old man here. There are too many trees. He might get hit by lightning." His face is resolute. The rain comes down in thrashes.

Liam looks from Logan to me, then back to the sky. He shakes his head, flinging water in all directions. His fear is like another dark cloud swirling around him.

"Come on, Liam!" I want to remind him that he owes me for destroying the courtyard and blaming it on me. He owes it to Gōnggong to help him, because he pretended to be Logan and gained my grandfather's friendship when he didn't deserve it. I have enough guilt of my own—it would be nice to get rid of some. But I know that it's not as simple as taking a brick out of my basket and giving it to Liam. He has to pick up and carry his own basket. So I just say, "I need your help!"

With both hands, Logan grips Liam's arms. "We'll do it together. I've got your back."

The two brothers look at each other, and Liam's shoulders straighten. He nods once, short and hard. Determination replaces the fear in his face. Relief washes over me even as the rain lashes my cheeks.

"We have to do this logically," Logan says. "We need a system. We can't keep running in every direction. We could miss a spot that way." He points. "Let's start over in that corner and work our way to the rear gate. Together."

We run down the aisles between the stones and the trees, searching for Gōnggong in his old khaki trench coat. The time between lightning cracks and the drumbeats of thunder gets shorter. The storm is getting closer. Then, in the pause between thunderclaps, we hear the thin wail of a siren. Logan catches my eye and nods grimly. It's not a tornado watch anymore. It's a warning. There's a twister coming our way.

The sky is almost completely dark, and we still haven't spotted Gōnggong. Gusts blow leaves and small branches off the trees. There's only one more section to check, the oldest part of the cemetery. We sprint, fighting against the wind, the sound of angry sky and sea dragons roaring in our ears.

Something slaps me in the face, and I shriek. It's cold and wet and clings to my nose and mouth, smothering me. Logan tears it away and is about to toss it when I grab his hand. "No, wait!" I uncrumple the dirty thing— it's a hundred-dollar bill from Monopoly.

"There!" Liam shouts. "I think I see him!" He points to a hunched form a few rows away. We race over to find Gōnggong kneeling in the mud in front of an old granite gravestone streaked with lichen. My grandfather's head is in his hands, and his shoulders shake. More Monopoly money is strewn around him.

"Gōnggong!" I cry, dropping down next to him. "Are you okay? What are you doing?"

He grabs on to the gravestone. The letters are worn and impossible to read. His face is so pale in the waning light, like the pearl inlay in one of Nǎinai's ebony hair combs. Rainwater streams down his cheeks, a waterfall of tears.

"Gōnggong," I shout over the wind. "We have to go. Let's go home." I tug on his arm while the twins try to shield us with their bodies. Logan keeps glancing at the sky.

Gōnggong turns to me, his eyes filled with confusion. "Sùzhēn? Shì nǐ ma?" I freeze. Sùzhēn is Nǎinai's first name. Gōnggong thinks I'm Nǎinai.

I shake my head. "No, it's me, Lan."

Gōnggong strokes my cheek with his work-roughened fingers. "Sùzhēn?" he says again, his voice so low I have to lean closer to hear. "Nǐ lái le. Wǒ bú pà."

"Yes, Gōnggong, I came." What does he mean, he isn't afraid? Why would he be afraid of Nǎinai?

Logan and Liam urge me to get Gōnggong up. "It's going to be on us any second!" Logan shouts. Liam says something and dashes away. Gōnggong grabs my hand.

With his other hand still on the gravestone, he pushes himself upright. I stand quickly, trying to lead him toward the rear gate. He won't budge.

"This way!" Logan yells, pulling at my other arm in the direction that Liam went. I take another step, but Gōnggong doesn't move.

"Please, Gōnggong." I squeeze his hand. "There's a tornado coming. We have to go!"

"Sùzhēn," my grandfather says for the third time. "Wǒmén xiànzài guòqù ma?" His face is no longer confused and anxious. He looks peaceful, as if he can't feel the wind whipping his hair and the rain pelting his face.

This doesn't make any sense to me, but I latch on to the word that means going. "Yes, we're going!" I tug him forward one step. And then, as another bolt of lightning arcs overhead, I remember the day Nǎinai died. Bàba had made the phone calls, telling family and friends that Nǎinai "guòqùle"—she had "crossed over," the polite Mandarin phrase for saying that someone has died.

I look down at my pale-blue raincoat, purchased at the thrift store by Māma and a couple sizes too big for me. The hem billows in the wind, and my jeans are nearly invisible in the gloom. Gōnggong thinks I'm his wife, here in ghost form to bring him over to the afterlife, where she is. He isn't afraid to die.

"No, Gōnggong!" I say. "I'm not Nǎinai! I'm Lan!" I have to make him understand. I have to make him want to live.

He turns toward me and smiles, but he still sees his beloved wife. "I'm Lan," I try again. "Nǐ de sūnnǔ. Your granddaughter."

There is a loud crack from overhead and I hear Logan shout, "Watch out!" He pushes us to the side as a large branch the size of a dragon's antler splits from a tree and falls, grazing Logan's shoulder. Logan collapses, the branch pinning him to the ground.

"Logan!" I try to lift the branch, but it's too heavy. Logan grunts in pain. I look around wildly for Liam, but I can't see anything through the rain and the debris blowing everywhere. "Liam! Help! Logan is hurt!" I yell. It's just like him to run off when things become difficult. So much for doing this together.

"Go!" Logan rasps from where he lies on the ground. "Get to safety! Head to that crypt!" He motions to one of the small stone houses. "The one that's in the little valley. We need to be as low as possible!"

Gōnggong looks so tired and weak. The wind lifts his

trench coat and blows it backward, making him sway. I can't risk having him fall, too. "I'll be back as soon as I can," I promise Logan, my eyes brimming with tears.

"Gōnggong, let's go!" I pull him toward the crypt. This time, he stumbles a few steps forward and leans heavily against another gravestone.

"Sùzhēn," he says. "Wǒ guòláile."

"No!" I scream. Gōnggong can't die. He lost Nǎinai, but I lost her, too. Lost so many other things. My best friend, my littlest cousin, my uncles and aunts, my school, my home, my name, everything. I can't lose Gōnggong, too. I have to snap him out of this nightmare. I have to make him see me, not Nǎinai. Me.

I cup Gōnggong's cheeks in my hands, force him to look into my eyes. "It's me, Lan!" I repeat. He stares blankly. "Meilan," I say, but it comes out as a faint croak. My name tastes strange in my mouth, bitter and sharp and sweet all at once. I scream my name above the shriek of the sea dragons, "Huā Měilán!"

Chapter Forty-One

As if rising from beneath murky water, Gōnggong's eyes slowly clear. He wipes the rain from his face with one hand. "Huā Měilán?" He looks around him at the cemetery and the plastic shopping bag in his hand. "Zhè shì zěnme huí shì?"

I almost laugh in relief. "I'll explain what's going on later. Come on, we have to go somewhere safe!" I keep speaking to him in Mandarin as we make our way down to the crypt, leaning on each other for support.

We get to the door of the small square building just as Liam yanks it open. He stuck around after all. "I finally busted the lock with a rock! Quick, go inside." He looks behind me. "Where's Logan?"

Panic blooms on Liam's face when I tell him about the branch falling on his brother. "I'll come help you as soon as I get my grandfather settled," I say.

"There's no time," Liam shouts as he sprints away.

I don't register how noisy it is outside until Gōnggong

and I are inside the tiny structure. All the trees outside are creaking and cracking, and the howling of the wind rises and falls like ocean waves. Pebbles and twigs fly through the open doorway and pepper my legs as I help Gōnggong sit down on the floor, propping him against the back wall. "Rest," I tell him in Mandarin. "I'll be right back."

"Xǐaoxīn, bǎobèi," he says, patting my cheek. *Be careful, precious one.*

Raising my arms to shield my face, I only make it five feet past the door when Liam appears out of the thrashing rain, half carrying Logan, whose arm is around his brother's shoulders. He hops along, one foot raised behind him. I rush to wrap Logan's other arm around my own shoulders. Propped between us, we get him into the crypt and lay him down on the floor next to Gōnggong. My grandfather looks from Logan to Liam and back again. His eyes widen, but he doesn't say anything.

Liam goes to close the heavy bronze door, which muffles the sound of the wind and the trees considerably, but also makes it really dark inside the crypt. Liam turns on his phone's flashlight. Gōnggong hands me his shopping bag, and I remember that he got a candle and matches from the variety store. Miraculously, they're still dry. I light the candle and set it near Logan, hoping that tiny flame will dispel some of the musty chill in the air.

"I'm so glad you're okay," I say to Logan, who is breathing heavily. Then I notice that one of his socks is bloody. "You're bleeding!"

He props himself up on his elbows and wiggles his foot experimentally. The pain makes him gasp and fall back. "I think my ankle's broken."

I bite my lip. I convinced him to help me look for Gōnggong. If he'd gone home when Liam wanted to, he would've been fine. Drinking hot cocoa with his family and waiting out the storm in comfort instead of here in this damp, chilly crypt. "I'm so sorry," I tell him. "This is all my fault." I feel like I've been saying that too much lately.

"Hey," Logan says. "I'll be okay. It's not your fault—I offered to help."

"Yeah, you didn't need that foot anyway," Liam says. I turn to glare at him but stop when I see the concern on his face. Maybe being snarky is his way of coping with stress.

Gōnggong speaks to me in Mandarin. "That's a good idea," I tell him.

"What is?" Logan asks.

"He says we should remove your shoe so it doesn't cut off your circulation when your foot swells. We should also stop the bleeding." I pause for a moment. "He learned that in the military." I motion to Logan's foot. "Can I?" Logan nods and swallows hard. Carefully, I untie his sneaker and spread the sides apart as wide as I can. Gripping his leg just above the ankle, I take a deep breath and pull with my other hand. Logan makes a sharp short cry as the shoe slides over his heel. "Sorry, sorry!" I say. "It's off now."

"My shoe or my foot?" Logan jokes weakly.

I ask Liam to slide the bottom of Logan's jeans up so I can inspect the injury. Blood trickles from a long, shallow wound running up his calf. His ankle is bruised and his foot is pale, but nothing else seems out of place. I breathe a sigh of relief. "Okay, your bone isn't showing or anything. The branch must have cut you when it fell." I look into Logan's eyes, dark and cloudy from the pain. "Thank you," I murmur. "For saving me and Gōnggong."

Logan glances over to my grandfather, who pats his shoulder. "I'm just glad we found him."

"Me too," I reply, although glad doesn't even come

close to describing how I feel. I'm proud that I found a way to reach Gōnggong, but I'm sad that he was so confused. I'm thrilled that we're safe and worried about Logan's ankle. I'm even thankful that Liam was enough of a beast to smash the lock on the crypt door, not that I'd ever tell him so. I don't think there's a shade of blue that expresses all that. I don't think there's a single version of myself that could've done everything I did today. I surprise myself by sliding over and giving Gōnggong a hug, something I haven't done in a long time and wouldn't normally do in front of people who aren't family. Gōnggong seems surprised, too, but after a moment his arms tighten around me, and instead of feeling breathless, I feel like I can finally breathe deeply again.

I let go to rummage in my backpack, coming up with a first aid kit. I didn't make the tree branch fall, and I didn't ask Logan to take the blow for me, but it still feels good to help a friend. I use gauze to clean the cut on his leg and stop the bleeding. I try not to think about how I'm touching his bare skin as I slather antibiotic ointment on the wound and stick several bandages over it. I take out a bottle of water and some Advil.

"Jeez, what else you got in there?" Liam asks. "Any food?"

Instead of being annoyed, I feel another little burst of

pride for being prepared. "Actually, yes. There's a couple more bottles of water and some granola bars. I thought Gōnggong might be hungry when we found him."

"I think he could use it now." Liam gestures to my grandfather, whose eyes are closed. "Here, I'll do that." He takes the water and pills from me and helps Logan sit up enough to swallow them.

"Watch out, you're being nice again," Logan teases. He doesn't sound angry with his brother anymore.

Liam rolls his eyes. "I'm going to stop if you're going to be such a dork about it." A half smile crosses his face.

I scoot over to Gōnggong's side. "Do you want some water?"

He opens his eyes and blinks. "Huā Měilán," he whispers. He sees the water and nods. "Hǎo."

I give him the bottle, and he drinks slowly. The weak light coming through the stained glass above the door fades away into nothing. We share the granola bars as the wind whistles through tiny crevices between the door and its frame. Stones and other unnameable objects ping against the metal like hail, and every now and then something large hits one of the walls, but we are safe here, protected by stone and steel and the dead. I wonder how the dragon tree is holding up and if the tree spirit is safe inside.

Liam stares at me. "Hey, is your name not Melanie? Your grandfather said something else."

I'm caught off guard, and I fidget under his gaze. Talking to him is still new and uncomfortable. "No. That was, um, Mr. Reynard's idea. He told everyone to call me that."

"No wonder you never respond to it. I just thought you were too full of yourself to talk to us." He pauses. "Your real name is . . . Meilan?"

"Yes," I say, torn between fear and pride. "Huā Měilán, if you say it in Mandarin."

"We name you," Gōnggong says, startling all of us.

"What? You mean Bàba and Māma named me?"

"Bù," Gōnggong says. "Nǎinai and I name you."

Chapter Forty-Two

Gōnggong's face registers my surprise. "You not know this story? Nǎinai never tell you?"

I shake my head. How is it that I don't even know the story behind my own name?

"This story better in Chinese. You translate." Gōnggong studies Liam. "First, what your name?"

"Liam," he says, clearing his throat. "I'm Logan's twin."

"Twins," Gōnggong says contentedly. "Very lucky. Nice meet you, Liam. Thank you for helping in garden. Sorry I call you wrong name. Right name very important."

Liam is startled, I think, that my grandfather realizes his mistake and that he can tell the twins apart. "I, uh, no problem. It's, um, nice to meet you, too."

Gōnggong turns to smile at me. "Ready for story?"

Am I? I want to hear the story, but do I want Liam to hear it, too? It's hard to forget that he's only ever called me by names that aren't mine—some of them he made up on purpose to hurt me. Now he knows my real name. What will he do if he knows the reason behind it? Will he turn it into a joke, or make fun of me with his friends? He helped rescue Gōnggong, but how do I trust that he won't be a bully once we're in school again? I know exactly what it's like to be different people in different places. Can he give up that version of himself so easily?

As if he can hear my thoughts, Liam looks up from where he's been staring at the floor. "I'm sorry for calling you mean names. You're from a big city, and Logan was so into you—"

"Dude," Logan protests. It could just be the candlelight, but it looks like he's blushing. My face feels hot, too.

"Sorry, bro, but I need to get this out." Liam holds my gaze. "I guess I was jealous he was hanging out with you and afraid you were convincing him that small towns like Redbud are bad and he should leave. I called you names and trashed the courtyard and told Mr. Reynard you did it. But then I got to know your family. Your grandfather was nice to me, and your dad makes the best pie and never kicks me out of the café. It's not what I expected. Can we just start over? I want to make it right." He stretches his right hand out toward me. "Please, Meilan?"

I want to believe him, but this boy has made my life so hard. I had to become Mist because of him. I avoided Logan because of him. I got suspended because of him. How can one "sorry" make everything "right" again? Why does he expect forgiveness from me so easily?

"Nǐ de ēnhuì bǐ tiān cháng," Gōnggong murmurs.

For a moment, I don't understand, and then it hits me that Gōnggong is quoting the last line of Nǎinai's family song—the line that I translated as "Your grace is longer than the heavens." Grace can mean forgiveness, too. Who is Gōnggong asking me to forgive? I could use some grace. From Third Aunt, from Xing, from Bàba and Māma. Perhaps even from myself. Logan's injury, Gōnggong's disappearance, Bàba's sadness about his siblings—they're all bricks weighing me down. But maybe I never needed to pick them up in the first place. I look from Liam's outstretched hand to his anxious face. I've been carrying the bricks of his actions, too, and it's time he took them back. I want to tell him thanks for helping me today. And that I appreciate his apology. But he's made my life miserable since I got to Redbud. For no reason. And it's going to take more effort than this, so we'll have to see how it goes. So I do.

When I'm finished telling him all that, Liam looks startled. "Uh, okay. Sure," he replies. He lowers his hand dejectedly.

From his spot on the floor, Logan clears his throat. "I'd like to hear the story." He shoots a look at his brother. "We promise not to tell anyone if you don't want us to. And I'll call you by whatever name you want."

His answer warms me. I smile at Gōnggong. "I'm ready now." As he speaks, I translate.

"'You remember the song I played on the tape recorder? Remember the lyrics you translated?'" Gōnggong pauses to look at Logan and Liam. Then he keeps talking, and I continue to translate for him.

"'This song talks about how, even though it is a small house, it is still the best, most wonderful place to be in. The family makes the home that way. The parents are kind and the brothers and sisters are all good to each other. The home is even better than heaven.

"'This song played on the radio all the time when Năinai and I were first married. She was from a wealthy family, and I had nothing. We couldn't afford the servants or the beautiful silk dresses she grew up with, but she never complained. We looked around our humble home, and it didn't matter that we were poor—we knew that we were rich because we had each other and soon, we would have children, just like in the song.

"'The heavens blessed us with your Bàba and his brothers and sister. They were so precious to us.'" Gōnggong chuckles a little, remembering. "'Maybe they didn't always get along as harmoniously as the children in the song, but we knew they loved each other and respected me and Nǎinai.

"'Taiwan had become so strict under Guómíndǎng rule. As our family grew, we wanted better education and more opportunities for our children. A new law in the United States and one of Nǎinai's relatives helped us come over and settle in Boston. We didn't speak English. We didn't know what kind of work we could find.

"'We left our house, our village, all our friends and family, and we came to this country. Did you know the bakery was Nǎinai's idea? She had a dream that the jade fènghuáng pin she always wore suddenly came to life and flew high up into the clouds. She searched for it everywhere, up and down all the streets and alleys. Finally, exhausted, she stopped and sat down on the front step of an empty shop. She heard a sound. When she looked up, the fènghuáng was standing right in front of her. The sunlight on the bird's wings made it glow like gold. The fènghuáng was holding something in its beak. Nǎinai held out her hand, and the bird dropped a pastry into it. It was a small mooncake shaped like a yuánbǎo.'" I pause to think for a moment. "That's, like, a gold nugget, but with a special shape. I think it's also called an ingot."

Gōnggong nods in approval, and we continue, "'When we searched for apartments in Chinatown, Nǎinai saw a vacant store just like the one in her dream. She knew then that it was a sign for us to open a bakery.'" Gōnggong laughs. "'I don't know if she really had this dream or if she just wanted to open a bakery because she loved to eat sweet things. I learned to bake and Nǎinai took care of the money. The family blossomed.

"'You were the first flower. Your Bàba and Māma gave us the honor of naming you. And when Nǎinai and I looked at the shape of your ears—so delicate, like petals—and the pink rosebud of your mouth, all we could think of were flowers.'" Gōnggong stops and so do I, my heart filling with love for my grandfather and embarrassment at being described that way in front of Logan.

Gōnggong takes my hand. He says, "'Our new apartment didn't have a garden, not even a patch of grass where we could stand and see the moon. The song says, 'Even though we don't have a good garden, the fragrance of spring orchids and autumn osmanthus floats in the air.' So we named you Meilan—Beautiful Orchid. You are our sweet spring orchid. You are our precious one. Your imagination and stories make our family richer, more fragrant.'" With his thumb, Gōnggong gently wipes the tears from my face. I hadn't even realized I was crying.

"'When your cousin was born, we named her Xīnggùi—Starry Osmanthus—because she was another flower in our family garden.'" His smile is sad. "'You didn't upset me, Meilan. This is not your fault. I have been in the dark a long time without Nǎinai. I couldn't bear that she left me behind, and I lost my way looking for her. But you found me. You reminded me of our family to bring me back home. Because that is what home is—not a house or a garden or a bakery—but family.'"

Chapter Forty-Three

There's absolute silence after I finish translating Gōnggong's story. It's my story, too, and I'm struck by the thought that it's the first one I've told out loud since the night I babysat for Tiffi and made up the disastrous fènghuáng tale. Gōnggong's last word, *family*, leaves an oily, bitter taste in my mouth, not unlike the raw black walnuts from the dragon tree. Because if what my grandfather says is true, that home is family, does that mean I don't really have a home anymore? The uncles and aunts and even Xing have forced the four of us out of the family unit. Until they take us back, will we forever be guest people?

But then Bàba's words from our lunch in the café come back to me. It was only five days ago, but it feels like months. *We all made our choices,* he said. I thought that he meant the uncles and aunts had chosen to kick us out of the family, but now I think Bàba was talking about his own choices. He is a free grasshopper, no longer bound to his siblings or the bakery. He chose to leave Boston. He chose to make a new home in Redbud, with Māma, Gōnggong, and me—the ones who love and believe in him the most. He chose his family. Maybe I can, too.

I look over at Logan and Liam to see their reactions to the story. To my surprise, they're staring at each other in what must be the "twin telepathy" mode that other people talk about. They both raise their arms simultaneously and bump fists. The last traces of the weird, tense vibe that I sensed between them when I first met Liam ease.

Logan suddenly sits up, and his eyes flare in the candlelight. "Did you notice how quiet it is? The tornado must have passed by us without touching down."

"Or we're in the eye of it," Liam mutters darkly.

Logan ignores his brother and digs in his pocket for his phone. The screen is cracked. "Crap. My phone is toast. Liam, you got any bars?"

Liam flips his phone over, and the beam from the flashlight swings wildly around the mausoleum. "Nope. Still no reception. Battery's low, too."

"The walls are probably too thick," Logan muses. "Go outside and see if you can get a signal. We need to get Meilan and her grandfather home."

Hearing my full real name come out of his mouth

makes my stomach flip in a way that has nothing to do with the beetles. "Gōnggong and I are fine. You need help," I say.

"I'll call Mom and Dad." Liam pushes open the door and disappears outside. Early evening light spills through the doorway, making me blink.

"Guess we won't need this anymore." Logan leans over to blow out the candle. "I'm never going to be able to smell cinnamon apple spice in the same way again."

I won't, either, I think.

Liam manages to get through to his parents. "They're sending an ambulance," he says after hanging up. Then he hands his phone to me so I can call Bàba, who says he'll pick up Māma and meet me at the hospital.

"I'm going to go wait at the gate for the medics," Liam says. "So I can lead them back here." He steps back from the crypt and laughs. "Hey, look at that! We couldn't have picked a more perfect place to ride out the storm."

I join him outside and stare up at the name carved above the heavy bronze door: FLOWERS. The English translation of my own family name. It can't be a coincidence. *Thank you,* I breathe, to Tao, to Mr. Shellhaus, to Nǎinai. Somehow, they led us here. They helped us find

Gōnggong and get us all to safety.

There are leaves and branches and random items scattered everywhere, but otherwise the cemetery has escaped major damage. I circle around, finding Gōnggong's dustpan, but not the broom or the Monopoly money. Lying against the base of one gravestone is a small photo album. I pick it up and see that it's filled with pictures of a family celebrating birthdays and holidays. Everybody is smiling. Nobody takes photos of the sad times.

I tuck the album into my coat pocket. Chances are the tornado swept through this family's home, stealing their things, their souvenirs. Maybe I'll be able to find these people and give them back some happy family memories. I've been sad and worried for so long, focusing on the bad times. Maybe this album is a sign for me to look through the Hua family photos and start remembering the good.

Liam shows up half an hour later with two EMTs. One pushes a stretcher and the other pushes a wheelchair. They insist on putting Gōnggong in the wheelchair, and he finally agrees. I follow them back into the crypt so they can check out Logan's ankle.

"Nice job with the bandages," the dark-haired technician says. She smiles at me. "How'd you know to take off his shoe?"

I smile back. "My grandfather. He learned first aid in the military."

"That's great," she says. "You must be proud of him."

Warmth spreads inside my chest. "I am," I say softly.

Māma and Bàba are already at the hospital when we arrive. They're standing awkwardly next to the twins' parents, who are looking everywhere else but at them. All four of them rush toward us as we get out of the ambulance.

Māma clutches my upper arms and searches my face. "You are not hurt, Lan?"

"I'm fine, Māma." Behind her, Mr. Batchelder has his arm wrapped around Liam's shoulders, holding him close. His wife leans over Logan, trying to hug him as he lies there on the stretcher.

Bàba waits until Gōnggong is helped down from the ambulance and sitting in the wheelchair. Then he goes to kneel in front of him. He takes one of Gōnggong's hands and only says, "Bàba," but the anguish on his face reveals so much more.

My grandfather raises his other hand and gently strokes

Bàba's head. "I was a little confused today," he murmurs in Mandarin. "Caused much trouble for everyone."

"No matter," Bàba replies. "You are safe, that is what is important."

"Huā Měilán and her friends saved me," Gōnggong tells him. "They are very brave."

When Bàba turns to me, the look in his eyes is as tight and warm as a hug.

The emergency-room doctor releases Gōnggong after taking his vital signs and telling him to drink lots of fluids and get more rest, but then she takes Bàba and Māma aside and says something that makes their faces turn somber. I make a note to ask them about it later. I have things to tell them first.

We go over to where Liam and his parents are waiting for Logan to return from having his ankle x-rayed, and I introduce my family. Stiffly, Mr. and Mrs. Batchelder shake hands with my parents and Gōnggong.

"You lucky to have two good children," Gōnggong tells them. "They have much courage."

Some of the ice melts, and Mrs. Batchelder says, "They do. And I'm glad you're safe." Mr. Batchelder just grunts.

Māma catches Mrs. Batchelder's eye. "We would like

to invite your family over for dinner next weekend," she says, pronouncing each word carefully. "To thank your sons for all their help, and to get to know you better, since we are neighbors." It's clear to me that she's been rehearsing it in her head.

"Why, that would be lovely!" the twins' mom exclaims. "What should I bring?"

Māma looks faintly horrified. "No, no, I will cook everything. You are our guests."

"And I will bake pie," Bàba adds. "Buckeye pie for you," he tells Liam. "And lemon meringue for your brother."

"Those are our favorites!" Liam says, surprised.

"Yes," Bàba says, smiling. "I know this already."

Chapter Forty-Four

The town cancels school the next day because many roads are blocked, so I sleep in. When I finally get up and raise my window shade, a shriek escapes from my mouth. I stare at the yard in horror. It had been nighttime when we finally left the hospital; a strange, quiet darkness hid all the devastation.

The tree. My dragon tree. Logan's walnut tree. Its great trunk lies diagonally across our yards, the fence and Gōnggong's new garden crushed underneath. A tangle of roots and dirt rises out of a gaping hole, like a giant bristly beast climbing out of the underworld.

Tao. Tao is gone. Where is she? Can a tree spirit survive without their tree?

My family joins me at the window, drawn by my cry.

"Shù yù jìng ér fēng bù zhǐ," Māma murmurs. Beside her, Bàba gives her a strange look.

"What does that mean?" I ask. "Something about a tree and wind?"

After a minute, when it becomes clear that Māma isn't going to answer, Bàba says, "Word for word translation is 'Trees desire peace, but wind never stop.'"

I think about this saying, about Tao trying to help me and then the dragon tree being knocked down by the storm's winds. "So does that mean that peace is impossible?"

"No," Bàba says. "It means that life changes, no matter if you want it to or not." To my shock, he puts his arm around Māma's shoulders, and she leans, ever so slightly, into him. They turn as a unit and leave the room without another word.

Gōnggong and I continue to stare at the damage in the yard. "Zhēn kěxī," he says.

This, I understand. "Yes, Gōnggong. It's a pity." I don't know if he means the dragon tree or his garden. Maybe he means everything.

I see movement from the twins' house. Liam steps out, holding the back door open for Logan, who walks slowly, on crutches. A white cast covers his lower leg and foot.

"I'm going to go look at the tree," I tell Gōnggong. "Do you want to come?"

We pick our way down the yard, watching out for

walnuts hidden under leaves and branches that threaten to roll under our feet and send us back to the hospital. On its side, the trunk is easily four feet high. Only Logan and Liam's heads are visible on the other side.

"Hi," I call out, waving.

Liam scrambles up and stands on the tree trunk, looking down at me and Gōnggong. "Hey," he says. "Isn't this cool?" He adopts a superhero pose, feet apart and hands on hips, as if he toppled the giant tree with his super strength.

Is that how he felt after destroying the courtyard garden? I shake my head. "No, it's not." I put my right hand on the trunk and walk along it, feeling the deep grooves in the bark, which form a diamond-like pattern. If these rough scales couldn't protect the dragon tree from the winds of change, then all of us are defenseless.

Logan appears around the side of the root ball just as I reach the flattened fence. He navigates the distance between us and stops, looking down at one of the split rails. "Never liked this fence anyway."

"Seems appropriate that it got smashed with a *massive log*, then."

He stares at me for a second and bursts into laughter. I feel the same fluttery feeling from that day by the pond when Logan compared me to a starling. Not the scrape and click of beetle wings, but the soft brush of feathers.

"That was the best," he says when he stops laughing. "I actually don't think I'll mind anymore when Liam calls me Log." His face suddenly turns serious. "It's a bummer about the tree, though. I've been climbing on it my whole life. It's like an old friend." He pats the bark and then looks sheepish. "You probably think that's silly."

"Not at all," I reply, thinking of Tao. "It felt like a friend to me, too."

"Come look at this." Logan turns and moves to a spot just in front of where the roots jut toward the sky.

I follow and find him staring into a large crack through the trunk. I peer into it and gasp. "It's hollow!" That must've been where Tao lived. I feel the sting of tears.

"No worry," Gōnggong says from beside me, making me jump. "She will find new home."

"Who will?" I ask.

"Tree spirit, of course," Gōnggong says with a wink.

Later, Logan and I sit on a plastic tarp on the grass, watching Liam and Gōnggong clean up what's left of the vegetable garden. I brought out my markers when Logan asked me to sign his cast, but now I don't know what to write. Everybody at school still thinks my name is Melanie. Finally, I settle on drawing a small bird with blue-black feathers and white speckles.

"You can draw, too?" Logan makes a *hrrmph* sound of mock disgust. "Is there anything you're not good at?"

I know he's teasing, but I decide to answer honestly. Tao would want me to, and out here, I am Blue, the one who is tired of keeping things to herself. "Talking. Cooking. Being a good daughter. Living up to my parents' expectations. I could go on and on."

Logan's eyes widen. "I think you're way too hard on yourself. I could eat a million of those curry pockets. And trust me, no one ever meets their parents' expectations. It's a fact."

His answer makes me feel a bit better. "Families . . ." I start to say, but then I stop. It feels like too long of a story. Where would I start?

Logan seems to understand anyway. He looks over at Liam. "Truth," he says.

Gōnggong and Liam finish picking up the branches and debris that had fallen or been blown onto the garden. A large corner still lies underneath the tree trunk. A few of the plants they uncovered have survived, but most have been crushed, their fragile stems broken and tender leaves ripped away. It's heartbreaking.

"My dad has a friend who makes furniture," Liam says. "And another one who runs a landscaping company. They're going to come over tomorrow and take the tree away. Then you can replant." Liam pauses and then adds, "I'll help you."

Gōnggong nods. "Good. Then you replant also."

Liam looks puzzled. "What?"

"School garden," Gōnggong says.

This time, all three of us gape openmouthed at Gōnggong. He smiles.

"Uh, yeah, okay," Liam stammers. His face is red. He catches my eye and looks away.

"Wow," Logan says. "Your grandfather doesn't miss much, does he?"

I smile. "I know this already."

I close my eyes and take a deep breath. The scents of wood and earth and the sky after a storm mingle together. The first thing I see when I open my eyes is the dragon tree. Tao is gone, and tomorrow the tree will be, too, but Gōnggong is here. Māma and Bàba are here, inside the house. Logan and Liam are here.

I am here, too.

Chapter Forty-Five

Two weeks later, the hubbub after the storm has died down and we have settled into our routines at the Cliff. Some things, however, are slightly different. Logan and Liam switched seats in Health class so Logan can sit next to me. Mrs. Shaughnessy hasn't said anything about it yet, and I'm not sure she will. What she did say, though, is that she's "disss-appointed" in the three of us for going out into the storm during a tornado warning. Mist was appalled at being humiliated in public even though many of the kids congratulated us for rescuing Gōnggong.

Today, when Mrs. Shaughnessy goes out to get the worksheets she forgot, Liam leans forward and taps me on the shoulder. Just a few weeks ago, I would've flinched from his touch. Now, I just turn around and say, "What's up?"

"You're probably going to get called to Foxman's office today," Liam informs me. At my shocked expression, he holds up both hands. "Relax, you're not in trouble. I confessed."

Logan smirks. "Yeah, he hasn't been able to sleep since Gōnggong revealed he knew who the true culprit was."

Liam gives his brother a sour look. "Well, now I don't have a guilty conscience anymore. Happy?"

"Kind of," I say at the same time that Logan says, "But you should. You *are* guilty."

"Jeez," Liam complains. "Just thought you should know."

Mrs. Perry delivers a note the next period, at the beginning of Social Studies. Ms. Brown's eyebrows raise when she reads the note, and she glances my way. After class, she tells me that Mr. Reynard wants to see me in his office during lunch. She looks concerned, but I just smile and thank her and head off to English.

Sneaky of Foxman, though, to use my lunch period. That way he keeps me from going out to the courtyard and makes sure I'm hungry and uncomfortable for the rest of the day.

After Art, I make my way to the front office, and Mrs. Perry shows me into Foxman's lair.

"Well, Melanie, I thought I should let you know that

Liam Batchelder has admitted that he is responsible for the events in the courtyard garden."

You mean the complete destruction of the garden and framing me for it? I nod.

The principal looks annoyed. "You've already served your suspension, so I can't undo that, but I will remove the suspension from your school record. Starting today, Liam will be working to clean up and replant the garden as his punishment."

Part of me thinks that Liam should get suspended, too, but I know he won't. Fox demons might be devious, but they take care of their family and friends. Liam is protected through his father.

There's a knock on the door, and Mrs. Perry appears, looking apologetic. "Ms. Brown is here. She says she'd like to speak to you."

"Not now," Foxman snaps. "Tell her I'm in the middle of speaking to Melanie."

"She says it's about Melanie, sir. She's quite insistent."

The secretary moves aside, and Ms. Brown bustles in. She gives me a quick smile before addressing the principal. "Mr. Reynard, I will be direct. The week after the storm, Melanie turned in a fascinating oral history paper about a veteran who happens to be her grandfather."

Foxman grunts. "I am well aware of who she chose to focus her project on, Ms. Brown."

"Are you?" my teacher replies. "Because I think you'd be very interested in what she discovered, as well as the additional research she did on her own." She turns to me. "Melanie, please give Mr. Reynard the highlights of your interview and research."

What? Mist recoils. But Ms. Brown is gazing at me encouragingly, and Foxman is glaring at me with his boiled sap eyes and wrinkled snout.

I try to recall exactly what I wrote. "My grandfather fought in the Vietnam War, which the Vietnamese call the American War."

Foxman makes a low, growling sound but quickly covers it by clearing his throat. I stop, distracted by the noise and the poster leaning against the bookshelf. Someone has taken the photos and descriptions of the veterans that used to be in a folder on his desk and glued them onto a large poster board, with the black-and-white photo of Raymond Reynard in the center.

I point to the photo. "That's one of your relatives, isn't it?"

Ms. Brown looks at the photo, at the principal, and at me. She doesn't say anything.

"My uncle." Foxman grits his teeth. "He has nothing to do with your project."

"You're right," I say. "But I think *you* think my grandfather has something to do with your uncle being captured. That's what POW means, right? Your uncle was a prisoner of war. See, I took your advice and spent my suspension thinking about *my people.*"

"How dare you," Foxman splutters.

Ms. Brown looks like she's finally seeing the sun through the fog. She motions for me to continue.

"You assumed that because I'm Asian my grandfather fought against the United States in that war. When he actually helped the US military." I glance at Ms. Brown, at her proud face and broad smile. "If you're honoring veterans who have fought alongside the United States, then he deserves to be included."

A series of strangled, garbled sounds come out of Foxman's mouth. My heart pounds, and I fight the urge to laugh. Fox demons hate to be laughed at. Ms. Brown stares pointedly at the principal and crosses her arms.

"For the record," Foxman finally manages to say. "I deny your accusations. But since Ms. Brown thinks you did a good job on your project, I give you permission to invite your grandfather to the celebration." He pauses, clearly expecting me to thank him.

I take a deep breath. Even though he's a fox demon, I see that he's carrying around a lot of weight, including the pain of what happened to his uncle. He's Basket in his own life, too. My Basket accepts, while his lashes out. Will he ever recognize that? Is he capable of seeing what we have in common?

"Good," I tell him.

"That's all you have to say?" Foxman practically snarls.

I realize that I do have more to say, and this is my chance. "I'm sorry that your uncle was a POW, but even if my family were Vietnamese, we are not responsible. Besides, in my research, I discovered that lots of people don't agree on which was the 'right' side. Many in this country protested the war. The soldiers who fought against the United States believed that they were helping their country. They were doing what their government told them to do, just like your uncle and my grandfather. Blaming all Asians does not honor your uncle's sacrifice. And let's remember that there are no heroes in war—everyone loses something."

If Mr. Reynard were a Western dragon, he would

probably flame me to a crisp. But I am Mist, and fire has no effect on me. I am water and air, and I drown fox demons with logic and suffocate dog-headed word-shadows. I stand my ground.

The principal grinds his teeth, dulling them. "Are you quite done, Melanie?"

"My name is Meilan," I say, then float out the door.

Chapter Forty-Six

The sound of the audience is a low buzz that carries down the hallway. Both of Ms. Brown's classes—which is the entire seventh grade—are lined up against one wall. The veterans stand along the other wall, dressed in their uniforms, shades of blue and tan and camouflage green. At my request, Gōnggong and I are the first in our lines after the drummers and flagbearers. Gōnggong stands very straight, intently watching the flagbearer in front of him. Suddenly, a familiar blond-haired boy darts out from behind me and does something to the flagpole. Cassidy, who is holding the pole, stares at him in surprise.

Ms. Brown hisses, "Liam Batchelder! What are you doing? Get back in line—the procession is about to start!"

The boy turns and grins at me. It's Logan. He just got his cast off yesterday and he's already running around. I roll my eyes. From somewhere in the back of the line, Liam protests, "Hey, I'm right here!"

Ms. Brown turns to look at Liam, confused and apologetic, while Logan trots back toward me. As he passes Gōnggong he raises his hand, and my grandfather mimics him. Logan gives him a light high-five and rejoins our class. Gōnggong glances at me, amused, and then studies the flagpole. His face breaks into a wide smile. The flag of Taiwan, printed onto a thick sheet of paper, sticks straight out from the pole.

Thank you, I mouth to Logan. Mist would never have done that.

Music starts playing in the auditorium, and Mr. Reynard's voice rings out, welcoming the audience and starting the ceremony. The drums beat, and we march behind the flagbearers in two parallel lines. Students and parents clap as we enter the room and walk down the aisle, coming to a stop in front of the stage. Ms. Brown takes the microphone and explains the oral history project and its significance to the audience. Then she beckons me to the stage.

I look at Gōnggong, suddenly panicked. He puts a hand on my shoulder, and we climb the steps to the stage together.

I stand in front of the microphone and stare out at the sea of faces. They stare back, and my heart pounds louder. What am I doing up here? This is school and I am Mist. I'm breaking the rules. Out of the corner of my eye, I see a hand. Gōnggong's hand, reaching out, palm up, as if he's going to pick up the handle of a basket. With him, I am Basket, too, and it's like he's reaching out to hold me and share the load.

I take his hand and stare at the cuff of his uniform. It's frayed and shiny where the fabric has worn thin, revealing the sleeve of his blue dress shirt. Blue. Another one of my names, my variations, but maybe not for much longer. I have friends now—Logan and Anita and maybe even Liam. I can tell stories about the meaning of my name and nothing bad happens.

I glance up into Gōnggong's warm brown eyes and feel the gray mist, the bamboo strips of the basket, and the creeping tendrils of blue swirl around me like my own personal tornado. The variations of me spin and weave together, coalescing into a shimmery human-shaped form. A me-shaped form. I know what to do. I close my eyes and inhale deeply, breathing in the silvery shape until it fills all the corners of my body.

Back in the cemetery, when I was trying to get Gōnggong to see me, using my real name was the thing that finally worked. Now I understand the ending of

A Wizard of Earthsea. The wizard Ged confronted the shadow that he had released and named it with his own true name. And by doing so, his friend Estarriol realized that Ged "had made himself whole: a man: who, knowing his whole true self, cannot be used or possessed by any power other than himself."

I stand on the stage, visible and vulnerable but also proud. I am not alone. And I know who I am. I am all of the meanings of lán and more.

I named my whole true self to Gōnggong, Logan, and Liam, and then again to Foxman. Now it's time to declare myself to everyone and take back my power. I use what air is left in my lungs and force the beetles out of my throat.

"Hi. Before I introduce my veteran, I want to set something straight." With each word, a beetle flies out of my mouth and disappears in a tiny spark. No one else seems to notice, so I press on. "Most of you know me as Melanie, but that's not my real name. Actually, it has never been my name. My true name is Huā Měilán. Měilán is my first name." I risk a glance at Mr. Reynard, who scowls at me from the side of the stage. Ms. Brown's mouth is open, but her eyes are shining. "My grandfather and grandmother named me."

Gōnggong lets go and puts his hand on my shoulder, and I cover it with my own, like I'm putting my hand on my heart. "Měilán means Beautiful Orchid in Mandarin. There are thousands of varieties of orchids, but there is only one me. I'm sorry I didn't respond to Melanie, but I promise I'll answer if you call me Meilan." Logan gives me a thumbs-up from his place in line.

I turn to Gōnggong. "Now let me tell you about my grandfather, Huā Xìnlóng."

By the time I'm done with Gōnggong's story, all the beetles have flown away, leaving my insides light and airy.

Gōnggong waves as the audience applauds. Liam gives a piercing wolf whistle that Ms. Brown quickly shushes. In the front row, Bàba and Māma wipe their eyes. I guide Gōnggong to his seat on the stage and head back to the students in line. Debbi grins at me as I pass her. She seems nice. Maybe we could be friends, too.

"That was great, Lan," Logan tells me, deliberately using my nickname. Beside him, his aunt gives him a puzzled look that makes me laugh.

Fiona and Anita say nice things, too, calling me Meilan as if it's the most natural thing in the world. Anita even gives me a quick hug. I'm surprised by how easy it is for them to switch over, to welcome the real me.

Two by two, my classmates and their invited veterans take the stage, where they are introduced and applauded. After the last veteran takes his seat, Mr. Reynard gets up and thanks them all for their service. Gōnggong beams.

Afterward, there is cake and juice in the cafeteria. Bàba tells me how proud he is of me, and Māma says, "See? Horse came back with other horses." She gestures to where Logan, Liam, Fiona, Anita, and Debbi are standing together.

"You're right," I admit. "I guess a bad thing did turn into a good thing. But my horse wants to be called Meilan."

Māma lifts one shoulder in a half shrug and says, "Qiān lù yī shī." Then she goes to get a piece of cake.

Think over a thousand times yet can still make one mistake. It's as much of an apology as I'll ever get from Māma. We all make mistakes.

Chapter Forty-Seven

Two nights before Thanksgiving, we are all in the kitchen helping Bàba make pie. The Redbud Café sells them for people to bring home for their own holiday dinners. Growing up in Massachusetts, we studied the history of the Wampanoag Nation in school and learned that the story people like to tell about Pilgrims and Native Americans celebrating the "First Thanksgiving" was mostly just that—a story, invented by colonists to cover up a more gruesome history. We also learned that all the dishes we think of as being traditional for the holiday, including our creamy pumpkin pie, were made popular by a woman writer in the 1700s, over a century after the English Pilgrims first landed in Plymouth. The power of stories strikes again.

Knowing all that doesn't change the fact that we have to make three kinds of pie: pumpkin, pecan, and apple. Three dozen of each, for a grand total of one hundred and eight pies. Plus, Samantha has asked Bàba to bake

Chinese pastries, so he's making a selection of traditional things like egg tarts and butterfly cookies as well as experimenting with fusion creations like bōluóbāo with a peanut-butter-flavored cream filling. Gōnggong has talked him into making walnut cookies, too. The whole house smells like spices and nuts, sugar and cream. A new version of the delicious aroma that used to fill my old apartment. And maybe, a new version of Thanksgiving dessert for Redbud residents.

Bàba's cell phone rings on the kitchen table. His hands are coated with flour, so he presses the button to put the call on speakerphone. "Wèi, Jiāyù," he greets his sister with a touch of weariness.

Tiffi's voice bounces through the speaker. "Hi, Jiùjiu! It's me, Tiffi!"

"Hello, Tiffi," Bàba's voice is cautious. "What can I do for you?"

"Can I talk to Meilan, please? She called me a long time ago and said she'd call me back soon but she never did so now I'm calling her," Tiffi says all in one breath.

"Of course," Bàba says, and he gestures for me to speak.

"Hey, Tiffi," I say. "Hold on a minute while I wash my hands."

But just like her mom, Tiffi doesn't follow instructions. "Hi, Meilan! I listened to my Māma and Bàba's conversations, just like you asked, and the only thing I found out that was interesting was that they were going to start a new business but now they aren't." Her cute voice reverberates around the room. "I don't really know why they changed their minds, but they said something about Third Uncle and then they started saying their alphabet letters."

"Alphabet letters?" I have no idea what she's talking about.

"I know the whole alphabet!" she announces. "And I can write it all, too. But Māma and Bàba were being boring and saying the same three letters over and over again. D-U-I-"

I finish drying my hands and snatch up the phone, turning off the speaker. "Third Uncle got a DUI?" I gasp. "Did they say anything else?" I look up and find that my parents are staring at me. Gōnggong is shaking his head.

There's a pause, and then Tiffi says, "I remember! They talked about court, and I wanted to know if there would be a king and a queen there and if I could go in my princess dress, but then they got mad and went into their bedroom to talk and shut the door on me."

I walk to the kitchen table and sit down heavily. I want to go to my room to talk, but then Māma and Bàba will think I'm talking behind their backs—even more than I already am. I lower my voice as much as I can. "I'm sorry, Tiffi. That wasn't very nice of them to do that."

"It's okay," she says cheerfully. "That's why I decided to call you, so you could tell me a story instead."

The beetles are gone. I'm free to tell as many stories as I want. "How about a princess story, then?"

"No, I wanna hear about the golden phoenix again. I fell asleep before the end last time, so I never found out what happened to the fènghuáng and the mommy she was looking for."

I suck in my breath. "Not that story, Tiffi. Any story except that one."

"Why?" she whines. "Why won't you tell me that story?"

What do I say? Because that's the one that tore the family apart? I look up, and Gōnggong catches my eye. He smiles and goes back to chopping walnuts. And I remember that I took that brick out of my basket. In my heart, I give it back to Third Aunt, where it belongs.

"Because I found out the real story behind the name of the bakery," I tell Tiffi. "And it's way better than the one I made up for you, because it's the truth. I'll tell it to you after Thanksgiving, okay? Right now I have a ton of apples to peel."

"Okay," Tiffi is cheerful again. "But wait, don't go yet! Someone else wants to talk to you!"

"Tiffi, who is it?" I ask, but she doesn't answer. Part of me wants to hang up, but I don't. If I can face a tornado, talking to Third Aunt will be a breeze.

"Hi, Meilan. How are you?" It's Xing. The other flower of our family. She sounds so normal. As if we haven't been on opposite sides of a vast ocean of silence for months.

"Um, okay," I reply. "Pretty good, actually."

"Yeah? That's great!" Her voice is too cheerful.

My heart twinges, and for a moment I'm afraid the beetles are back, but there are no more pinches. Beetles or not, I don't know what to say, so I don't say anything at all.

"Meilan? Are you there?" Now Xing sounds hesitant, nervous. I must make some sort of sound, because she continues. "I just . . . I wanted . . . You know, I hope you have a happy Thanksgiving."

That's all she wanted to say? I find my voice. "Same to you," I say. Even though I want to be friends with Xing again, I'm still hurt by our last conversation. The silence swells, neither of us knowing how to cross it. I can't keep the chill out of my voice when I finally say, "I should probably get going. Bye."

"Wait! Meilan, I'm sorry," Xing says with a hitch in her voice. "Please don't hang up."

I think about all the things we leave unsaid. I think about Tao telling me to listen, to stick to the core. I think about Năinai's song, about the grace of family. "I'm still here."

"Thanksgiving isn't going to be the same without you," she says. "It's going to be the first time we've ever spent the holiday apart. I miss you. I've missed you for a long time. I'm sorry I said all those things." Her voice is soft and sad, melting the icy fear in my heart.

"I've missed you, too. So much." I sit on the bench in the mudroom. "Are you babysitting?"

"Yeah, and Tiffi made sure to tell me that I'm not as fun as you are." Xing laughs a little.

"You'll be her favorite after I tell you where Third Aunt hides the fancy chocolates," I say, and then I do just that.

The next morning, Māma, Gōnggong, and I wake up early and go to the café with Bàba to help out. Our oven at home is too small, so we'll bake the rest of the pies there. I box pies while Māma and Gōnggong fill big baking trays with the traditional Chinese pastries and Bàba's new creations and put them in the display cases. I especially like the eggnog-flavored custard tarts.

People come in all morning to pick up the pies they ordered. Most of them buy some Chinese pastries, too. I'm surprised by how many people greet Bàba by name. He introduces me as Meilan, and the pride on his face warms me. It's not the Golden Phoenix Bakery, but for a moment, it feels like it.

Ms. Brown stops in and buys a dozen walnut cookies. "Can't have too many desserts!" She laughs. "These will go great with my great-grandmother's Tausenblättertorte."

I blink. "Your great-grandmother's what?"

She laughs again. "It means Thousand Leaves Cake in German. It's a yellow layer cake filled with custard and topped with meringue and sliced almonds. My family immigrated to Ohio from Germany in the 1930s and brought the recipe with them."

"That sounds delicious," Bàba says. "Perhaps you would not mind sharing her recipe?"

"Of course!" my teacher replies. "I'll give it to Mei-lan next week." I finish tying red string around the box of cookies and hand it to her. She wishes us a happy Thanksgiving and waves on her way out the door.

Around lunchtime, the line of customers dwindles and Bàba says I can take a break and eat. Samantha tells me to help myself to anything in the kitchen, so I dig around in the giant refrigerator and make myself a chicken salad sandwich. With cheese. I sit on a stool next to the oven, enjoying the time alone, knowing my family is just past the swinging kitchen door.

Bàba peeks in a little while later and looks relieved that I'm done eating. He puts an arm around my shoulder and guides me through the doorway. "Come, come. I need your help. Logan and Liam are here. Logan cannot decide which pastries to get, and Liam is asking for free samples of everything."

I laugh and head to the pastry case. Logan and Liam are bent over it, bickering about what to buy. Through the windows behind them, the sky is a crisp, brilliant blue. Suddenly, a flock of starlings cartwheels through the clouds and comes to rest in the parking lot, their dark bodies shimmering with green and blue and purple. Logan turns and sees them, then catches sight of me. A smile lights his face, and I feel aglow, too.

The stories in the making are even better than the ones I already know.

Author's Note about
Transliteration of Mandarin and Chinese

Meilan and her family speak Mandarin, which is transliterated into the English alphabet using the Pinyin system. Pinyin is the official romanization system of mainland China (PRC) but is also used in Taiwan (ROC) along with other systems. I chose to use Pinyin because it is how I learned to transliterate Mandarin, and also because it is widely used to teach Mandarin in the United States. I wanted to include the tone marks so Mandarin speakers and students could read along. As you may have gathered from the book, speaking the same syllable in different tones can result in wildly different meanings.

Mandarin learners may also notice some differences in pronunciation or vocabulary, which can be attributed to differences between Mandarin spoken in mainland China and Mandarin spoken in Taiwan, where Meilan's family is from. I have also incorporated colloquialisms used in my own family, who were born on the mainland but grew up in Taiwan.

bìng cóng kǒu rù—"sickness enters from the mouth"
(literal); be careful what you eat (figurative)

bù yí yú lì—"do not leave extra strength behind"
(literal); to spare no pains or effort; to do your best/
utmost (figurative)

jié zú xiān dēng—"quick foot is first to climb" (literal);
the swift-footed arrive first, similar in meaning to
"first come, first served" (figurative)

mù yǐ chéng zhōu—"the trees have already become boats"
(literal); it's too late to change anything (figurative)

qiān jīn nán mǎi yì kǒu qì—"a thousand pieces of gold
cannot buy one breath" (literal); a living person must
not ruin their life (figurative)

qiān lǜ yī shī—"consider a thousand times yet can still
make one mistake" (literal); similar in meaning to "to
err is human"

rù xiāng súi sú—"when entering the country, follow the

customs" (literal); similar in meaning to "when in Rome, do as the Romans do"

sài wēng shī mǎ, yān zhī fēi fú—"when the old man lost his horse, how could he have known it would not be fortuitous" (literal); similar in meaning to "every cloud has a silver lining"

shù yù jìng ér fēng bù zhǐ—"trees desire peace, but wind never stops" (literal); things change no matter if you want them to or not (figurative)

yī tiáo shéng shàng de mà zha—"like grasshoppers tied to one rope" (literal); we're all in it together (figurative)

yìng jī lì duàn—"should opportunity arise, act decisively" (literal); to act on an opportunity, to take prompt advantage of a situation (figurative)

zǎo qǐ de niǎo'ér yǒu chóng chī—"only the early bird has worms to eat" (literal); those who are late to act, arrive, or get up tend to miss opportunities already seized by those who came earlier, similar in meaning to "the early bird catches the worm" (figurative)

A Wizard of Earthsea by Ursula K. LeGuin.

Chinese Proverbs and Popular Sayings: With Observations on Culture and Language by Qin Xue Herzberg and Larry Herzberg.

"Home Sweet Home" (Nǎinai's Family Song): *http://castleofcostamesa.com/song-list-trial-page/song-list/chinese-childrens-songs-about-family-and-home/chinese-childrens-songs-home-sweet-home/*

Books about the Vietnam War

Patrol: An American Soldier in Vietnam by Walter Dean Myers.

10,000 Days of Thunder: A History of the Vietnam War by Phillip Caputo.

Books about Veterans Day

The Poppy Lady: Moina Belle Michael and Her Tribute to Veterans by Barbara E. Walsh, illustrated by Layne Johnson.

The Wall by Eve Bunting, illustrated by Ronald Himler.

Books about PTSD

Finding My Way: A Teen's Guide to Living with a Parent Who Has Experienced Trauma by Michelle D. Sherman.

The War That Saved My Life by Kimberly Brubaker Bradley.

ACKNOWLEDGMENTS

One of the most beautiful and unexpected things I discovered about bringing a book into the world is that it creates a family. A large, extended family where everyone's contributions are valued. This book would not exist without you all.

Boundless gratitude to my book family's revered leader, editor Joanna Cárdenas, who believed in Meilan from the beginning, when all she'd read was a few chapters. Thank you for your insight and for challenging and inspiring me to make this book (and Meilan) as fierce as I could. I look forward to many more awesome conversations where we *get stuff done*!

Heartfelt thanks to my agent, Erin Murphy of the Erin Murphy Literary Agency, for being the best book shepherd, career coach, and matriarch a Gango could ask for. Your unwavering belief in me keeps me motivated (and the driveway snowblowed).

To my Crumpled Paper critique group family: Lisa

Robinson, Maria Gianferrari, Lois Sepahban, Sheri Dillard, and Abby Aguirre, who have been there since the beginning of my writing journey, your astute advice, thoughtful feedback, and steadfast friendship have been invaluable. Nothing makes me happier than to see our books keeping each other company on my shelves.

To Debbi Michiko Florence, sister in spirit, I don't know how to thank you for your insight and cherished friendship. This book will forever remind me of a glorious retreat in Maine, full of writing sprints and chocolate and laughter.

Hugs and thank-yous to longtime friends who have become family—Dawn & Jim Dentzer, Stacey & Tony Mastromatteo, Taiji Saotome, and Isabelle & Jason Zee. You never failed to ask about my writing, and that has kept me going too many times to count.

To my #AsianAmChildLit family, Betina Hsieh, Jung Kim, Sarah Park Dahlen, Mike Jung, and Paula Yoo—thank you for all the important work you do to ensure that Asian Americans are represented in children's literature. You inspire me to raise my voice even when the beetles are blocking it. #AsianAmAF forever!

Every family has bedrock members, and for me they are the Lesley University MFA faculty, particularly my mentors, David Elliott, Susan Goodman, and Pat Lowery Collins. Thank you for giving me a solid foundation of craft to build this book on.

Thank you to the amazing Team Kokila—Namrata Tripathi, Zareen Jaffery, Sydnee Monday, Jasmin Rubero, Ariela Rudy Zaltzman, and Natalie Vielkind, for your support, feedback, and encouragement. A special shout-out to Katie Radwilowicz, Theresa Evangelista, and Violet Tobacco for designing and creating the most meaningful and gorgeous cover. To the entire Penguin Young Readers family, in the production, design, subsidiary rights, publicity, marketing, school & library, and sales departments—thank you for taking Meilan under your wings!

To Dr. Lan Dong, Elise McMullen-Ciotti, and Chinese copyeditor Yilin Wang, my deepest gratitude for your wisdom and expertise.

Everlasting love and thanks to the extended Lee, Chan, and Wang/Wong families, who have supported and encouraged me all along the way. Extra-special thanks to Ezra Chan, the best 哥哥 I could have wished for (I appreciate you now); Anita Ung, partner in book nerdery and baking sprees; and Feodor Ung, master of post-prandial alkalosis. I'd want to be your family if we weren't already related. I'm also incredibly grateful to my in-laws, Cathay and Judy Wang, who made it possible for me to get a degree in writing—truly a progressive Chinese parent act if ever there was one.

Tim, you're my North Star, my steady guide, my staunchest supporter. Thank you for indulging my whims and making sure I get out of the house sometimes. I love you. Evan and Bennett, wǒ de bǎobèi érzimen, thank you for being my joy, my inspiration, my source of dubious teen slang. Seeing who you've grown to be gives me hope for the future.

And for my dearest family members who have crossed over—Māma, Bàba, Wàipó, Wàigōng, Joshua—your grace is indeed longer than the heavens.